Rave Reviews for CRUSI

"*Crush* is an unforgettable, stimulating romance that will have you reeling in astonishment when the unthinkable strikes in Cami's world! Which of these characters will come out of this deceitful web carefully designed by this wonderfully talented author, Lacey Weatherford! I give this book my thumbs up!" ~*Jessica Johnson, Book End 2 Book End*

"Once again, Lacey Weatherford has delivered a romance so exhilarating, you'll be left in a puddle of swoony sighs. *Crush* has it all – romance, suspense, angst, humor . . . not to mention amazing one liners from a guy so deliciously sexy, it'll leave you breathless and blushing for hours to come! I don't just have a crush . . . I have an addiction!" ~*Belinda Boring, Bestselling Author of The Mystic Wolves*

"I absolutely loved, loved, loved, this book! Lacey takes us on an electrifying ride—there were so many times I could feel my heart beat faster in anticipation wondering what was going to happen next! *Crush* is a 5 star page turner full of passion, secrets and intrigue...A MUST read!!!" ~*Holly Malgieri, I Love Indie Books*

"*Crush* is AH-MAY-ZING. Sparks were flying off the pages throughout the entire book. The romance isn't the only thing going on, it has many different levels to it. I absolutely loved the plot—I was amazed once all the pieces started coming together. I soooo did not want this book to end!" ~*Tishia Mackey, Paranormal Opinion*

"*Smitten*, the sequel to *Crush*, was definitely worth the wait! The way that Lacey Weatherford is able to capture the love between Hunter and Cami is magical. No wonder Lacey has been named The Queen of Hearts!" ~*Lisa Markson Reviews*

"Ms. Weatherford has done what I thought impossible and given us a sequel that is just as enjoyable, if not *more* enjoyable than the first book. With *Smitten*, Lacey Weatherford has cemented her place among my favorite authors. I can't wait to see what she comes up with next!" ~*Melissa Simmons, Girls Heart Books*

"Find a comfy place on the carpet, because the romance will leave you a melted puddle on the floor, and while you're down there, the next scene will have you rolling around in laughter." ~*Irene Hunt, Third Eye Tight Editing*

SMITTEN

Lacey Weatherford

ACKNOWLEDGMENTS

This book was written for my readers after they read Crush and begged for more. I hope you will love it too. I know I do!

This book got way behind schedule due to a myriad of horrible life-threatening health issue. I'd like to thank my friends and family for all their support during this trying time. You took good care of me, let me cry on your shoulders, and helped me make my way back into the land of the living again. I love you all so much! I'm blessed to have such an amazing support system.

I'd also like to thank my agent, Jane Dystel, for her patience in getting this book from me, and for her encouragement to concentrate on getting better too. I appreciated your kind words and taking the time to check in on me. I hope we can get together again soon!

Most of all, I'd like to thank my editor, Irene Hunt. She puts in tireless hours helping to polish these stories. Sometimes I have an immediate hit, and other times I have to do a little rewriting to hit the mark just right. I appreciate knowing I can hand you a manuscript, and you'll give an honest, straightforward opinion. Thank you for all you do and for "squeeing" excitedly with me when amazing things happen. (Please don't hit my shoulder anymore when you're excited. I have to explain the bruises to other people! Haha Love you!)

I hope everyone will have as much fun reading this book as I did writing it. Hunter, Cami, and Russ always manage to leave me with a big grin on my face! I hope there will be one on yours as well!

Thanks so much,

Lacey

DEDICATION

For Jace.

Thanks for dropping everything, at any given moment, to discuss plot lines. I love you so much! It's an honor to have such a wonderful son!

CAMI ♥

CHAPTER ONE
Cami-

Watching from my dorm room window, I couldn't help staring dreamily as Hunter got out of his Camaro and jogged along the sidewalk below. His body never ceased to impress me, his quick lithe actions causing his sinewy muscles to ripple underneath his clothes—muscles I loved to run my fingers over all the time.

As if he heard my thoughts, he glanced up, catching me spying on him, and that thousand-watt grin of his made an appearance. His dark hair rippled slightly in the breeze, and he tapped the watch he was wearing. Instantly, the butterflies, which had temporarily gone missing, were back in my stomach. For a moment, I'd forgotten where he was taking me tonight—to meet his parents.

I gave a little wave of acknowledgement and signaled I'd be right down. Going to my bed, I grabbed my handbag before checking my appearance in the full-length mirror one last time. I hoped I was dressed okay. My thin, white blouse with short-capped sleeves hugged my figure nicely and overlapped the top of my gray trousers. I'd paired gray sandals that showed off my nice summer pedicure, complete with my French tipped toenails.

Sighing, I appraised my thick red hair I'd left hanging in the naturally curly waves Hunter liked so much. A knock at the door interrupted me, and I hurried to open it.

"Hey there, gorgeous," Hunter said, eyeing me appreciatively before he entered the room and swept me into his arms. "You look amazing!"

I blushed, laughing before I realized he was holding me in *both* his arms. "Hunter! Err . . . Dylan, you're not wearing your sling!"

He grinned as I traced over his bicep to his shoulder, resting my hand gently there—the memories of him being shot still too fresh in my mind.

"I went to the doctor today. I don't have to wear it anymore. Everything is healed nicely." He bent to lightly kiss my forehead. "And I told you before . . . , call me Hunter if you want. It's still my middle name, and it doesn't bother me one bit."

"I worry it'll be awkward around your family. They won't know who I'm talking about." I gave a small laugh and shook my head. "I've been trying to retrain myself, but it's been difficult."

Ever since I'd found out my boyfriend was

actually an undercover cop posing as a student at my high school, I'd struggled to switch from using his alias, Hunter Wilder, to his given name, Dylan Wilcock. The problem was, my mind had firmly implanted him as Hunter. He continued to reassure me it was okay to call him that, but I felt a little weird since no one else did. Well, no one else besides Hunter's best friend, Russ, that is.

Russ had thankfully made a full recovery after being nearly poisoned to death by my previous best friend, Clay. He was very grateful to Hunter and the role he'd played in saving his life. It seemed he was almost Hunter's shadow now—moving here, to Tucson, for school as well and continuing their friendship as if nothing between them had changed.

I liked having him here too. Granted, we'd only been at U of A for a week and had spent most of that time settling in to our new places, but it was still nice to have a familiar face on campus to hang around with occasionally.

"Don't worry about it, Cami. Relax and be yourself tonight. My family is going to love you." Hunter leaned in closer, quickly placing a soft kiss against my cheek, and I gave him a questioning look. "What?" he asked with a laugh.

"A kiss on the cheek? Really? I must be losing my touch."

He flashed me another incredible grin. "I didn't want to mess up your makeup. Besides, there will be plenty of kissing later on tonight." He winked at me.

"You seem pretty sure about that," I teased back, running my index finger over his amazing lips. He grabbed my wrist, stilling it, and sucked my finger into his mouth. Laughter escaped, and I bit my lower lip.

Slowly he released my finger, and the grin was back as he bent toward the side of my head, his warm breath brushing against my ear. "I'll let you in on a little secret. I have something special planned for you later at my place."

Goose bumps flared over my skin. "Special?" I managed to squeak out.

He nuzzled his face into my hair. "I'm finally out of that damn sling, and my muscles are feeling good after therapy. I figured you and I could celebrate together. What do you think? Maybe cuddle on the couch and watch a movie?" He paused, pulling away to look at me. "Or we could skip the movie and make out instead." He grinned.

Mental images of the two of us tangled in each other's arms flashed through my mind, and my heart rate kicked to about a thousand. "Why do I get the idea you're hoping I'll choose the second option?" I smiled, loving the excited look on his face.

"Am I that obvious," he replied with a laugh.

I nodded. "Pretty much, yeah."

"And that's why I love you. You know me so well." He lifted his hands and cupped my face stroking my cheeks with his thumbs. "My family is going to love you too." He leaned forward and lightly kissed me. His chocolate-colored eyes, with their flecks of honey, looked warm and caring as he locked gazes with me. I didn't doubt his love. I could see it shining there.

The butterflies resurfaced at the mention of his family. "I'm worried they'll think I'm too young for you."

"They already know how old you are, Goody," he said, using his pet name for me. "I've explained everything to them. My mom didn't even bat an eyelash. She thinks it's all terribly romantic."

"Really?" Hearing that made me feel better.

Hunter chuckled. "Really. They're very excited to meet you. Chris has told them how wonderful you are too. He and my sister will be there as well. You have allies."

I had fond memories of the few times I'd been able to visit with Hunter's brother-in-law, Chris. Not to mention he'd saved both our lives during the incident with Clay, so that gave him huge brownie points in my book.

"Are we good?" he asked. "No more nerves."

I gave a short laugh. "Oh, I still have plenty of those. I don't want to screw anything up."

"You'll be perfect. Don't worry."

"How can you know? Have you added psychic abilities to your impressive resume?" I teased him. "Because unless you've suddenly become all-knowing, I don't see how you can predict something like that."

"I know because you're perfect. Everyone who meets you loves you. Why would my family be any different?"

"I bet Gabby would beg to differ with you."

An image of the gorgeous brunette from high school popped into my head. "She was very clear about wanting me out of the way so she could have you."

Hunter groaned. "Please don't ruin our nice evening by mentioning her. I've quite enjoyed leaving her in the past—where she belongs."

"Really? That's too bad. I was thinking of dying my hair dark-brown and purchasing a much sluttier wardrobe. I thought you might like it." I bit my lip in anticipation of his reaction.

"Don't you dare touch your hair. Ever. It's perfect like it is." He picked up one of the lose curls and twisted it around his finger.

"Ever?" I asked, faking confusion. "It's going to be awful messy if I can't touch it *ever.*"

He laughed and gently tweaked my nose. "You know what I mean, Miss Smarty Pants."

"Smarty Pants? Is that an upgrade or a down grade from Goody-Two-Shoes?"

His eyes were positively sparkling with mirth. "Neither. You'll always be my Goody." He leaned in and lightly kissed my lips, before giving me a half-cocked grin. "Do you know how good you make me feel?"

I slid my arms around his neck and hugged him tightly. "You make me feel good too." Popping higher on my tiptoes, I kissed him—lipgloss forgotten. A soft moan escaped him and he wrapped an arm around my waist, his other hand slipping to my neck, tangling into my hair.

I sighed happily at the contact, loving the feelings his touch evoked inside me. He made me feel the craziest things. I'd never experienced this kind of intense emotion for another person before.

He suddenly broke away with a heavy sigh, leaning his forehead against mine. "We better get going I think, or I might be tempted to skip dinner. My mom wouldn't be too happy about that I'm afraid. She's been very anxious to meet you."

The ball of nerves bounced back into my stomach. "Okay. Let's get this over with."

He laughed heartily. "I'm not taking you to be executed, you know. I really do think you'll like them."

"I'm sure I will . . . especially if they're anything like you." I was doing my best to be positive. I wasn't sure why the idea of meeting his parents was so terrifying. Of course, I'd never been in love before. Hunter . . . Dylan . . . was my first love. Making a good impression was a must for me. It was obvious he was close to his family by the way he lit up when talking about them. What if they felt I wasn't good enough for their son? Horror stories of relationships ending because the family didn't get along with the newcomer floated in my mind. That couldn't happen to us. I couldn't lose him.

Hunter grabbed my hand, leading me out of my dorm room, downstairs, and to the parking lot. He opened the passenger door of the Camaro, and I slid inside. I dug through my purse to find my lip-gloss while he went around to get in his side. He climbed in beside me and watched for a second as I leaned forward to look into the visor's mirror.

"You don't really need to wear that, you know."

I glanced over at him. "What do you mean?"

"I mean you might as well save yourself the trouble because I plan on kissing you all evening. You're going to be constantly reapplying." He winked at me.

"You're incorrigible," I replied with a small smile and a shake of my head before I finished.

He shrugged. "Just trying to help you out."

I recapped my makeup and dropped it into my bag, leaning back against the seat. "At least let me make introductions first. Then you may kiss to your heart's content."

"Is that a promise?" He grinned as he started the car. "I'm going to hold you to it."

"Does it really matter? You know you're going to do what you want anyway."

He chuckled as he backed out of the space. "Yeah, I am. You really do know me too well."

I smiled. "So how far away is your parent's house?"

"It's not too far. About fifteen minutes from here, if we hit all the lights right." After he had merged out onto the road, he reached over to take my hand in his, squeezing it gently. "I can't wait for them to meet you."

A small time later, we pulled through the open gates of a private drive. My jaw fell open. "This is where you grew up?" I asked in amazement.

"Yep. Pretty, huh?"

I didn't know what to say, but pretty wasn't

the word I would've chosen—opulent, maybe, or astounding. The house was an incredible Spanish styled mansion with cream walls and a red tiled roof. It stood, towering three stories high, at the end of the driveway. Tall Sycamore trees bordered the drive and disappeared around behind the structure. At the end of the drive, a large, russet concrete fountain sprayed water about two feet into the air from the top tier, before falling and running into a small, sparkling pool around the bottom. A well-manicured patch of lawn, edged with beds full of riotous-colored flowers, surrounded the pool, spreading out to create a little island in the middle of the brick-laid driveway.

My nerves skyrocketed. "I didn't know you were related to Donald Trump." I was joking, but there was suddenly a lump in my throat I couldn't seem to swallow.

Hunter laughed loudly as he parked the Camaro. "This place would be a quaint cottage for Donald." He eyed me, flashing his perfect grin again. "Relax, Cami. I'd never take you anywhere that'd make you uncomfortable."

My voice didn't seem capable of making any sound at the moment, so I merely nodded. He hopped out of the car and jogged around to my door. I could tell he was excited as he held his hand out and pulled me from the car.

I followed him up the red tiled steps, which led to the massive double front doors. Hunter pushed one side open, practically dragging me into the house behind him.

It was time to meet the family.

CHAPTER TWO
Cami-

My eyes gravitated to the middle of the soaring foyer where a giant wrought iron chandelier, layered with antique glass and small crystal prisms, hung. The curve of an equally impressive staircase, which boasted a beautifully sculpted wrought iron banister, accentuated the placement of the fixture. Large paintings, depicting the Spanish countryside, graced the golden-washed walls, complimenting the orange-red color of the Saltillo tile on the floor. It was easily the fanciest house I'd ever been in.

"Nice place," I muttered under my breath, feeling my distress intensify a notch.

Hunter squeezed my hand reassuringly. "Don't be intimidated. You'll get used to it."

I didn't have time to reply. A tall man with black hair, slightly graying at the temples, entered the room. He was dressed in a linen shirt unbuttoned at the neck, with dark pants and shoes. I immediately assumed this must be

Hunter's dad from the warm smile that crossed his face when he saw us.

"Hello, Dylan," he said in a rich, low voice, and I thought I detected a slight accent. "I'm sorry I didn't hear you arrive, or I would have greeted you at the door." He hugged Hunter affectionately before turning to me. "And you must be Cami. It's such a pleasure to meet you. Dylan has spoken nonstop about you."

I mustered a somewhat nervous smile. "It's nice to meet you too, Mr. Wild . . . err, um, Wilcock," I stammered out, feeling like a fool for almost calling him the wrong name.

Both he and Hunter laughed, and I felt my skin flush.

"This isn't my dad, Cami," Hunter said. "This is José. He's . . . well, he's like the butler, for lack of a better word."

"I prefer house manager," José said with a nod, extending his hand.

I shook it. "Nice to meet you, José." I was sure my face was a lovely shade of red.

"He's trying to take your bag for you," Hunter whispered in my ear.

"Oh, sorry," I said, feeling my skin heat even more as I slipped my purse off my shoulder and handed it to him.

"Your parents are on the back patio with Chris and Sheridan. They opted for a more relaxed environment and decided to do a barbeque for dinner tonight. You know how much your dad loves grilling."

"I do," Hunter said with a grin. "And he's good at it. This will be fun."

He gave me a quick squeeze as if he were trying to reassure me. I relaxed almost immediately. A barbeque? And Chris was here. I knew he was on my side. This shouldn't be too bad.

Hunter led me down the long hallway, which was as equally ornate as the foyer, with doorways and arched openings that branched off into other areas of the house, allowing me a peek at the richly decorated rooms. This family was loaded.

We reached a wall of wood and glass-paneled French doors. One set was open to the outside and Hunter led me through to one of the most lavish patios I'd ever seen, set next to a large, sparkling pool.

Wood beams crisscrossed over our heads, draped in fragrant honeysuckle vines, which artfully hid the misting system cooling the hot desert air. Plush, brightly-colored cushions decorated the wrought iron furniture arranged in a cozy seating area next to a large, wooden dining table and chairs.

At one end of the space, an unlit stone fireplace stood adjacent to a large built-in barbeque grill. A brown haired man in a white t-shirt and khaki colored pants stood with his back to us, a large metal spatula in his hand. Delicious aromas filled the air, and I felt my stomach rumble slightly. A large granite counter ran beside the grill, and behind it was what appeared to be a full bar. Chris and a woman with long brown hair sat on barstools sipping what looked like martinis. A beautiful woman stood behind the counter shaking drinks and talking to them. Her black hair, cut in a trendy A-line bob, shook in unison with the motion of her hands. I knew instantly this was Hunter's mother. She was definitely the one he got his dark looks from. She spied us then.

"Dylan!" she called out, a wide smile gracing her lovely features, her dark eyes flashing in delight. Everyone turned to look. She set the shaker down and hurried over to us, giving Hunter a hug.

"Hi, Mom," he replied, releasing my hand to return her embrace tightly. She was slightly taller than I was, and her figure was both shapely and curvy, shown off nicely in the sporty orange-striped tank top, white shorts, and matching sandals. Somehow, she still managed to make the casual outfit seem fancy. I couldn't help but notice the large diamond wedding ring that graced her finger. It caught the light every time she moved her hand to pat his back.

She let go of Hunter and turned to me, clasping me warmly. "And you must be Cami. I'm Consuela, but everyone calls me Connie. We are so happy to finally have you here. Dylan has spoken so fondly of you."

"What she actually means is he never shuts up about you," Chris interjected with a laugh as he joined us.

I smiled at Connie when she pulled away. "It's nice to meet you, Connie. Hun . . . um, Dylan, speaks very loving of all of you too." I blushed over my blunder of Hunter's name again. "I'm sorry. I still have a hard time calling him Dylan. Old habits die hard."

"No worries," a new voice interjected, and I glanced behind Connie to see Hunter's dad coming to join us. "We call Dylan lots of names around here. Troublemaker, Stinker, Pain-in-the-butt are some that come to mind. Wouldn't you agree, Dylan?" he asked with a grin.

"Cami, this is my dad. Watch out for him—he's quite the jokester. You can never believe anything that comes out of his mouth."

"Weston Wilcock at your service, my dear," Hunter's dad said, stepping forward to shake my hand too. "It's a pleasure to meet you. I see Dylan wasn't exaggerating about your looks."

"Well, you *can* believe that," Hunter added with a wink.

I blushed again. "It's nice to be here. Thank you for having me." Hunter definitely got his teasing personality from his dad.

"You might need to lay off the charm a bit, Dad, or Cami will be blushing all night long," Hunter said, laughing.

"I'm simply reaffirming what you've been saying all along." Weston smiled. "Please excuse me, Cami. I'm going to burn the food if I don't get back to my grill."

"Come on," Hunter said, dragging me past his mom and Chris. "You've got to meet Sheridan."

His sister had turned on the barstool and was facing us, showing what I had missed before—her slightly rounded belly. She was pregnant. My eyes automatically flashed to the martini glass beside her on the counter, and she let out a little giggle.

"I see you've quickly assessed my condition. Don't worry. Only virgin drinks for me. It's great to finally meet you, Cami." She brushed her long brown hair over her shoulder and extended a slender hand toward me. "Chris and Dylan have both told me so much about you."

"Well, I hope it was all good." I wondered what they could've possibly been saying as I flashed her a smile and shook her hand. For some reason, I felt an instant connection with her, but I wasn't sure why, other than knowing how much Hunter loved her. She resembled Weston more than Connie—a softer, more feminine, version of her father.

"Only the best. Dylan's quite smitten with you, which I'm sure you're aware of. I've never seen him this happy before."

I locked eyes with Hunter, and he wrapped an arm around my waist, pulling me closer to him. "Is that true?"

"Yep."

"Well, I'm glad. You make me feel pretty great too."

"I bet he does," Chris joked from behind me, and Hunter turned to punch him in the shoulder.

"You're one to talk. We can hardly stand to be in the same room with you and Sheridan. You can't keep your hands off her." He gestured toward Sheridan. "Which is plainly evident,"

Chris laughed, running his hand through his short blond hair. "Can you blame me? Look at her. She's hot!" He slid back into his seat beside

Sheridan and leaned over to kiss her cheek. I was happy to see I wasn't the only one here subjected to blushing skin. It was clear these two were crazy about each other.

It was interesting to see Chris in this kind of environment. I hadn't had the opportunity to interact with him much when Hunter was undercover, and lately all contact with him had been related to the case they'd been involved in. He held a place of tenderness in my heart because he'd been the one to save Hunter's life when Clay had attacked him. I realized I identified him as an all-business kind of guy, but that wasn't the case when he was with his wife. He was a total romantic.

"Is there something I can do to help?" I asked Connie when she stepped back behind the bar. I looked around to see if there was more food that needed preparing.

"No, just take a seat and enjoy yourself. The kitchen staff is taking care of the rest."

Staff? How many people work here? I wondered as I slid onto a barstool next to Chris. I couldn't quite wrap my head around having hired help around all the time, but I guess the house was big enough it only made sense.

Hunter scooted his barstool closer to me and then sat down.

"What would you like to drink, Cami?" Connie asked, returning to her role of bartender.

"Do you have any soft drinks, or juice?"

"We have both. Anything in particular you'd like?"

"An apple juice if you've got it."

"Perfect. We're having apple martinis, so you can have your apples too." She smiled and reached into a mini refrigerator under the liquor shelf behind her.

"I'll take an apple juice too, Mom. I'm driving tonight, and I need a clear head," Hunter said. He slipped his hand over and patted my leg affectionately. The sweet gesture made warmth spread through me. I was excited we were getting to spend the whole evening together. I placed my hand top of his, and he turned to link his fingers with mine.

"See, nothing to worry about," he whispered softly against my hair.

"I like them all," I replied in the same fashion, and he flashed a smile before giving me a tender kiss on the cheek.

His mom slid two apple juices in fancy martini glasses in front of us, interrupting our private moment. "Dylan tells me you're a music major. We'd love to come hear you perform sometime."

"That would be great. I've started classes, and we'll have our first concert next month. I'll be sure to invite you."

"Wait until you hear her, Mom," Hunter interjected. "She'll blow you away. I've never heard anyone better."

"Why don't you sing something for us now?" Weston asked from the grill, and I choked on my apple juice.

Hunter patted me on the back. "Let's not kill her all at once, okay, Dad? Give her a minute to get used to all of us. I'd like to keep her around a while longer."

"I bet you do," Chris said with a knowing wink, and I coughed again.

Hunter shot him an amused glare. "Cami, would you like to walk by the pool with me?"

"Sure," I replied, grateful he was attempting to rescue me. We took our drinks and walked hand in hand toward the water. The pool was as impressive as the rest of what I'd seen. A hot tub was at the far end of one side, and large boulders were around the backside with a slide fashioned to match the rocks. Water sluiced down the slide and various places over the stones, creating mini waterfalls, which fell into the sparkling Pebble Tec pool. Large and small palm trees dotted the surrounding area, as well as a few padded lounge chairs for sunbathing, which looked more like something one would find at a five-star resort rather than a private residence.

"Your home is very beautiful," I said when we stopped at the edge of the pool. "I had no idea your family was so wealthy."

Hunter took a sip of his drink before he shrugged. "It's all I know. I always thought this was a normal life for most people."

I snorted. "Hardly. I can't even fathom what it would be like to grow up with this kind of money."

"I'm glad you didn't."

That comment surprised me. "Why?" I stared at him, anxious to hear his answer.

"Because you're perfect the way you are right now—wholly unspoiled, sweet, real. I like all those things about you." He pushed a strand of hair, blowing in the warm breeze, away from my face.

"You think having money would change those things about me?"

"Not now, because you're already you. But it could've if you had it your whole life."

"You seem to have turned out okay," I reminded him.

"Only because I met Chris. I was much crazier before then." He grinned. "My dad wasn't completely kidding when he said I had lot of names. He called me his wild child. That's how I came up with Wilder as my alias. Chris helped me change that lifestyle."

I gave a slight chuckle. "You must've been thrilled to find out your sister was getting married to a cop."

"He definitely wasn't the type of guy I expected her to end up with. He's perfect for her, though."

We both turned and glanced at them.

"They seem really happy together," I said. "Love does crazy things, doesn't it? It can step in and change people's lives completely."

"Tell me about it. Look what it did to mine." He stared at me now, a smoky heat glinting in his eyes, and he stepped closer. "I thought I was going to go crazy trying to stay away from you."

"Now you don't have to." I couldn't look away.

His heated gaze flared. "No I don't." He took my drink from my hand and placed it on the ground with his before straightening to wrap his arms around my waist.

I slipped my arms around his neck, and he bent to kiss first my forehead, then my cheek, before pressing his lips to mine. He held me tightly, kissing me deeply, his tongue exploring my mouth as the fire instantly flared between us. One of his hands drifted downward, pressing us closer together.

Laughter echoed through the air from the group back at the bar, and I broke away. "Hunter." I slid my hands to his chest as I pushed back. I could feel the blush stealing across my skin. "Your family is watching."

"Cami," he said, holding me tighter.

I pushed harder—embarrassed at the show I was sure we were putting on for everyone.

"Cami, stop," he demanded again, but it was too late. I lost my balance, falling backward. Hunter tried to hold me, but the momentum was too much, and both of us tumbled into the pool.

CHAPTER THREE
Hunter-

My head broke the surface of the water, and I gasped, quickly scanning for Cami. I breathed a sigh of relief when I found her sputtering behind me. I closed the distance between us as laughter filled the air from the edge of the pool. I ignored them as I grabbed Cami's arm and gently tugged her to me. She wiped her hair away from her face, and thin black rivulets of mascara streamed down her cheeks.

"Are you okay?" I asked, concerned. I'd fallen on top of her when we'd hit the water.

Her skin immediately flushed a lovely shade of pink. "I will be after the humiliation settles."

I allowed myself to grin then. "I tried to warn you."

She grimaced. "I know, but I didn't realize what you meant until it was too late. Sorry."

"Are you two all right?" My mom's concerned voice floated above us.

"You know they have suits you could've

borrowed in the pool house. You didn't have to shove her in," Chris drawled out in a joking manner.

I glanced up at him as I started leading Cami toward the steps. "You're hilarious. Why don't you do something useful—like get us some towels?" I didn't think Cami had realized her white blouse was practically transparent now. While I was enjoying the view, I wasn't too thrilled with the idea of everyone else seeing it. She'd be embarrassed if she realized.

Sheridan and Chris appeared at the end of the pool with stacks of the fluffy, white towels my parents always kept in abundant supply. I helped Cami up the steps, and Sheridan had her quickly wrapped in a towel, for which I was grateful.

"What happened?" my mom asked, joining us as I tried wringing the water out of my pants.

"I took a step backward, not realizing how close I was to the water," Cami stated mournfully. "Hunter tried to catch me, but I took him down with me, I'm afraid."

"Forced into taking the plunge, eh?" Chris added with a laugh.

"Something like that." I chuckled. "Sheridan, is it okay if I go raid any clothes you have left in your closet? I think you're probably the closest size to Cami."

"Of course you can. They may be a little outdated, but she's welcome to anything."

"Thank you," Cami said, graciously. "I'm so sorry for the trouble."

"No trouble whatsoever."

I quickly used a towel to sop the worst of the wet before taking my shoes off. "Follow me," I said with a nod to my heavily-bundled girlfriend whose hands were buried somewhere beneath a couple of fluffy towels.

She followed me into the house. "I'm so embarrassed," she whispered once we were out of earshot of the others.

I wrapped an arm around her shoulders and hugged her. "Don't be. Accidents happen. Besides it gives me the opportunity to have you all to myself for a bit."

She smiled a little then. "But I'm a chlorine mess now."

We climbed the staircase. "That's okay. My old room has a private bathroom. You can get showered while I find something for you to wear in Sheridan's closet."

"Is there any chance she might have a hair tie or something I can put my hair in a ponytail with? It'll be a frizzy mess without all my hair products to calm it down."

"I'll check. I'm sure I can find something somewhere," I replied, stopping to open the door to my room. I gestured for her to enter and stepped in behind her.

She stopped suddenly and glanced around. "This isn't a bedroom—it's a suite." She stared at me with wide eyes. "Half my parent's house could fit in this space."

I chuckled as I tried to look at it through her eyes. I supposed to someone who'd never been here it would seem overwhelming. I stared at the sitting area with black leather furniture, complete with my own television and gaming system, then glanced over the shelves on the gray walls, which held my trophies, awards, and pictures from my years in school. I paused when my gaze fell on my large bed covered in a black-and-red checkered bedspread, and I briefly wondered what it would feel like to see Cami in that bed with her gorgeous red hair spread out over my pillows. Heat streaked through me at the thought. I wanted her there.

I cleared my throat, knowing I needed to clear my head as well. "Um, the bathroom is through this door." I ushered her into the large gray-and-black tiled space. "Help yourself to whatever you need, and I'll go find you some clothes. If you'll leave the door unlocked, I'll leave them here on the counter for you."

She smiled. "Thank you. I'll hurry so you can shower and change too."

I was having a hard time controlling my thoughts. "You know, they say showering together can conserve water," I replied, lifting an eyebrow suggestively. She blushed the deepest shade of red yet, and I couldn't help my chuckle. I was teasing, mostly, but if I were being honest, I'd jump right in if she gave me the okay. I couldn't seem to resist tempting her.

"Uh." She faltered as her gaze traveled over my wet clothes, and I knew without a doubt she wasn't immune to me either. "Are . . . are you serious?"

"Are you seriously considering letting me join you?" I responded with my own question.

She shook her head and smiled. "No. Your

whole family is waiting for us downstairs!"

I sighed. "Then I was *totally* joking—not serious at all."

She laughed. "I see how it is."

"Do you?" I laughed. I knew I was way more daring than she was. She was right, though. I needed to stick with our plans. I'd be able to have her to myself later tonight. "You're right, as usual. I'll be a good boy." I gave her a wink, and she looked a little skeptical.

"Why do I doubt that?" She bit her lip as she took off her wet towels and laid them on the counter, bringing her wet shirt back into view.

My blood roared. "Probably because you do know me." I didn't even attempt to hide my appreciative stare over her clinging, white blouse. "I better go."

She gave a little wave of her fingers, and I had to force myself to shut the door before I was tempted to grab her and kiss her again. I leaned my forehead against it for a moment, taking a deep breath.

The simple thought of spending time with her tonight made me smile. I continued to think about her as I made my way to Sheridan's room. I couldn't believe how quickly Cami had gotten under my skin and into my heart. I'd never been what I considered a romantic—more like a player in my teen years—but she brought all that out in me. It had been such a struggle to stay away from her at the beginning, but it was nothing compared to what I felt now. I wanted to be with her always, and that was a subject I intended to approach her with this evening.

Rummaging through Sheridan's old clothes, I found a sunny-yellow tank top I knew would make Cami's red hair glow beautifully. I chose it and a pair of tan shorts before realizing she wouldn't have any under things. I didn't relish the idea of going through my sister's underwear drawer, but Cami was going to need something. I quickly chose the first pair of panties and bra folded next to each other, hoping they might fit her okay. There was no way I was holding them up to look. Some things a guy shouldn't know about his sister.

Remembering her request for a hair band, I dug through the drawers in Sheridan's bathroom and picked out several before heading back to my room.

I knocked on the bathroom door. "It's me— bringing your stuff in," I called out as I entered.

"Okay, thank you. I'm almost done," she replied over the noise of the shower.

I placed the items on the counter and opened my drawer to get out a comb and hairbrush for her, placing them on the counter. I closed the drawer and glanced into the mirror.

Immediately, I recognized my mistake, but I couldn't look away from the outline of her body behind the frosted glass of the shower door. It hid enough to protect her privacy, but what I could see made my imagination run wild. I closed my eyes and swallowed hard, clenching the edge of the counter. I needed to cool off in a big way. "Hey, I'm going to go shower real quick in Sheridan's bathroom so you don't have to rush. Go ahead and rejoin the others when you're ready. I'll meet you there shortly."

"All right. See you in a few minutes." She was completely oblivious to the effect she was having on me.

I didn't even bother to turn on the hot water, climbing straight into the cold spray. My skin prickled, and I couldn't help letting out a little gasp of surprise followed by a shiver. I braced my hands against the wall and hung my head as the chilly liquid sluiced over me for several minutes.

When I felt sufficiently frozen, and much calmer, I finally turned some of the hot on and quickly finished washing. As I stepped out and dried off, I realized I hadn't bothered to grab any clothes in my rush to get away; I was so intent on putting some distance between us. So, tucking the towel around my waist, I headed back to my room.

I wasn't expecting the sight that greeted me, and I stopped in the doorway. Cami stood with her back to me, studying items on my shelves, looking at pictures of me through the years and trophies I'd won. The clothes I'd picked seemed to fit her nicely from this angle, hugging her curves and showcasing her long, pretty legs. She'd pulled her curly hair into a loose, messy bun of sorts with several wild tendrils escaping to brush the creamy skin of her neck.

She turned and instantly locked eyes with me before allowing her gaze to travel hungrily down my towel-clad form. Instantly, the effects of my cold shower were null and void.

"Sorry," she said, apparently completely

oblivious to the way she was making me feel. "I couldn't resist the opportunity to see pieces of your life from before I knew you."

"No reason to apologize. I'm happy to share them with you." I shut the door behind me. I went to my dresser and grabbed some clothes, and she gave me a smile before she turned back to the shelves. I dressed quickly and went to join her, wrapping my arms around her from behind and resting my chin on her head.

"Where was this picture taken?" she asked, pointing to one of me in my red and white football gear.

"That was after the state championship my senior year."

"Wow! State? That's awesome! I can understand why you're smiling so big. It's a huge accomplishment. I'm assuming your team won?"

"Yep," I pointed to the hat sitting on the shelf beside the picture. "We got these after the game and this too." I picked up a small box and flipped the lid to show her my championship ring inside.

"Holy cow! That's enormous! I didn't know they did that kind of stuff for high school football. Have you ever worn it?"

I laughed. "Heck yeah! I wore it the rest of my senior year clear until I started the police academy. I had to take it off for training, and I never put it back on, but I still love it. We made it to the playoffs all four years, but this was the only time we got to the state game. It was pretty awesome."

"I wish I could've known you then." She leaned her head against my shoulder, and I hugged her tighter.

"How come?" I was curious to know why.

She shrugged. "I think I really would've enjoyed getting to experience all these things with you." She picked up a picture of me in my basketball uniform and ran her fingers gently over it.

"Did you have a girlfriend?"

I snorted. "Several," I answered honestly. "And not one of them can hold a candle to you." I kissed the top of her head.

She turned and wrapped her arms around my neck. "I think you're just trying to butter me up now."

"Always." I grinned. "But it happens to be the truth too. No one has ever made me feel the way you do."

"And what way is that?" We swayed together naturally.

"Like I might come apart at the seams if I don't kiss you right now." I lowered my mouth to hers, kissing her gently at first. Her lips parted, and I eagerly took advantage of what she offered, deepening the contact between us. I loved having her here in my old room. She was the first girl I'd ever had in here, and it was like a fantasy come true.

"Will you do me a favor?" I asked in between kissing her lips and drifting down to her neck.

"What?" she replied in a breathy voice.

"Come lay on my bed with me."

"What about your family?"

"Just for a few minutes. They won't even know the difference." I pulled her in the direction of my bed, and she didn't resist, so I took that as her consent.

She lay down, and I crawled beside her holding my arms open for her to slip into them.

"So what brought this on?" she asked, running her finger over my chest.

"You'll think it's stupid." I kissed the top of her head again.

"No I won't. Tell me," she urged.

"You're the first girl I've had in my room besides Sheridan or my mom. I wanted you in my bed."

She laughed. "Technically we are on your bed, not in it."

"That's something I'd be more than willing to remedy if you want."

She continued to smile at me. "Pace yourself there, killer. It'll give you something to look forward to in the future."

I chuckled and rolled her over, bending to kiss her softly again. "I love you, Cami."

There was a knock on the door. "Dylan?" Chris's voice came through and Cami stiffened.

I didn't want to interrupt this moment with her. "Not now, Chris. We'll be down in a couple of minutes," I said turning my attention back to her.

"I'm sorry to . . . uh . . . disturb you, but it's work. They've been trying to reach you."

"It's my day off. Take a message." I kissed Cami's lips again.

"They said it was an emergency. They want

both of us to come in right now."

I sighed heavily and sat up, kneeling beside her. "I'll be right there," I said, wishing I could stay with her. "I'm sorry about this," I apologized as I got off the bed. I offered her my hand and pulled her after me.

"It's all right. I understand."

I bent to kiss her neck. "Please believe me when I say I'd rather be here with you than anywhere else."

She smiled. "I know, but it sounds like they need you. I'm okay with that."

I wanted to keep kissing her, but I made myself turn around and walk away, going over to where I'd dropped my wet clothes by the door. I quickly fumbled through my pants pockets.

"Here're the keys to my apartment. I want you to take my Camaro. Go there and wait for me after dinner, okay? I still fully intend to finish our celebration together."

She nodded and accepted the keys. "Sounds great, but do I have to stay for dinner? It'll be a little awkward for me without you and Chris here."

"You don't have to do anything you don't want to." I slipped a dry pair of shoes on and went into the bathroom to quickly comb my fingers through my damp hair, trying to straighten it. When I came out, I found her holding our folded wet clothes in her arms. She'd slipped her shoes back on.

"I'll wash these at your place," she explained. "Sorry about your wallet." She handed me the wet leather with my ID and money. "I'll get you a new one."

"Don't worry about it," I said taking it and tucking it into my back pocket. "You ready to go?"

She nodded, and we made our way downstairs, finding Chris and José waiting by the front door. José had apparently anticipated Cami leaving with me, because he held her purse in his hand.

"Please make our excuses to my parents and Sheridan," I asked him as he handed Cami her bag.

"It was very nice meeting all of you," Cami added. "I hope I'll be able to come back soon."

José smiled warmly at her. "I'm sure you will if Dylan has anything to say about it."

I grinned and shuttled her out the door. "Sorry to rush, José. Thanks for everything."

"Be safe!" he called after us.

"I'll see you later," I whispered, giving Cami a quick kiss as I deposited her beside the Camaro. "I love you."

"Love you too. Be careful."

"I'll call you as soon as I know what's going on, so you'll know when to expect me."

"Okay." She watched me climb into Chris's car before she turned to get into the Camaro.

"Sorry about this," Chris said as he started the engine.

"Dude, don't you know better than to answer your phone on your day off?" I grumbled as I slumped down into the seat. I glanced at Cami longingly as we drove past, knowing I wasn't really mad at Chris because I would've done the same thing. "I hope this doesn't take forever."

CHAPTER FOUR
Hunter-

"We need you to go undercover again," my police chief said, folding his arms across his broad chest as he leaned against the window in the interrogation room he'd pulled us into.

I gave a long drawn-out sigh. "When?"

"Right now," he replied seriously.

"No. Not a chance. I'm busy. Get Johnson or somebody to cover it," I said referring to the other young cop my age on the force.

"That's why we need you. This is Johnson's case. He's been working on infiltrating a group of suspects and was supposed to make contact tonight. He's in the hospital with acute appendicitis. We can't mess this up and wait for him to get better. It'll look too suspicious. We have to send someone else in."

I wanted to bang my head against the table thinking about Cami waiting for me at home. "I don't know anything about this case. I'd be walking in blind."

"Another reason why we called you in. We're going to prep you for the next three hours on the particulars and get you ready to go out and meet your new girlfriend."

"Excuse me?" I said leaning forward to rest my arms against the table. "I like the girlfriend I have. She's currently sitting in my house waiting for me to finish the romantic evening we had planned."

Chief Robson had the decency to look apologetic. "I'm sorry to spring this on you, Wilcock, but we need you. You've already been undercover, so you know the drill, and you match the look we're going for. We've been trying to get a lead on this case for a long time, and now we have an insider feeding us information."

Chris interrupted. "He's only now been cleared after being shot. Do you think this is good timing for him?"

"We think it will lend credibility to his story, actually. We can fabricate something about him being involved in a shootout perhaps. It'll make him look like he's already been in with a rough crowd."

I knew the department had been really careful to keep my name and pictures out of the news when things had gone down with Clay in New Mexico. There was no reason for anyone in Arizona to know who I was, and I could see they weren't going to let me out of this.

"What's the case?" I asked with a defeated sigh.

"It's actually a missing person's case; Manny

Perez is the name. He worked for a local garage as a mechanic and tow truck guy. His partner on the job was Jack Rivera, also known as Ripper by his friends and the locals. Jack's sister came forward and asked for help. She believes her brother may have killed Manny. They allegedly had a heated argument at work, and no one has seen him since."

My first reaction was suspicion. "And why would she want to turn in her brother?"

"Manny was her boyfriend. She wants to find his killer."

"And now I'm supposed to be her new boyfriend? Wouldn't that seem a bit callous of her?"

"Manny's been missing for almost a year. There were no leads during the previous search for him, and foul play was suspected because all of his belongings were still at home. He simply disappeared.

"Jack's sister, Roberta Rivera, has recently come forward with information that her brother and Manny organized a car theft conspiracy using the tow trucks from the auto body shop. They haul the stolen cars to an undisclosed location, chop them, and sell them for parts—unless they're high-end vehicles. Those they've been reselling on the black market.

"Johnson's been building a relationship with her. They text regularly and have met a couple times, but he hasn't been introduced to her brother yet. We want you to step in and take over where he left off—try to get in close with Jack, and see if you can gain any information about Manny. This car theft ring he's got going on sounds like a lucrative operation and needs to be brought down too. The charges need to stick, so get all you can on Jack before we bring him in. Plus, it appears he could be the small guy at the bottom of a much bigger car ring. We'd like to see where he could lead us, if anywhere."

"Sounds like a dangerous guy," Chris added.

Chief Robson nodded. "I agree. You're gonna need to watch your back, Wilcock. For the time being, we want you to cut all ties to your current life. No contacting your family, your girlfriend, or anyone who could make Jack suspicious of you. You're going deep under. It'll be safer for your friends and family this way."

I clenched my jaw, not caring for this scenario at all. It was one thing to go undercover, another to completely abandon my life to do it. I didn't say anything.

"Officer Napier, we have plans for you too," he continued, looking at Chris. "We're going to establish you as Dylan's older foster brother who has a drug problem and issues with holding down a job. You'll have a house in the general vicinity—it's not going to be very pretty, I'm warning you. It's far enough away to be out of Ripper's social circle, but close enough for you to go back and forth. As far as your alias, you'll be keeping your first name, but you'll use the last name of Myers."

"Sounds wonderful," Chris said sarcastically.

"Well, it'll be better for you than him," the Chief responded, nodding toward me. "You'll be able to check out often. He won't."

"How long is this supposed to last?" I asked, wishing I could take something for my impending headache.

"As long as it takes. We need to bring this guy down."

"Can I at least go home and tell my girlfriend what's going on?"

He shook his head. "No, we need to finish filling you in on all the particulars. We've got to make new identification, get you set up with the appropriate clothes, and into a new car."

"A new car?"

"Another Camaro actually—one that was seized in a drug raid. We've changed the plates and registered it under a new name, but that's when Johnson was working the case. He was using the name Gage Jackson."

"Has this Roberta chick given that alias out to anyone yet?"

"I don't know. Why?"

"Can you find out? Because if she hasn't, I prefer using Hunter Wilder as my alias. It took me forever to get used to answering to it before. I'm comfortable with that name, and there shouldn't be any issue using it again here in Arizona."

"I'll look into it and see what we can find out before you leave tonight."

"Great." I patted my pockets feeling for my phone before realizing I'd left it charging in the Camaro. "Hey Chris, can I borrow your phone?"

He reached into his pocket and tossed it to me.

"We need you now, Wilder. No time for phone calls. Make it fast." Chief eyed me sternly.

I stared at the phone, hating the need to rush. I quickly decided on a new plan, dialed a different number, and waited for an answer.

"Hey Russ," I spoke when he answered. "I got a favor I need you to do."

I pulled into the parking lot of the club called Racers and got out—being sure to arm the alarm system. I paused to admire the vehicle in the dim lighting of the parking lot—cherry red with a black hood, spoiler, side skirts, and rims. Short, black, double racing stripes ran from the hood to the front tire well. The souped-up engine purred like a kitten and raced like a dream. I'd long been a fan of Camaros, but I was in love with this car already. I glanced around casually as I walked toward the building, knowing I was in the land of car thieves. I truly hoped no one would steal it before I got to enjoy it.

My transformation had been completed at the police station. I'd been given the phone Johnson had been using. My name, Hunter Wilder, had been programmed into it after my contact, Roberta, confirmed she hadn't given the name of Gage to anyone yet. I wore black lace-up work boots, covered by baggie tattered jeans, a belt cinched low on my hips so the top of my underwear showed if I lifted my shirt, as was the current fashion. A white wife-beater tank covered by an open black-and-gray plaid shirt with the short sleeves rolled a little to accentuate my biceps, completed the ensemble.

My left ear still throbbed a bit from the new piercing, and I now sported a small diamond stud. I wasn't too thrilled about that, but apparently, it was a detail Johnson had arranged with Roberta, so I had to comply. I grumbled internally. I sure hope the department appreciated all the crap I had to go through for them.

I flashed my new ID at the big, burly bouncer who stood by the door. He was a scruffy looking tough guy, a combination of muscles and extra weight. I sized him up; figuring he could probably bulldoze me over in a heartbeat. He scrutinized my license carefully before looking back at me. "You new around here?"

I nodded. "Yep. Moved here a few weeks ago," I said, falling back on my fabricated life story, which had been drilled into me for the last several hours.

"Well, keep it clean. We don't want no troublemakers." He handed me the card back.

"Not planning on making any trouble—just looking for a hot woman, that's all." I flashed a knowing grin at him.

He didn't smile. "You'll find plenty of those in there," he said blandly, as if he were completely uninterested. It seemed he took his job very seriously. Good to know. The thumping music grew louder as he opened the door, allowing me to enter.

It took a second for me to quickly scan the layout of the place. The room was large and dark, lit mostly by the neon accents on the walls around the dance floor depicting racecars, checkered flags, and other racing paraphernalia. Tables and u-shaped booths lined three of the walls, and the bar—which ran almost the entire length of the back wall—was a glowing, white surface with neon racing stripes along the side. The place looked pretty packed. Evidently they had a menu too, because there were several waitresses running around in different colors of extremely tight, low-cut jumpsuits, serving food and drinks to people.

I scanned the bar area looking for my contact, Roberta. I'd been told she'd be wearing jeans with a bright-pink top and would have her dark hair pulled back in a ponytail. I spotted her instantly, and was surprised no one had prepared me for how beautiful she was.

She was sitting on a barstool, leaning back with her elbows on the bar as she faced the door. Observing her staring at me with a very pleased, appraising expression on her face—much like I was probably doing to her—I realized Cami would pitch a fit if she saw me with this girl. She wouldn't like it at all, not that I liked it either.

This girl was a player, that much was evident from her trendy heels, super tight jeans, and handkerchief-style shirt—its triangle covering the bare necessities in front. She turned and set her drink on the counter, briefly exposing her bare back with a couple crisscrossing ties before turning toward me. Her giant silver hoop earrings caught the light as she flipped the end of her long, sleek ponytail over her shoulder.

Her figure was smoking, and her face was gorgeous—big dark eyes, straight pretty nose, and full pouty lips. She wore a lot more makeup than Cami, but it was tasteful enough and highlighted her features well.

I smiled as I would if I were seeing someone I already knew, and she returned the gesture, adding a flirty wave of her fingers. I sauntered across the room toward her, feeling sick about the role I knew I had to play. Cami was supposed to be the girl wrapped in my arms tonight. Now I didn't even know when I'd see her again. Hopefully, this case would end quickly.

"Hey, baby. You're looking pretty hot," I said as I sidled up beside her, leaned in, and gave her a kiss on the cheek.

The girl next to her turned and stared at me, her mouth open in awe. "Is this the guy you've been keeping under wraps, Roberta?" she asked, barely blinking as her gaze wandered over me.

"This is him. Hunter Wilder, meet my friend, Cherise." Roberta smiled and slid her arms possessively around my waist, and I slipped mine loosely around her shoulders.

"Nice to meet you," I said with a polite nod in the direction of her cute blonde friend.

"No wonder you've been hiding him! Shoot, I'd never get out of bed if I were dating him! Why are you even here?"

Wow, this girl was forward.

Roberta laughed casually. "You rarely get out

of bed anyway." Even her voice was sexy. I bet she had guys constantly clamoring all over her. I loved the way she'd managed to turn the conversation back around on her friend.

Cherise shrugged and looked at me hungrily. "What can I say? I like sleeping in after work . . . and other things."

"Let's dance," Roberta said, reaching for my hand. She dragged me out to the crowded floor. I shot Cherise a grin and followed dutifully after Roberta. Her heels made her significantly taller, but still she was a couple inches shorter than my shoulder.

When she reached a spot big enough for us, she faced me, stepping so close I could feel the heat from our bodies mingling together. She popped up on her tiptoes and spoke in my ear.

"Nice to meet you. Thanks for your help."

I briefly glanced around to see if anyone was looking at us. I wrapped my arm around her, dragging her the rest of the way against me. "Nice to meet you too. Sorry about the switch-up tonight. Johnson had an emergency."

"So I heard. It all worked out okay, though. I'm sure you'll do fine."

She slipped her arms loosely around my neck, and we began swaying back and forth even though the music was fast, and the heavy beat made the floor vibrate beneath us. We looked like two people who were really into each other, and this made it much easier for us to talk.

"Fill me in on what I need to know—starting with your real age. I have a hard time believing you're twenty one." I leaned back and arched an eyebrow at her.

She gave me a wide innocent stare. "That's what it says on my ID Would you like to see it?"

"I know all about fake IDs and how easy they are to get." I wasn't falling for her routine.

She sighed and gave me a slight grimace and a short laugh. "Yeah, I guess you would, wouldn't you? I'm actually twenty."

I stared at her again, pursing my lips.

"Okay, okay. I'm nineteen, but I'll be twenty in four months, and that's the truth." She watched me closely, waiting for my reaction.

"I believe you. The first thing you need to know is I have to be able to trust you. We both need to have each other's backs in case things get dangerous. I don't want any surprises thrown at me."

She glanced away before nodding. "All right, but the street goes both ways."

"I'll tell you everything I'm able," I replied seriously.

"What does that mean?" she asked, looking a little put out.

"It means that when it comes to information I get from the department, you're on a 'need-to-know' basis. That's all I can promise. I won't compromise the investigation."

She pondered this for a moment before giving me a slight nod.

"Who is this guy, Roberta? Is he bothering you?" A male voice broke in, and a pair of hands shoved of us apart.

"Calm down, Ripper," Roberta said, pushing

him away and cuddling back up next to me. "I told you I was dating someone new and he was meeting me here tonight. He's not bothering me."

Great, I was hoping Roberta would have a chance to fill me in on things better before I came face to face with this guy. I'd have to do my best winging it.

"You looked upset," Ripper said, glaring at me. He was a couple inches shorter than I was and leanly muscled, his dark hair shaved into a very short buzz cut. He wore a folded, gray bandana around his forehead, and a black t-shirt with skulls that ran from his stomach over his shoulder. I didn't pay much attention to his baggy pants or shoes, deciding it was wiser to keep my eyes on him while I judged his aggression level.

"She was mad because I told her she should change her top." I glanced at Roberta appreciatively before turning back. "I mean I love it and all, but I don't really like the way every guy in the place is ogling her."

Ripper's attention was successfully diverted away from me to his sister. "Roberta, what the hell are you wearing? It looks like a damn napkin or something!"

She looked extremely frustrated. "I keep telling you I'm not a little girl anymore. You have no say in what I wear."

Uh-oh. It seemed as if I'd managed to hit on an already touchy subject.

Ripper stepped closer. "It is when you're out flaunting the goods for anyone to see. You want to end up in some alley on your back? You're gonna get labeled a slut by every guy in here."

I wasn't sure if Ripper had any idea about how active his sister might be, but I certainly didn't judge her as an innocent by any standard. She might only be nineteen, but it was obvious, even after a few short minutes, she was used to getting what she wanted when it came to men. I could already tell by the way she handled me.

"Oh blow it out your ear!" she continued. "I'm sick and tired of the overprotective act. Now lay off. We both know you don't give a damn about my reputation."

Ripper made a move to get even more in her face. I needed to diffuse the situation.

"Hey, man. I got this." I shrugged out of my plaid shirt and offered it to Roberta. "Why don't you wear this?"

Roberta glanced back and forth between Ripper and me. I could see the hesitation before she finally sighed. "Fine," she spat, grabbing the shirt out of my hand. She headed toward the large hallway with a sign pointing to the restrooms.

Ripper chuckled as he turned back toward me. "She's saucy, isn't she? You sure you want to date her?"

I grinned. "I like 'em with some fire." I stuck my fist out. "Hunter Wilder."

Ripper stared at it for a moment before he reached out and bumped it. "Ripper Rivera. Thanks for looking out for my sister tonight, man. Sometimes I wonder what the hell she's thinking."

I laughed. "If you figure that out, then clue me in. It might be helpful."

Ripper gave me a half smile. "You're new around here?"

"Yeah, I moved here with my foster brother a couple weeks ago. He supposedly has a lead on a new job. Maybe he'll be able to keep this one too . . . if he can stop snorting everything he earns up his nose."

Ripper chuckled. "You're not a fan of the powder, huh?" he asked.

I shrugged. "I like partying as much as the next guy, but I don't think it needs to happen twenty four/seven like my brother does. I'd be hard-pressed to remember a time he wasn't high. It gets a little old when he keeps crawling to me for money."

"What do you do for a living?"

"I'm a mechanic. I like cars—building, restoring, or doing pretty much anything with them. My boss at my last place let me use his tools and stuff to soup up my Camaro. I'm still looking for a garage or something that's hiring around here. I haven't found one yet."

Ripper looked me over. "You like cars, huh? Come on. You can come hang at our table. I'll introduce you to Seth and Nick. Then maybe you can take us out and show us this car of yours."

I tried not to grin as I followed after him. Hook, line, and sinker—I was in.

CHAPTER FIVE
Cami-

My hair and makeup had been properly fixed and my clothes changed after dropping by my dorm on the way to Hunter's. Call it vanity, but I wanted to look good for him when he arrived. I was looking forward to spending the evening cuddled in his arms.

I'd let myself into his apartment and was surprised by what I found. There were fresh red rose petals scattered through the apartment, from the front door to the small dining table. More petals were scattered around several unlit candles of all shapes and sizes grouped together on the tablecloth. A silver tray held an ice bucket with a bottle of sparkling cider chilling inside, and two crystal wine glasses sitting next to it.

I noticed a folded piece of paper on the table with my name on it. I picked it up, wondering if I should read it now or wait until he got home. My curiosity got the better of me, and I peeked at it, recognizing his handwriting immediately. "Cami, I love you more than you'll ever know. Thanks for being part of my life. Hunter." I smiled as I replaced the note and glanced around, noticing more candles on other surfaces around the living room. There were several movies laying out on the coffee table—all romantic comedies from the looks of it. I laughed to myself. He'd certainly pulled out all the stops. I loved that he'd gone through all this trouble to create a special evening for the two of us. He made me feel things I'd never felt before. Every time I'd glance up and see him staring at me, my stomach would do little flip-flops of excitement. I couldn't believe he'd chosen me.

Remembering the plastic bag I had in my hand, I made my way into the hall and opened the folding closet doors that hid the washer and dryer. I emptied our wet clothes from the pool into the washer and gathered more dirty clothes from his hamper in the bathroom to complete the load. I added the soap and started it, closing the cupboard and wondering what to do next.

The rest of the apartment, which I now knew was decorated in the same tastes of his bedroom at his parent's house, looked pretty clean. I was sure he'd straightened everything up for tonight. Having missed dinner with his family, though, I was hungry, so I went into the small kitchen to search for some food.

There was a delicious-looking strawberry cheesecake in the refrigerator, and I was positive it was a dessert he planned on sharing with me later. He knew strawberries were one of my favorite things. I sighed, biting my lip as I smiled. I loved him.

A short time later, I had a peanut butter and jelly sandwich on a small plate and was curled up on the couch with my e-reader. I browsed through my books, looking for something to read while I waited. I needed to occupy my mind with something besides checking the clock every thirty seconds to see how much time had passed.

About thirty minutes later, I was a few chapters into my novel when I heard a knock at the door. My pulse rate instantly shot up. I briefly wondered who could be here until I spied Hunter's keys lying on the table. I forgot I had them.

I set my e-reader on the coffee table and stood, self-consciously running my hands over myself to smooth my clothes and check for crumbs. I silently cursed myself for not bringing my toothbrush with me. I was sure I had peanut butter breath now. I hurried to my purse and grabbed a mint before going to the door and opening it.

"Hey, Cami. You look nice tonight," Russ drawled as he glanced over me, a knowing grin which revealed the cute dimples in his cheeks, plastered across his face.

"Oh. Hi, Russ," I replied, surprised to see him. I leaned my head out the door, looking for Hunter.

"If you're looking for Romeo, he's not here. Can I come in?"

I faltered, not knowing what he'd think of

seeing all the rose petals scattered everywhere.

"I know about your plans tonight. I helped Hunter set things up, and I was supposed to come light all the candles before you two got here. But then your plans changed."

"Ah," I said, stepping back so he could enter. Hunter had definitely thought this out.

Russ went and plopped himself down on the couch. He stretched before running his fingers through his short brown hair and then locking his hands behind his head. It made his biceps pop out, and I could tell the results of working out with Hunter were already starting to show. He was staring at me now, his blue eyes twinkling mischievously. He was up to something.

I closed the door. "So what brings you over?"

His grin widened. "I'm here to date you."

I choked a little as I searched for words. "Uh . . . excuse me?"

He laughed and patted the space next to him. "Come sit down and relax. I won't bite. I promise to take it easy on you."

I shook my head. "Not until you tell me what you're talking about." I folded my arms and stared at him.

He chuckled again. "Your superhero called me with some bad news. Apparently, he's been detained and will be unable to join you this evening. He asked me to order a pizza and see that you got something to eat since you missed dinner at his parents. He wants me to fill you in on what's going on."

My heart fell in disappointment. "You don't have to order a pizza. I made a sandwich," I replied as I walked over and sat down dejectedly next to him.

"Too late. I already ordered it and some wings before I came over. It should be here any minute."

I nodded absently. "So did Hun . . . Dylan say when he'd be back?"

He shook his head. "No. He doesn't know. Cami, he said to tell you he's really sorry, but he's been called undercover again. They needed him and Chris right away. He doesn't know how long the assignment will last, but due to its dangerous nature, he's been told not to contact any of his friends or family. He said it's for our protection, so no one can trace him back to us."

I suddenly felt the urge to cry. I didn't like the idea of him being placed in that kind of danger. "Do you know where they sent him?"

"He's here in Tucson somewhere, but he didn't say where he was going. He did say, if for some reason we ever do happen to run into him, we need to pretend we don't know him. He said he doubts that will happen, but just in case, he wanted us to know."

"Did he tell you anything else?"

Russ sighed. "Yeah, he said to let you know that his contact is a girl, and he has to pose as her boyfriend. I'm to reassure you he'll only be thinking of you the entire time he's away, though."

I wrung my hands together nervously. I didn't like any of this. "Did he know about this beforehand? It seems awful sudden for them to throw him in the middle of all this without any warning."

"No. I guess another officer was supposed to handle the case, but he had to have emergency surgery or something. They sent Dylan, uh, Hunter in this case, in his place. Apparently, he's still using his same alias."

I stood and paced toward the kitchen, feeling completely helpless. I wished there was something I could do, and I hated not knowing when I'd see him again. How was I supposed to sleep, or even function normally, knowing he was in a dangerous situation? I was still having the occasional nightmare about Hunter being shot. This wasn't going to help.

"Don't worry, Cami. Chris is with him. You know he'll have his back. He's a smart cop, and he's good at what he does. He's been undercover before, so he knows what he's doing."

"That's what scares me. He got shot trying to save my life last time. No one had any clue how dangerous Clay was. Now he's saying, up front, that this situation is worse. It's kind of putting me into panic mode."

Russ got up and came over, placing both hands on my arms and stilling me. "You're gonna have to get use to stuff like this, Cam. It's the nature of his business. He's a cop. He could get shot giving a traffic ticket."

I blew out a frustrated breath. "You aren't helping things."

"I'm only trying to be practical. You love

someone who has a dangerous job. It's a job he loves too. If you can't handle that, you might need to reevaluate your relationship."

"I don't need to reevaluate. He's everything to me. I may not have known who he really was when I fell in love with him, but I still thought he was involved in a dangerous lifestyle. I was willing to accept that to be with him. I didn't like it, but I did it. There's no way I'm backing out now."

"Good girl." Russ smiled and gave me a quick hug. "Hunter wasn't happy about the interruption at all. He's crazy about you, and I know he'll do his best to hurry and get back to you. But until then, you're gonna eat pizza and watch a movie with me. Relax and let me take care of you until he gets back."

I snorted and gave a half smile. "I don't need a babysitter. I'm a big girl."

"I know you are, but I gave my bro my word that I'd watch out for you, and I intend to keep it. I owe him you know."

"You know he doesn't think you owe him anything. He feels your . . . overdose . . . was all his fault. If he hadn't been around, you wouldn't have been accidentally poisoned by a drink meant for him."

"All I know is that it isn't his fault Clay was a screwed up, crazy bastard, and if it hadn't been for Hunter's quick actions, I wouldn't be here now with you talking about it." He let go of my arms and went back to the couch. "I owe him my life."

I went to sit beside him, placing my hand on

his arm. "I'm so sorry about what Clay did to you."

He stared hard at me. "Would you quit apologizing for that freak, Cami? You're not responsible for his behavior."

I sighed. "I feel like I am. He was my friend, and he was obsessed with me. If I hadn't been in the picture none of this would've happened."

"If you hadn't been in the picture, he'd have been fixated on some other girl. Look, I know you two were friends most of your life, but I can't say I'm sorry he died. He's the kind of guy who could've come to school and killed everybody. He was a ticking time bomb. I know you've got to see that now."

"I do." I slouched down onto the couch beside him. "I wish I'd seen that side of him sooner, though. Maybe I could've done something to help him before he got as bad as he did."

"You're too sweet. I know Hunter loves that about you, but it kinda scares me. You trust people too easily." He gave me a pointed look.

"I've never had a reason to not trust anyone until this whole thing with Clay blew up in my face. Honestly, I still think I'm in shock over it all. Sure, it's made me more nervous around people, but I'd like to think most of the world is inherently good."

Russ laughed loudly. "Girl, I can't believe you, and I even grew up in the same town and went to the same school. Your world sounds completely different than mine."

There was a knock at the door, interrupting

us.

"Pizza's here," Russ said, hopping up. He opened the door and paid the delivery guy. "Come get some more to eat." He carried the box into the kitchen. "Should I light the candles still?"

I snorted, knowing he was trying to lighten the mood. "Sure, why not? Might as well have a romantic night with somebody."

He laughed. "So you know—I draw the line at the candles. I may have promised Hunter I'd make sure you were taken care of, but there will be no cuddling or making out."

I opened my mouth to reply, and he raised his hands to halt me. "Stop right there. You should know that no amount of begging is going to get me to change my mind."

I grinned, folding my arms as I gave him a pointed look.

"I see I've made you speechless," he continued as he grabbed some plates from the cupboard. He set them on the counter and glanced at me again. "Don't worry. It happens to most females that meet me. They can't seem to handle all of . . . this." He made a wide sweeping gesture over his body and then paused to flex his arms in different poses.

I burst into laughter and punched him in the shoulder. "You're such a dork!" It was impossible to stay unhappy when Russ was around.

"That's why you love me," he said with smile. He slapped two slices of pizza on a plate and handed it to me with a bow. "May I present your dinner, milady?"

I shook my head as I took the plate. "Thank you."

He grinned. "Happy to come to your rescue, fair maiden. Now eat up. When we're finished, you and I will clean up all these rose petals and watch a movie together. You can pick it."

"Sounds great." I gave a sigh as I turned toward the table, still wishing Hunter would reappear, but I was glad he'd sent Russ in his place. It sounded like he was going to be a big part of my life for the next little while.

CHAPTER SIX
Cami-

I bit my lip for a second, my heart pounding as I scanned down the list on the auditorium door. I paused when I got to my name and let out a tiny squeal. Quickly pulling my phone from my pocket, I tapped out my message to Hunter.

Got the SOLO!!!!! I hit send before the wind was suddenly sucked out of my sails. I had Hunter's phone. Not him. There was no way for me to even get a message to him. This was the second time I'd done this today. I felt stupid. He was going to get his phone back and there was going to be a bunch of outdated messages from me on it. I couldn't help it. He was always the first one I shared things with. It almost felt like he'd died or something—disappearing from my life the way he had. I was having a difficult time adjusting.

Giving a dejected sigh, I turned and started walking toward the parking lot where I'd left the Camaro. I stared at the sidewalk, lost in my own pity party.

"Why so glum, chum?" Russ's voice interrupted my gloomy thoughts. He draped an arm around my shoulders and gave me a squeeze.

I glanced up and gave him a small smile. "Nothing really. I'm just being a baby."

"Missing our boy?" he asked, his voice full of concern.

I nodded and sighed. "I keep trying to text him things before I remember he won't get it. It's weird to have him completely disappear from my life. He was there one second, and then he wasn't. It makes me feel like he's dead. I don't like it."

"You aren't being a baby. You miss him. It's natural. If it makes you feel any better, I started to send him a text today too."

"Really? That does make me feel better. It's nice to know I'm not the only one."

"Yeah, well, I'm sure it's harder for you. It's not like I want his tongue down my throat or him groping me the way you do."

I snorted and shoved him away from me. He laughed and fell back into step beside me.

"Will it help if you tell me whatever you needed to tell him? Unless it's that gushy love stuff you two are always spouting off to each other. I don't need to hear any more of that." He scrunched his face and made a shiver suggesting he was totally grossed out.

"It was some news I had, and we aren't *that* bad!"

He raised his eyebrow in shock. "Excuse me,

but I beg to differ. I practically need a mind wipe after spending any time with you two. It's almost like watching porn or something."

I slapped his arm. "Whatever! We are *so* not like that!"

"Hunter, I love you," he said in a high-pitched voice. "You're my world, Cami," he mimicked in an overly deep tone before he wrapped his arms around himself and started making moaning and kissing sounds.

I couldn't stop the laughter. "We don't ever do that!"

"Note to self: Videotape Cami and Hunter the next time they're together for proof and blackmailing purposes."

I shook my head. "You're such an idiot. You can leave now."

He draped his arm around me. "Sorry, I can't. I've given my word to be your personal idiot until Hunter rematerializes into the land of the living. I'm all yours, Cami—your own personal beck-and-call boy. Now tell me this news. Is it good or bad?"

"Good! I got the big solo I auditioned for! I'll be performing it in our next concert." I could feel the excitement pulsating through me again. I couldn't wait to call my mom and tell her. She'd be thrilled.

Russ snorted. "Please. How is this news? No one can compete with your pipes, girlfriend. Surely you know that by now."

"This is way different than high school, Russ! This is one of the best musical theater universities around! The competition is much greater. There are some really talented performers here. I was competing against twenty other girls for this song."

"Which completely proves my point, don't you agree? You're among the best, and you're still the best."

"You're too sweet," I replied, appreciating his support.

"Not sweet, simply telling it like it is," he answered as we approached the Camaro.

"Do you have any more classes today? I thought maybe we could hang out together tonight—get another pizza or something."

"Sounds great to me. I was actually going to ask if you might be willing to put that giant brain of yours to use and help me out with our math assignment. Some of us mere mortals aren't as intellectually gifted as you are."

I laughed again and rolled my eyes. "I guess I could be persuaded to stoop low enough to mingle with the common minds," I jokingly replied. "After all, you are my self-proclaimed, personal beck-and-call idiot. It's the least I could do."

He swept off his ball cap and made a dramatic bow as if he were greeting royalty. "The common minds thank you, great lady."

I snorted and glanced around the parking lot. "Stand up straight before someone sees you." I couldn't stop laughing. He was such a goof.

He straightened immediately. "As you wish." He winked at me. "See you around six? I'll bring the pizza, you bring the brain."

"Deal," I replied still chuckling. "See you then."

I watched for a moment as he turned and jogged across the lot. He was a great guy. I couldn't imagine it would be too long before some girl snatched him up. Whoever she was, I hoped she would like to laugh.

I unlocked the Camaro and climbed inside, grateful to have a friend like him in my life. Closing my eyes, I breathed in deeply, the faint sent of Hunter's cologne still in the vehicle. I loved the way he smelled, and the scent somehow made me feel closer to him again.

Smiling to myself, I wondered what he'd think if I went and stole his cologne from his apartment and sprayed it on my pillow. It would be a totally girly thing to do, but it would give me something to hug that smelled like him. I missed being next to him.

Sighing, I started the car and headed home—my heart and mind full of aching thoughts as I drove. I parked when I arrived and grabbed all my things before trudging to my room and letting myself inside.

I glanced around the space, seeing little pieces of my life with Hunter scattered everywhere. I'd been so excited to move here so we could spend more time together—he had too. Now we were stuck right back where we'd been over the last couple months—apart. I was happy for the distraction Russ was providing me, and I mentally thanked Hunter for being so considerate about my wellbeing. He hadn't left me alone, but I wondered if he was. I wished I knew how he was faring.

I took out my phone and dialed his number even though his phone was sitting on my desk. It went straight to message.

"Hey, you've reached Dylan. Leave me a message." The phone beeped, signaling it was time to speak.

"Don't laugh when you get this. I miss you, and I wanted to hear your voice. It's been hard not being able to talk to you. I hope you're okay. I love you." I hung up and flipped through my photos, putting a new one as my screen saver. "I hope you'll be back soon," I said to his smiling face.

CHAPTER SEVEN
Hunter-

I tossed my phone and keys onto the nightstand and collapsed onto the bed. My phone buzzed, signaling a text message, but I ignored it. After a week of texting with Roberta, I didn't care if I ever saw another message from her again. To say she was really getting into the part of playing my girlfriend was a bit of an understatement. We'd decided early on to do whatever was needed to maintain appearances. I didn't realize that would consist of her texting me about *everything*—from shoes to her gal pal gossip. I'd learned way more about her in a week than I ever wanted to know in the first place. The girl seriously stuck to me like glue.

I closed my eyes, wishing for the millionth time I could call Cami. I ached to hear her voice again. There was nothing to remind me of her— no pictures, messages, nothing—only the memories in my head. That's what had saved me so far, lying in bed every night and closing my eyes while I let all the things we'd done together replay in my head.

"How's my lovesick baby brother?" Chris's voice asked, and I opened my eyes to find him leaning in the doorway.

I sighed. "Exactly that. Are we done yet?"

He chuckled. "I wish. Your parents and Sheridan send their love. They said to tell you they miss you, and they hope we wrap this thing up soon. I'm guessing you have nothing new to report?"

"Nada," I replied. "Not one damn thing—still hanging out and getting to know the guys. I'm sick of going to that blasted club."

Chris nodded. "I get it, but when in Rome . . . ," he let his sentence drift off.

"I'd rather *be* in Rome. It's got to be better than this."

"Hang in there, man. It'll get better, I'm sure."

"I'd be fine if I could check in on Cami once in a while. Hell, at this point I'd settle for sitting in a parking lot and watching her walk by. I just want to *see* her. This no contact thing is killing me."

"I know, but you have to remember it's also protecting her."

"I do. That's the only thing keeping me from breaking the rules." I sighed. "So, anything new from the department?"

He shook his head. "Nope, more of the same—continue on with what you're doing. I guess Randolph was in a fender-bender while he was responding Code 3 to a call. He's okay, but the whole department had to sit in on a mandatory reteach of the defensive driving course. They made us watch all the videos and take a test on it again. So perk up, you got to miss all that!"

I chuckled. "That's something, I guess. Nice of Randolph to put everyone through that."

"Yeah, the guys have been ribbing him pretty hard." He glanced at his watch. "You have any plans tonight?"

"Yep," I replied, drawing out the word and glancing at him with an eye roll.

He laughed. "Let me guess? The club?"

I made a shooting gesture with my fingers. "Pow! Chris gets a bulls eye. How'd you manage to guess?" I let my hand drop lifelessly to the bed.

"Cheer up. It could be worse. Besides, weren't you the one who used to love using your fake ID and hanging out in those places? I clearly recall you telling me about picking up girls there when you were younger."

"That's before I met Cami. There's no reason to go to a club now unless she's there, and in case you haven't noticed, clubbing isn't really her scene."

"So take her with you sometime. You never know, she might like it," he suggested.

I shrugged. "Maybe, but I'm not going to be able to find out for a few years. She won't be twenty-one for a while, and it would probably look bad for me to get her a fake ID since I'm a cop and all."

Chris chuckled and nodded. "Yeah, I can see

how that might be a problem. I guess that's what happens when you choose a teenager to be your girlfriend, though."

"Spare me the age lecture please. I've already given it to myself a billion times, and I come to the same conclusion every time."

"Which is what?" he asked.

"I don't care how old she is, obviously. She's the one. Period. End of discussion."

Chris sighed. "Well, if there's one thing I know for certain about you, it's that you're bullheaded, and when you make up your mind about something, you're not very likely to deviate from that course."

"Are you saying you don't approve of my choice?" I could feel the tension knotting in my shoulders as I prepared to defend myself.

"Not at all. I quite like your choice, honestly. Cami is a beautiful, good girl and way better than any of those other girls you used to amuse yourself with."

I chuckled. "So you're saying she's too good for me?"

He laughed. "No, I'm saying it's about time you started dating someone worthy of you."

I couldn't help but smile. "You're my brother-in-law. You have to say things like that."

"Don't delude yourself. I don't have to say jack to you if I don't want to."

I groaned. "Can you please not use the term Jack around me? I've had about all I can handle of the elusive Mr. Ripper."

"Jack the Ripper . . . ," Chris mulled the words over. "He sure seems full of himself. Do you think he has the instincts to match the pseudonym? Was Manny his first victim, or are there others we don't know about?"

"All good questions I don't have the answers to, I'm afraid. So far, the only thing I can accuse him of is drinking and driving. There hasn't been one word of stealing or selling cars, or chopping parts. All we've done is drink beer and talk about women and building custom cars. I'm really not even sure if he trusts me yet. He keeps staring at me and squinting, like he's trying to see through me or something. It's a bit nerve wracking to be truthful."

"You'll get it. Keep being yourself—people naturally gravitate toward you."

I glanced at the clock and sighed. "Guess I better go get ready. My *girlfriend* likes to show me off to everyone."

"I love that there are guys on the department who'd kill to be in your shoes right now, and you're grumbling about it. Try to enjoy yourself—hang out, have fun."

I gave him a noncommittal grunt and headed for the shower. "I'll try, but it's kind of difficult when the girl rubbing herself all over you, isn't the one you want. I'd happily trade places with you, if you'd like."

He raised his hands in surrender. "That's perfectly okay. You keep your job. I get to see my wife, thank goodness. Besides, I'm way too old for either of your teenage girlfriends."

I chuckled and shook my head. "You're such an ass."

He grinned. "It's a gift."

CHAPTER EIGHT
Cami-

I stared down at the text from an unknown number on my phone.

I can't take it anymore. It's been 3 weeks & I might actually die if I don't get 2 C U. I knew exactly who it was from, and my heart skipped a beat. Was I dreaming of him again? Another text beeped in before I could respond.

I'm going 2 send U an address & I want you 2 meet me there. It's an automotive store. Drive my car & park 2 the side of the building. Lift the hood & sit in the car with the door locked.

Lift the hood? That's a weird request, I thought. I waited for more.

Write down the address & then delete these texts. I'm taking a big risk with this.

The phone buzzed one more time and an address appeared. It was across town and would take me a while to get there. It looked like I was going to miss my class tonight. I'd need to call in.

Got it. I texted back. It'll probably take me 30

minutes 2 get there.

C U soon.

I waited for a few moments in case he sent anything else, but nothing happened. Quickly looking up the address on my computer, I took a moment to memorize the driving instructions. It was freeway most of the way there, and the automotive store was a couple blocks away from the exit. It would be easy to find.

My pulse raced as I grabbed the keys and my purse and headed to the car. I was so excited to see him. It felt like it had been ages, although Russ had dutifully filled in for him, checking on me several times a week and in between classes occasionally. I smiled as I remembered the dinner and movie we'd gone to last weekend. I'd teased him about how having me around all the time was going to seriously cramp his style with other girls.

"What other girls?" he'd replied with a laugh, brushing off my comment.

Living in a single dorm room, I hadn't really had the opportunity to become well acquainted with any of the girls at school since I was always at class, studying, or doing my work-study hours in the library. What free time I had, had been spent with Hunter before this, and now Russ. I was happy to have someone to fill the time with.

The freeway was busy with the evening rush hour traffic. Coming from a small town, I always forgot to take that kind of stuff into account, and I tapped my fingers against the wheel, hoping it wouldn't slow me down too much.

In the end, it wasn't too bad—only about 15 minutes later than I said. Parking, I glanced around the lot and realized Hunter wasn't here. At least, I wasn't sure if he was, since I'd forgotten to ask him what he was driving.

Getting out, I went to the front of the vehicle, released the hood, and glanced around the parking lot one more time. There was no sign of him, so I got back into the car. It was slightly nerve wracking sitting here alone. From the looks of all the graffiti on the buildings, this was a much rougher neighborhood than I was used to. Suddenly I recalled Hunter telling me to lock the doors. I quickly pushed the button, feeling safer when the loud click sounded.

I checked the phone, to see if I'd missed any texts while I was outside, but there was nothing. I couldn't help watching the parking lot behind me through the mirror, trying to catch his arrival. It was pretty dark when a flashy red-and-black Camaro pulled up beside me. There he was in the driver's seat, and I felt my pulse rate jump into high-speed.

I quickly climbed out of the car, not even bothering to close the door behind me, running over. Hunter got out to meet me, pushing me back in front of the vehicle where the hood was raised. He glanced around quickly, before hugging me tightly.

"Man, I've missed you so much," he said, burying his face into my hair. "I'm sorry to drag you all the way out here, but I couldn't take it any longer."

"I miss you too. How much longer do we

have to do this?" I wrapped my arms around his waist squeezing him tightly, not wanting to let go. It felt so good to be back in his arms.

"I don't know—I wish I could tell you, but I won't be able to stay here long." He released me and stepped away with a longing look in his eyes, before he ducked his head under the hood and started looking at the engine. "Stand over here with me and pretend you're watching."

I did as he asked, wondering what was going on.

"Just in case I was followed here, we need to make this look believable. Do you have your phone on you?"

"I do," I replied, pulling it out of my pocket.

"Great. I need you to send me a text asking for help with your car."

"Give me your number again then, I deleted it with your texts."

He rattled it off to me, and I quickly added it to my phone contacts.

"Russ said you're going by Hunter Wilder again, is that correct?"

He reached out and jiggled a hose while he studied it. "That's right. It should be easy for you to remember, don't you think?" He glanced over at me and winked casually brushing his hand over mine as he set it down and linked our little fingers together.

"Yeah, that might be true, but it'll also make it harder for me later." I smiled at him.

"I can see how that might happen, but whatever you do, don't start calling me anything else now." He gave a short laugh and glanced back down at the engine before straightening. "Come into the store with me."

"What are we going to do?"

"We're going to get something to clean your jumper cables. You're going to be one of those helpless women whose car isn't running right, to find out it was only dirty cables."

"Ah, so I'm a stupid damsel in distress."

"Yeah something like that." He laughed. "Sorry."

He opened the door for me and we walked into the store toward one of the aisles. I followed and watched while he appeared to study and look at different items. It was so nice to see him in person again. I drank in the sight of him, afraid to blink for fear he'd disappear before my eyes.

"So what's been going on with you? Can you tell me anything?"

"No, not really. This is a dangerous group of people. I don't want you getting involved with them."

"You can't drop things like that in my lap, Hunter, and expect me to be okay with it. Do you know how many sleepless nights I've spent worrying about you, wondering if you were okay, or if you were shot in an alley somewhere? I need a bit more to go on, something that'll help put my mind at ease." I crossed my arms as I looked at him intently.

He gave a short chuckle. "Are you always this demanding?"

"Only when it comes to you and your safety. I take that very seriously, and after what happened with Clay, I want to make sure there isn't a repeat performance."

Hunter glanced around again before grasping my hand and squeezing it slightly. He pulled me around the end of the aisle toward the back of the store, gathered me into his arms, and held me tightly. It felt so good to be there again.

"Cami, I'm so sorry to put you in this situation. You know if I could change it, I would. In fact, I begged not to be sent on this assignment. There was no one else to go. All you need to know is that I'm doing okay. No one has attempted to harm me, and I don't plan on giving them any reason to. Chris is involved in this case as well and watching out for me. I know it's still risky, but I'm doing my best to stay safe. I promise."

I hugged him tighter, never wanting to let him go again. "I just miss you. I want you back to myself."

He gently kissed the top of my head. "I want that too, Goody. More than you could possibly know."

He held me for a few seconds longer before he released me and stepped away, continuing to look over items in the aisle before selecting one. I followed him to the register where he paid for it, and then we went back outside to the car.

Removing the item from the package, he revealed a round, steel brush of sorts. He proceeded to clean the jumper cables, which didn't appear to be dirty at all, in my opinion.

"What are you doing?" I asked.

"Keeping up appearances while we talk." He

continued on with his task.

"Isn't there somewhere we can go to be alone together—away from prying eyes that might be watching?"

"As much as I would love that, I don't think it's safe. I'd be too tempted to spend all evening with you, and it would raise questions to my whereabouts." He glanced around. "This location is too far away now as it is, but I didn't want you anywhere close to these guys."

"Where do they think you are?"

"I'm supposed to be meeting my girlfriend at a club across town right now." He studied me, clearly waiting for my reaction.

I couldn't help my sly smile. "Well, you *are* meeting your girlfriend."

He chuckled. "You know what I mean, Cami. My other girlfriend."

"I'm not sure how I feel about you having another girlfriend," I teased. "I'm not really big on two timing."

"Trust me, there is no actual two timing going on."

"So, you're saying you got stuck with an ugly girl?" I couldn't help letting a small giggle escape.

He gave a noncommittal grunt. "Hardly."

His reply caught me off guard, and I opened my mouth to question him some more, but a car playing very loud music pulled next to us.

"Damn," Hunter said, as he glanced at it. "Whatever you do, follow my lead. He's probably been watching us this whole time."

I knew we were in serious trouble by the

way he was acting. This was obviously one of the people he was worried about. A tall Latino guy—near Hunter's height, maybe a couple inches shorter—climbed out of the fancy sports car.

"Hey there, my man," he called out in a friendly enough tone, but I noticed he narrowed his eyes, his dark gaze scrutinizing both of us. "What're you doing way out here?" He walked up beside Hunter and clapped him on the back, squeezing his shoulder. "And who is this sexy little number you have with ya? You know my sister is the jealous type, right? You aren't cheating on her already, I hope." He laughed, revealing a set of perfect white teeth that lit up his face, but there was still a rough edge to his demeanor. He pounded Hunter against the back again. "If you are, I may have to break your legs."

Hunter laughed too and shook his head, but I certainly didn't see what the joke was. If this guy was serious, then he was a freak.

"Dude, you know I'd never cheat on Roberta. That girl is a hot mess, and I can't get my fill of her."

Hunter didn't look at me at all, and I tried not to feel hurt by his remarks. I knew he was playing a role, but it was still hard to hear him talk about someone else like that. The new arrival checked me out as he sauntered over to my side, and it didn't escape my notice that Hunter hadn't made any effort to introduce us. It was obvious he didn't want this guy anywhere around me.

I took in his appearance as well, albeit it was more discreet than how he was observing me. He was good looking and he knew it, short black hair cropped close to his head, dark eyes, perfect skin, and sporting casual, but nice clothing. There was something about him, though, that felt off to me—like he was putting on a show. He lifted his hand and twirled a bit of my hair around one of his fingers. I saw Hunter's knuckles turn white beside me as he continued to grip the edge of the car.

""What are you doing here?" Hunter asked casually. "I thought you were meeting Seth and Nick."

"Just out for a drive," the newcomer replied noncommittally. "What's your name, sugar?" he asked with a wink and a grin.

"I'm Cami." I didn't know what else to say. Hunter hadn't had time to coach me at all. I was totally tongue-tied, feeling a little paralyzed by fear. I was clearly out of my element.

"Well hi, Cami. I'm Ripper." He held out his hand, and when I accepted it, he raised it to his lips, placing a light kiss on the back. He didn't release me either, and I resisted the urge to yank it away and wipe it against my clothing. "How exactly do you know our Hunter over there?"

"Man, lay off her dude. She's my sister, all right?" Hunter jumped in, saving me from trying to invent a feasible reply. "There's no need to give her the third degree. She was having some car trouble and called me for help."

"Sister, really?" He glanced back and forth between us. His gaze narrowed as I gave him a faltering smile, wondering what the heck had possessed Hunter to say such a thing. There was no way we could pretend to have any kind of family resemblance. "What seems to be the problem? Cars happen to be one of my specialties." He looked away, leaning in to stare at the engine.

"No problem, just some dirty jumper cables. She wasn't getting a good connection. I cleaned them and she's set to go." Hunter sounded slightly irritated.

Ripper chuckled. "That's women for you—not very mechanically minded."

I didn't appreciate his condescending tone. "Well, I'm glad that's all it was. I can't really afford a bunch of repairs right now. Thank you, Hunter." I could see the tenseness in his eyes. "I better be getting along now."

"No problem. Happy I could help. Here, you can keep this too in case you need it again sometime." He placed the brush in my hand and turned to close the hood of the car.

"Where you running off to so fast?" Ripper asked, trailing me to the driver's door and quickly reaching around to open it for me.

I didn't know what to say, so I went with the truth. "Um, I'm late for a class."

"Oh, you're a student." He glanced over me again. "Yeah, I can see that. You look like the student type—all put together and ready to learn." He paused as he glanced between Hunter and me again. "What you don't look like, is

Hunter's sister. I was under the impression he didn't have any close family around here, other than his brother."

I froze, my mind searching for something, anything I could say that would diffuse the situation.

"She's my foster sister," Hunter said with a scowl from the sidewalk. "And she recently moved here for school. What is with you tonight, Ripper? Why the twenty questions?"

Ripper faced Hunter. "Chill out, will ya? I wanna know more about her. She's a pretty girl. You don't need to get all protective." He looked back at me with a sly grin. "I only wanna play with her a bit."

"She's too young for you," Hunter replied in a matter-of-fact tone. "Get the thought out of your mind, and let it go."

I was starting to get worried that Hunter might bash Ripper's head into the car. He seemed really angry.

"How old are you, baby?" Ripper asked, his appreciative gaze roaming over me once more.

I tried to laugh, but it came out as more of a strangled gurgle. "I'm only eighteen."

"That's perfect," Ripper responded, turning to Hunter. "She's legal, so quit sweating it."

"You're twenty-four, man. That's six years difference. It's practically robbing the cradle."

Ripper shrugged. "What can I say? I like them young." He grinned and winked at me again, and I resisted the urge to shiver from that creepy remark. "Cami, why don't you skip class and join Hunter and me for a bite to eat?

My treat."

"I really can't," I said, inching my way closer to the car so I could get inside. "I wasn't planning on this delay, and I'm already really late. Thank you anyway," I tacked on, trying to sound polite.

"Where's your class at?" he asked.

"U of A," I answered automatically without thinking that perhaps I should've shielded my answer.

"Shoot, by the time you drive all the way back over there, you'll have missed most, if not all, of your class. You're going to be marked absent anyway. Let me take you two to dinner."

I glanced over at Hunter, sending him a pleading look for help, unsure what to do. He gave a sigh and hung his head for a moment.

"Let him feed you or he's gonna bug me about it all night. But don't let him try to seduce you. He's a total player."

"Aw, come on. I'm not that bad once you get to know me. Leave your car here. You can ride with me, and I'll drop you off later."

"Like hell," Hunter said with a menacing growl. "There's no way I'm letting you alone in a car with my sister. Cami, you get in with me."

Ripper laughed as he got into his vehicle. "Touchy, touchy. Meet me at the diner. Shall we race?"

Hunter waved him off, and Ripper grinned as he threw his car in reverse and gassed it out of the parking lot, clearly showing off.

I slid into the passenger seat of the red Camaro, and Hunter got in on the driver's side.

He locked eyes with me. "Goody, you and I just fell into some seriously hot water."

CHAPTER NINE
Hunter-

"What are we going to do now?" Cami said looking at me with concern as I started the car.

"Give me your phone."

She fumbled for it in her pocket, and handed it over. I quickly punched in the number for my police chief. He answered on the second ring, and I filled him in on what had happened.

"Wilcock, you better be glad I'm not with you right now. I'd be tempted to strangle you. What part of "no contact" did you not understand? Hang on."

He was angry with me. *I* was angry with me. Wisely, I kept my mouth shut, knowing he wasn't truly looking for an answer. His voice was muffled for a few seconds as he spoke in an angry tone to someone else. Sighing, I waited.

"You're going to need to put her in your plan," he said when he returned. "I'll notify Chris, and we'll set Cami up as a younger foster sister of you both. That should be easy enough to pull off. We'll say she was placed with the family as a baby."

"No freaking way!" I practically yelled into the phone. "I don't want her getting involved in this at all!"

"Well, you should've thought of that before you met her! Don't place this on the department, Wilcock. You brought this on yourself, so now you need to fix your mess." He sounded extremely annoyed, and I couldn't blame him. He'd told me not to contact my family or friends; that we needed to keep them safe. I'd broken the rules, determined I could get away with it. Now I was going to pay the price by dragging the person I loved the most right into the middle of everything.

"Well, then let's send her somewhere else. There has to be some place safer for her."

"Hunter! I have school. I can't leave. I'll lose my scholarships!" Cami looked desperate. I knew this was upsetting her, but I didn't want her anywhere near the situation.

"I think you should leave her where she is," Chief Robson said. "She's living on campus, isn't she? That should be far enough away from what you're doing. Try to keep her out of things from now on. No more contact after this!"

"You don't understand, Chief. He likes her, and I think he wants to get to know her better. I can't allow that to happen."

"I can't make her disappear now," he replied with exasperation. "That would definitely look suspicious. We have limited time to deal with this. You're both going to have to make the best of this situation. I'll get to work right away making sure your story checks out with Chris. Until then, you're both on your own. My hands are tied."

I growled in disgust and ended the call, handing the phone back to Cami.

"What did he say?" She looked scared, and I hated knowing I was responsible for putting that look there.

"He says we're on our own. I made this mess, and they'll do their best to help, but we'll have to keep the pretenses going and work things out. I screwed up everything." I sighed, mentally kicking myself. "As of now you're officially my foster sister." I beat my hand against the steering wheel of the car. "Dammit!"

"Hunter, I'm so sorry. I shouldn't have come. I knew I should've said no when you texted. But I missed you so badly." She was wringing her hands together like she did when she was nervous.

"Don't you even try to take the blame! This is my fault. I knew better than to ask you to meet me, but I couldn't take it any longer."

I stared at her, my heart breaking, unable to stay away anymore. I grabbed her, pulling her against me, and kissed her, roughly sinking my fingers into her hair as I held her head next to mine. I felt like I was drowning in the sensation, like it'd been years since I held her like this. I couldn't get enough.

She melted against me briefly and then resisted, sliding her hand against my chest—and pushed me away. I looked at her in surprise, unable to believe it.

"Hunter, I'd give anything to stay here and keep doing this with you right now, but he's waiting for us. We've got to be careful. We can't do anything to make him suspicious."

I knew she was right. I snarled and turned back, put the car in reverse, and peeled out of the parking space. I didn't speak as we turned onto the road and headed toward the diner, a place Ripper and his friends Seth and Nick frequented often. I'd spent a lot of time there lately with them and Roberta.

"I need to know some of the details of our foster home," Cami said as I drove. "Ripper is going to question me, and I want to be able to answer him appropriately without blowing your cover."

Dragging a hand through my hair, I blew out a deep breath, trying to calm myself. I needed to get in control and think like an officer. She was right, and we only had a few minutes to get our story down.

"Chris is supposed to be my older foster brother. He'll be your older brother now too obviously. They're going to say you were placed with the family as a baby. It'll explain why you have a different last name than either of us. His family raised me from the time I was placed in foster care at the age of ten. They weren't the best family in the system, but there was love and respect. His parents wanted to adopt, but due to legal issues and lack of sufficient money, they were unable to.

"Chris left home and got involved in the drug

scene. He became a crack head. Even though he was the blood child of our foster parents, the family disowned him. But I couldn't forget the relationship we had growing up—he'd been the big brother who looked out for me, so I decided to start looking out for him. We moved in together and have been floating around the country as he goes from job to job. I've been working as a mechanic in the different towns we've lived in. I used those jobs to customize the car I'm driving now."

"Do you even know anything about cars?" Cami looked worried.

"Fortunately, yes. Auto shop was one of the classes I took every year in high school. My teacher happened to love rebuilding old cars, so my education works perfectly for this situation."

"I find it hard to believe a rich kid like you would have been interested in taking automotive classes."

I laughed and glanced over at her. "Are you calling me a snob?"

"Maybe." She grinned. "But not intentionally. It just seems funny to me. Most kids take classes they think will further their job career in the future. I can't picture you wanting to be a mechanic."

I shrugged. "I don't know that I ever thought I would be, but I do like working with cars. Besides, rebuilding them would be an amazing hobby for me. My dad has always loved cars too. I remember he built one of those kit cars once when I was a kid. I loved going for rides in it. I might have to get into that someday." I paused, thinking about how I'd enjoy this possibility. "My parents may have money, but they're self-made and doing what they love," I continued. "They believe in the value of hard work. They may have spoiled us with things, but they taught us a healthy respect for a good work ethic."

"So I'm guessing that's why they didn't have a problem with your sister marrying a police officer and you following in the same career yourself?"

I nodded. "I am sure that's part of it—but remember, I told you I was a wild child. I think they were happy to see me correct that and gravitate to a more stable future."

Cami snickered wryly. "You call this stable?"

I gave a slight roll of my eyes. "Yeah . . . I see what you mean. This probably wasn't exactly what they had in mind."

"What else do I need to know about what's going on?"

"We don't have much time, but here's the deal. This is a missing person's case. The department believes Ripper or some of his friends might be involved. His sister, Roberta, is my contact. She's helping to feed us information on Ripper and giving me a reasonable cover to approach them. That's why I'm posing as her boyfriend. Ripper and his gang are believed to be stealing cars too, and reselling them on the black market. I'm to gather all the information I can about how they run their operation and who they sell to, while trying to find any information on Manny, who is still missing."

I turned into the parking lot of the restaurant.

"Why would this Roberta go against her brother?"

"Manny was her boyfriend, and Ripper's business partner. He and Ripper had a fight one night, and no one has seen Manny since. Roberta thinks Ripper may have killed him."

A stricken look crossed her face. "That's scary. How long ago did this happen?"

I parked the car and turned off the engine before staring at her. Finally, there was the fear I wanted to see in her eyes. She needed to realize how dangerous this was. "It's been almost a year. Do you see why I don't want you here?"

"I do, but you're stuck with me now." She grabbed my hand, gripping tightly. "I'll be careful, but I'm not leaving you alone."

I grasped her hand even tighter. "Cami, I can't live without you. This is going to be hard. I'm hoping after tonight you won't have to be involved. But if you are, you're going to need to remember—you're my sister, not my girlfriend. You're going to have to change the way you act around me."

"I understand. I want to help if I can."

"If you really mean that, then do your best to disappear." I wasn't trying to be mean, I just wanted her as far from the situation as possible. I quickly released her hand when I noticed Ripper moving toward the car. "It's show time, Goody."

Cami gave a quick nod, and reached for her

purse. "I'm ready, let's do it." She plastered a happy smile on her face, opened the door, and got out.

I quickly joined them on the sidewalk, trying to take my own advice and appear at ease when Ripper casually draped his arm around Cami's shoulders. I couldn't blow this now. The friendship was still new and fragile between Ripper and me, and I needed to prove I could be trusted. I hoped I'd given Cami enough details for her to fake her way along tonight. I needed to be on my guard and pay attention to everything that was said.

The hostess seated us at Ripper's preferred booth in the corner. She handed us the menus and left to fill our waters. I tried not to drum my fingers against the table, which would be a sure sign of nerves—not that Ripper was paying any attention to me. He seemed fully mesmerized by Cami and intent on playing a game of "getting-to-know-you" as he tried to learn all he could about her. His first question, of course, was, "Do you have a boyfriend?" I wanted to punch him in the face.

Cami handled everything like a pro—too well, actually. She was answering everything appropriately, blushing in all the right places, being perfectly charming, and I knew Ripper was going to fall for her. How could he not?

"Why didn't you tell me you have a sister like Cami?" Ripper gave me an accusatory glare. "I would've had you invite her over long before now."

"That's precisely the reason I didn't tell you,"

I replied, sending a glare right back at him. "I know you're a player, and I didn't want you playing with her." I tossed my menu on the table, wondering where in the heck the waitress went as I looked around for her. I needed someone to help interrupt this love fest.

"Don't be telling her stuff like that about me," Ripper said with a laugh. "I'm trying to make a good impression here."

I wasn't going to make it easy on him. "Cami needs to concentrate on school right now. She has enough on her plate without complicating it with a guy."

Ripper turned toward Cami, giving her an appreciative glance as he ran his hand suggestively over her forearm. "I bet a smart chick like you can multitask, can't you?"

I tried not to groan out loud as I picked up the butter knife beside me, casually handling it as I briefly contemplated stabbing it through Ripper's eye. I hoped I could get through the rest of this meal without committing a murder of my own, but right now, it wasn't looking too promising.

CHAPTER TEN
Hunter-

My life was a mess. Could things be any worse than they were right at this moment? I was currently sprawled out in a recliner in my fake house. Roberta sat on my lap, nuzzling my neck, and I attempted to appear into what she was doing while resisting the urge to drag Ripper off the couch, away from Cami, and beat him to a pulp.

Cami was having a hard time keeping her eyes from wandering over the display of affection Roberta was putting on, but Ripper was doing his damnedest to divert her attention with small strokes and touches while he talked to her. I thought my head was going to explode. Where in the hell was Chris?

As if on cue, the door burst open and Chris stumbled in. While I was relieved to see him, I had to work hard not to laugh at his appearance. Gone was the well-dressed police officer I was used to, and a red nosed, sniffing, drunk guy stood in his place.

"You're home late," I said, staring at him with disgust.

He gave a loopy, lopsided grin and banged the door shut behind him. "I ssstopped sssomewhere for a bit of. . . refreshment after work."

"I can see that," I replied, gently pushing Roberta off my lap. She settled back into the chair behind me. I folded my arms, facing Chris with a determined expression. "Don't you think it's a bit early in the week to be doing this? You've got to work tomorrow, and you barely started this job. I don't think you should be blowing it already. You're running out of references, man, and I still haven't found any steady work. We can't afford to live off my savings forever."

Chris waved his hand at me in dismissal. "I don't wanna talk 'bout thiss right now." He stumbled across the room, pausing to stare toward the couch with a grin. "'S that my pretty baby sisster? What . . . no hug for your big bro, Cami? You haven't even been to sssee me sssince you moved here. Or have Mom and Dad brainwashed ya againsst me too?"

Cami stood and smiled as she walked toward him. "I'm always happy to see you, Chris."

He grabbed her in a big bear hug, and she wrinkled her nose in distaste, pushing away from him.

"Ugh, you've been drinking . . . a lot."

Chris frowned as he released her. "I'snot as bad as it ssseems. I ssspilled ssome on my shirt." He went over and dropped down on the couch, right next to Ripper, leaving the only seat for Cami on the other side of him. I loved how quickly he'd read the situation. I wanted to hug him too.

I made a big show of sighing loudly, turning to Roberta. "Be back in a minute, baby. I need to go get some coffee for Chris."

What a nightmare. I needed to get Cami out of here, but I wasn't sure how to safely execute her departure. Ripper seemed really into her, and I didn't want him to follow her home.

"Mmmm, coffee," Chris said, staggering into the kitchen after me. "What's the plan?" he whispered as he banged some of the kitchen cupboards looking for a mug.

"We need to get her out of here, but I'm afraid he'll follow her."

"I think you're right. Don't worry. I'll take care of it."

"How?" I glanced at him before pouring the coffee into the mug.

He winked. "Trust me. You'll like my plan."

I took the cup and grabbed him by the elbow so I could shuttle him into the other room.

"Come on, bro. Let's get you set back down and pour some of this coffee into you—see if we can't sober you up again."

"'Mnot drunk," he replied, slurring his words.

Ripper had slid closer to Cami again, and I almost laughed when Chris nearly sat on his lap as he wedged himself back in between them. Ripper looked slightly put out as he scooted away to give him more room. He glared at me.

I gave an apologetic shrug. "Sorry, man. He's a little out of it."

"You think?" he said with an eye roll. "He needs a shower too. He reeks."

"I can hear you," Chris said, giving him a swaying look. "'M sssittin' right here."

"Chris," I said, pretending to try and get his attention, but he kept leering at Ripper. "Myers!" I shouted, using his last name alias, and his head snapped to me. "Listen to me. I need you to drink this coffee." I carefully placed the mug in his hands, and he shakily lifted it to his mouth. "Be careful. It's hot."

I glanced between Roberta and Ripper. "Hey, I hate to cut the night short, but I'm gonna need to get this guy cleaned up and safely to bed so he can make it to work in the morning. I'll get with you two tomorrow, okay?"

Ripper looked relieved. "No worries." He glanced at Cami. "Come on, Cami. I'll give you a ride back to your car and make sure you get home okay."

"No!" Chris said, waving his coffee and sloshing some over the rim onto Ripper's leg.

Ripper winced and jumped from the sofa. "Damn, dude. Watch what you're doing!" He glared at Chris. "You burned me!"

"Want my baby sisss to ssstay here. I haven't ssseen her in agesss." Chris glanced at Cami with an adoring look in his eyes. His lip quivered like he was going to cry.

I gave an exasperated sigh. "You feel like staying here and helping me out with him tonight? It'll be like old times."

She gave a sad smile and patted Chris on the leg. "I'd hoped you were doing better by now."

He smiled. "'Mbetter now tha' you're here."

"Why don't you spend the night since it's so late. I'll take you to get your car in the morning. You can have my room and I'll sleep on the couch."

She stared at Chris for a moment. "I guess I can do that."

I turned to Roberta. "I'll see you tomorrow after you get off work, okay? Maybe we can go out for dinner or something."

She gave a sigh, and climbed out of the chair. "Fine. Don't keep me waiting."

I glanced over her slowly before looking at her face with a grin. "Never."

"Hey, man. Call me tomorrow when you get a chance," Ripper spoke as I opened the door. "I may have a lead on a job for you."

I clapped him on the shoulder as he walked past. "Will do. Thanks for looking out for me. Have a good night."

Roberta paused and wrapped her arms around my neck, dragging my face down to hers and kissing me full on the lips. I released the door and wrapped my arms around her, picking her off the ground as I kissed her back heartily. It was killing me to do this in front of Cami.

"Have a good night," she said when we broke apart, trailing her finger down my chest.

"See ya," I replied with a smile. I watched them walk out and get into their cars and waved as they drove away. I shut the door and dragged my hand across my mouth as I tried to wipe off Roberta's lip-gloss.

"I thought they'd never leave," Chris said, setting his coffee on one of the end tables and standing. He started unbuttoning his shirt. "Good to see you, Cami. Welcome to the madness. Now if you two will excuse me, I need to go take a shower so I can stand myself again. Then we'll talk and try to figure out this mess the two of you have got us into." He gave as both a stern look.

Neither of us replied, and he finally shook his head and hurried out of the room.

I stared at Cami, who suddenly seemed awfully quiet.

"I'm sorry." I didn't know what else to say to her. I'd made a mess out of everything.

She gave me a half smile. "That was hard to watch. I know you aren't actually cheating, but it still feels like I'm being stabbed in the gut."

My heart twisted in my chest. I sat down and wrapped my arms around her. "Goody, I'm so sorry. I know that doesn't help, but please know I love you and only you. I'll do anything required to protect you—even kiss another girl. It has to look believable. I've wanted to tear Ripper apart all night. I couldn't stand seeing his hands on you."

She gave a soft laugh against my neck. "I know. I can read you better than the others. I could tell you were wound tighter than a kite."

"You could?" I asked with a chuckle and she nodded against me.

"Hunter?"

"Yeah?"

"Don't let go of me. I've missed being in your arms."

"I've missed you too." I hugged her tighter for several moments before I stood and pulled her up with me. She didn't ask me where we were going, but I was sure she knew.

I didn't flip on the light when we entered my room, instead closing the door behind us and leading her to the bed. I stroked her cheek with my thumb, the dim glow from the window highlighting her sweet features.

She gave a quiet moan and nuzzled into my palm.

"I've missed you so much," I said softly. "Every night I lie in this crappy house and wish you were with me."

"And now I'm here." She smiled.

"Yeah, and now you're here." I trailed my fingers along her arm and over her shoulder, moving until I held her face in both my hands.

She stared at me expectantly, and I bent to place a light kiss against her lips.

"Stay with me tonight. Let me hold you in my arms. I need to feel you against me. I'll safely return you to your life tomorrow and leave you alone until this whole mess is wrapped up. Then I promise to continue right where we left off and give you all the love and romance you really deserve."

"What if I don't want you to leave me alone?" She searched my eyes.

"I can't have you here, Cami."

"Why not? I'm already involved. I think I

played along okay. Maybe I can help you get the information you need quicker."

"You can't stay because I don't do well hiding my emotions for *you*. It wouldn't take long for people to realize I want my 'sister' to be the one in my arms."

"I want to be there too," she replied.

I battled with the warring desires inside me—the one that wanted her with me, and the one that wanted to keep her safe. The longer I stood there, the more muddled my mind became. I only knew one thing for sure—I was going to make the most of these few stolen moments with her.

CHAPTER ELEVEN
Cami-

Hunter gave a loud groan, and I squealed when he suddenly scooped me off my feet. I kicked my shoes off, hearing them hit the floor as he laid me on the bed. It only took a mere second before his body was draped over the top of me, his mouth seeking mine in the darkness.

He kissed me hotly, his tongue invading, as I slid my fingers into his hair, holding his face to mine, returning his affection with everything I had. One of his hands drifted down my body, slipping underneath me as he held me closer, causing goose bumps to rise on my skin. His mouth drifted to my neck, and his warm breath teased near my ear.

"I've missed you so badly," he whispered before sucking and nipping lightly at my neck.

I leaned my head to the side, loving the feel of what he was doing. I understood exactly what he felt. My hands ran up and down his shirt, enjoying the feel of his muscles bunching in his back.

"Can we stay like this forever?" I breathed out and he chuckled.

"I'm positive there's got to be better places to hang out together than some old crack house."

I grinned, staring into his eyes that twinkled in the dim light from the window. "I keep telling you—I don't care where I am, as long as I'm with you."

"I realize that, but you deserve the best of everything, and I want to be the one to give it to you. You shouldn't have to follow me in crazy places like this."

There was a knock at the door. "You two decent? We need to talk about some things."

"Damn Chris to Hell," Hunter muttered with a slight laugh. "Can't anybody leave us alone for five minutes? We'll be out in a minute," he called out louder. "I'm helping Cami get ready for bed." Hunter grinned as I raised an eyebrow at him. "What? It's true. Just not in the sense I allowed him to believe."

We both sighed heavily. Hunter moved from the bed and pulled his shirt off. "Put this on. You can sleep in it."

I was happy to accept it. He always smelled so good. He sat on the bed and started taking his shoes off. I went to the end of the bed and took my blouse off, slipping his shirt on. It fell to my thighs. I quickly slid my jeans off and folded them together with my blouse.

"You're so sexy." It was dark, but I could still see the appreciative stare he gave me and heat crept into my skin. "I like seeing you in my clothes."

"I'm sorry we got interrupted," I replied, stepping closer, so I could run my hands over his bare chest. I loved the way it felt.

"Me too, but Chris is right. We need to get some things settled first."

He kissed me again, his hands running down to my waist, pressing me harder against him before he abruptly stepped away. "Go ahead into the living room. I'll meet you there in a second. I need to grab a couple things."

"Okay, hurry."

He smiled. "Of course."

Chris gave me a curious glance when I entered, but I just smiled sweetly at him and sat down on the couch. Hunter came into the room, holding a pillow and dragging a blanket with him.

"You're really going to sleep on the couch?" Chris asked in surprise as he settled into the recliner.

Hunter nodded. "It would be wise to keep up appearances. You never know when Ripper might come here."

"True," Chris replied.

I couldn't help feeling disappointed. I'd been looking forward to spending the night wrapped in Hunter's arms. Apparently, he'd changed his mind.

He sat beside me, tossing his bedding to the side before draping his arm behind me on the couch. "So what did you need to talk to us about?"

Chris picked up a manila envelope resting on the coffee table. "The chief had a new ID packet made for Cami—driver's license with a new home address, birth certificate matching our story, and registration for your car in her name."

Hunter didn't look too pleased about any of this. "Why did they go to all this trouble? I'm not planning on her being involved after tonight."

Chris shrugged. "Covering all their bases, I guess. Cami, the chief . . . his name is Dan Robson, by the way, he asked me to give you a few pointers."

"Okay, like what?" I asked, taking the envelope from him.

"He wants you to be aware of things in your dorm room—pictures, letters, cards, anything like that—from Hunter that would suggest he's something other than your brother. He'd like you to put those things away, for safety reasons, until Hunter is done handling the case."

"This seems a bit extreme," Hunter grumbled. "He better not ever be in her room."

I patted him on the leg. "No, I think it's a good idea. We can't be too careful. I'll do whatever's needed to help you both keep your cover. Is there anything else I should do?" I'd never done anything remotely covert in my life. Even though Hunter had been undercover before, I'd had no idea what was going on until everything was over. Being a part of this was both a bit scary and exciting.

Chris shook his head. "No. Go about life as usual. The three of us have permission to exchange phone numbers now, since it would be normal for us to have you as a contact, seeing that you're our sister and all."

"Well, that's something at least," Hunter said. "The no contact thing was killing me." He squeezed me to him and placed a kiss on my forehead.

"Still, be aware of what you're texting to each other. Phones are easily read by other people. It probably wouldn't hurt us to have a few decoy texts talking about family matters, in case that were to happen."

"I can do that. We left our phones in the bedroom, though," I replied. "Let me go get them."

"Don't worry about it," Hunter spoke, keeping me hugged close. "I'll program everything in for you later. Is there anything else you need to tell us, Chris?"

"Chief is wondering if you've found out anything new."

Hunter sighed. "So far, everything has been on the up and up. All I know is that Ripper works for Charlie's Garage as a tow truck driver, and he likes to rebuild cars and sell them. I've only seen a couple older cars in the shop at the warehouse he stays in, but I'm thinking that could be a front for something else. The place looks deserted from the outside, and with the windows blacked out, it constantly looks abandoned. No one who happened by would have any idea what's going on inside."

"I checked into the building owners like you suggested," Chris said. "It's actually owned by a great uncle of Ripper's. The man is old and in a nursing home. As far as I can tell, no one else in the family has any interest in the place, so he's not really breaking any laws by living there."

"He lives in a warehouse?" I asked, surprised by this information.

Hunter nodded. "He and Roberta both do. They have quite the setup in there. At least the little bit I've seen of the living quarters and bedrooms."

I shifted uncomfortably at the thought of him in Roberta's bedroom. She might be his contact, but I had the definite feeling she loved her role with Hunter. I didn't harbor any tender feelings toward her.

"All right. I guess just keep your eyes peeled. If we don't get anything else soon we may have to heighten our game a little, push some buttons, so to speak."

"Please be careful—both of you." I glanced between them. "I don't want anything to happen to you. I don't think I could live through that again."

Chris smiled sadly. "I'm sorry for what you went through before. We'll do our best to keep everyone safe this time. We know better what we're up against this go around."

"Let's get you to bed," Hunter said, quickly changing the subject. "You have school tomorrow, and you need your rest. Come on. I'll tuck you in."

"Goodnight, Chris. Thanks for everything," I added, standing to follow Hunter.

"Goodnight." Chris smiled and stood too,

passing us as he headed to his room.

Hunter followed me into his and retrieved both our cell phones. "I'll get these programmed tonight."

I stared for a moment at his bare chest before glancing to his eyes. "You know you can stay in here with me, right? I don't mind. I thought that's what you wanted."

He gave a heavy sigh. "I do, but I don't trust myself to behave. You get me a little excited sometimes, in case you haven't noticed."

"A little?" I teased and he grinned.

"Okay, a lot."

"What if I promise to behave for the both of us? I really miss you—even if you don't touch me. I just want to be in the same room with you."

He bent down, kissed me lightly on the lips, and then headed toward the door.

"Hey, I thought you were going to tuck me in." I felt completely disappointed.

"I am. Wait a second." He disappeared for a couple minutes, and I sat gingerly on the end of the bed while I waited.

He reappeared shortly. "Sorry. I needed to make sure all the doors were locked. And I fixed my bed on the couch, to keep up appearances. Let's go to bed."

I smiled widely. "You're going to stay with me?"

"Yes, and I promise to be good. But I am going to hold you."

I sighed. "I can't think of anything better."

We crawled under the thin blankets,

naturally scooting toward the middle of the bed. He opened his arms, and I slid happily into them. He cradled me close, his breath warm against my hair.

"I love you," he whispered.

I closed my eyes, feeling more relaxed than I had in a long time, and concentrated on soaking in the warmth of him. "I love you, too."

CHAPTER TWELVE
Cami-

I slid the framed photo of Hunter and me embracing into the drawer. Glancing around my room, I felt satisfied I'd removed any mementos that might not support our new supposed relationship. I hated putting those things away—hiding pieces of our time together—but I knew I needed to do as Chris had asked. Safety was the most important thing.

There was a knock on the door, and I was surprised to find Russ on the other side.

"Where were you last night?" he asked, looking worried. "I tried calling you, but I never got an answer."

"Sorry," I apologized. "I didn't always have my phone with me. Last night was a little crazy. Hunter called me to meet him, and things got a bit weird when the guy he's tailing showed up."

"Wow. That's kind of scary. Did it blow his cover?"

I gestured for him to enter and closed the

door behind him. "No, thankfully. But now I'm officially his 'foster sister.'" I made quotation signals in the air. "He's hoping I won't have to be involved anymore, but the police gave me a new identity anyway—just in case."

Russ grinned. "So you're undercover now too? That's so cool. I wanna help."

I laughed. "It's nothing as glamorous as all that. They needed to make me fit into their story is all. Hunter seemed really worried that Ripper was into me, though. He's convinced he's going to start following me around. They had to work at getting me out of there this morning without him seeing. Chris ended up driving me to Hunter's car on his way to work, while Hunter kept Ripper occupied."

"Ripper? That's an interesting name."

"Yeah, it is, I guess. It was actually strange to talk to him. I mean, yes, I could tell he was a total player, and at moments he had this tough edge about him, but he was nice too. He was pretty easy to talk to. It's hard to imagine he could be involved in something bad, or might even be a killer."

"Hmmm, I can see why Hunter doesn't want you around him if that's the case."

"He wasn't thrilled about it."

"I thought he wasn't supposed to contact any of his family and friends while this investigation was ongoing."

I sighed and pulled a chair out from my desk for him. "He wasn't. He broke the rules, and I let him."

He sat down. "And now he's kicking himself

for it, I bet."

"You got that right."

"Well, I guess I'll have to keep a better eye on you then. Gotta make sure you're safe. I don't want Hunter coming after me if I don't protect you like he expects."

"You don't need to babysit me," I said laughing. "I'm a big girl, and I can take care of myself, regardless of what Hunter thinks."

"That may be," Russ replied, leaning back onto his elbows as he stared at me. "But I'm not taking any chances. Hunter would slit my throat if something happened to you."

I rolled my eyes and shook my head. "He loves you too much to do anything like that. Especially after he saved your life once already. He'd never do anything to hurt you—you know that."

He shrugged. "Would you risk his full wrath to find out if that's true?"

I laughed heartily. "Point taken."

"Did you get your math homework done?"

"I did. Are you ready for the big test?" I went to the bed to get my bag and books sitting there.

"No, but then again, I doubt I ever will be. I'll walk with you to class, though—might as well get the torture over with." He gave a hefty sigh of defeat.

I chuckled again. "I'm sure it won't be that bad."

"I beg to differ," he replied. "Not all of us are mathematical geniuses like you. The rest of us humble folk have to be content to wallow in the shadows of people like you, Oh Great One."

I couldn't help my snort. "Whatever! You're so full of crap! You're amazing and you know it!"

He gave me a warm stare. "You know, I wish we would've known each other better in high school. You're a pretty awesome chick. I totally see why Hunter digs you so much." He opened the door, and I followed him out.

"Yeah, it's too bad everyone is so worried about cliques and social status."

"That wasn't why I didn't talk to you."

"Really?" I asked, surprised. "Why then?"

"You were too intimidating."

I laughed. "Excuse me? How?"

"You were this gorgeous, smart girl. What girl like you would pay attention to a guy like me?"

I stared at him, my jaw hanging open. "You're not serious, are you? Have you looked at yourself in the mirror? You're a great looking guy, with a spectacular personality. Any girl would be lucky to have you!"

"And that right there is precisely why I couldn't talk to you. You use words like spectacular. That's intimidating to us hard-to-educate people. Big words are hard to comprehend."

I laughed. "Comprehend is almost as big as spectacular. There's only one letter difference."

He shook his head. "You're only proving my point more. Who knows that kind of stuff? Besides, one letter makes a world of difference!"

"You're sure about that?" I couldn't help laughing when Russ was around. He always brought a smile to my face.

"Positive."

"How do you figure?"

He paused and put his hands on his hips staring me down. "You don't need a reason. It is because I say it is. That's all that matters."

I bit my lip, unable to hide my smile.

"What?" he asked.

"You sounded like my parents."

He hung his head in defeat and gave a sigh. "You've completely deflated my ego."

"Well it's a good thing I happen to enjoy spending time with the ego-less then, isn't it?" I linked my arm through his and started dragging him toward the lobby door. "Come on. We're going to be late for class."

My phone vibrated in my pocket as I stepped out of class into the warm desert air. I checked it, finding a message from Hunter, and opened it while I hurried toward the parking lot, eager to get into the air-conditioned Camaro.

Miss U, Sis.

Miss U 2, Bro, I answered back, happy to hear from him. How R U?

It had been a week since I'd last seen him. He didn't contact me too often, and I never sent texts to him unless he texted first. I was too worried I'd mess things up. Occasionally, he'd call me, usually late at night when he was at his house alone with Chris. He told me he was spending several nights with Roberta now at Ripper's to help keep appearances. They wanted him to think the relationship had progressed to the next level.

I couldn't help the jealousy that flared in my heart, and I'd remained silent, not knowing what to say. He'd read my thoughts correctly and rushed to reassure me that nothing was going on, and I could trust him. That was the problem. I did trust *him*; it was *her* I wasn't too sure about.

Ok. Working. How's school? I remembered he'd told me Ripper had gotten him a job as a tow truck driver with the auto body shop he worked for.

I continued my memorized path to the car while I started texting him back.

"You're a difficult one to find, you know that?"

Simply hearing his voice made me freeze in my tracks. I looked up to find Ripper leaning against the hood of the Camaro, arms folded, and his legs stretched casually out in front of him. He glanced over me appreciatively and gave a low whistle.

"Girl, you look better than I even remembered, and that's saying something. I guess you are worth all the effort I've put into tracking you down."

My voice was stuck behind a knot in my throat as I struggled to think of something to say. I forced a smile to my lips. "Hi, Ripper," I managed to choke out as I glanced around. "Is Hunter here with you?" I sent a silent plea heavenward, hoping he was even though I knew he wasn't. There was no way he'd leave me alone with this guy.

"No. Your brother is working. He's very elusive when it comes to extracting information about you." He chuckled as he stood and walked to me. He was too close—way too close. I had to force myself not to step away and run screaming for help. He lifted a strand of my hair and ran it between his fingers. "I don't think Hunter wants me to date you, but that doesn't matter." He leaned in next to my ear. "I pretty much always get what I want."

I couldn't help the tremble that ran through me at his words, and I wondered if he could see my pulse pounding in my neck. My heart was racing so badly I felt like I might be having a heart attack.

Get a backbone, Cami, I silently spoke to myself. "My brother has no say about who I date, but you might want to talk to *me* about it. I don't go out with just anyone. I'm a little picky." Slipping back into the role I'd played the other night seemed appropriate in this situation, and I hoped I sounded self-confident and sure of myself like I had then. It was a lot harder without Hunter at my side.

"Hmmm . . . is that so?" He kept his face close enough to mine I could feel his breath blowing against my cheek. "I'm always up for a good challenge."

"Cami!" Another voice interrupted us and Ripper stepped back, breaking the closeness between us. I couldn't help release a sigh of relief when I saw Russ jogging toward us. He stopped beside me, giving me a hug before loosely draping his arm around my shoulders.

"How're you doing?" he asked, with a concerned stare.

"I'm good. How are you? I was just getting ready to call you," I lied.

"Who's this?" Ripper interrupted. He glanced between the two of us, eyes narrowing.

I decided my best option was to go with the truth in this case. It was easier than trying to remember everything I'd been told and fabricating a lie on the spot. "I'm sorry. Ripper this is Russ. He's one of Hunter's and my best friends." I hoped to high heaven I wasn't messing anything up. "Russ, this is Ripper Rivera. He and Hunter work together now. Apparently they bonded over their love of cars."

Russ made no move to shake hands with Ripper, instead giving him a nod. "Nice to meet ya, man," he said cordially. "Hunter told me he had a new car buddy. That's cool. I hardly see him these days between all my schooling and work."

I tried not to look shocked. Russ was a cool liar under pressure. Evidently, I was the only one who didn't have this talent.

"I wasn't aware you knew our Cami here too, though," he continued on, keeping his arm draped around me possessively.

"We've only met once," I said. "I was quite surprised to find him here today."

Ripper smiled smugly. "What can I say? You made a good impression the other night. I haven't been able to get you out of my head since." He was making his intentions extremely clear to Russ.

"I've got to say, I'm surprised Hunter told you how to get hold of her. If there's one thing I know about him, it's that he's very overprotective of his little sister. He's run off every guy who ever wanted to date her—at least the ones I know of."

I gave an exaggerated eye roll. "Hunter is a bit of a control freak—I'll give you that. He's always been there for me when I needed him, though." I paused, narrowing my eyes at him suspiciously. "But you said he didn't tell you how to find me—so how did you?"

Ripper grinned, showing off his perfect smile. He really was a good-looking guy. I was sure many girls had fallen prey to his charms.

"I'm great at sniffing people out," was all he offered.

"Meaning what exactly?" Russ asked, clearly unsatisfied with that response.

"Meaning, I drove around campus several times until I found her car. I was unsuccessful the first couple of tries, but today was my lucky day. Once I found it, I just sat here and waited for her."

Russ turned and glanced over my shoulder, giving a cough into his fist. "Stalker much?" he whispered before turning back to Ripper. "How long have you been sitting out here?"

Ripper glanced at an expensive looking watch on his wrist. "Oh, about an hour and a half."

Russ raised his eyebrows. "Wow. You're determined."

"Very," Ripper replied. "So how about it,

Cami?"

I was confused. "How about what?"

"How about a date? I'd like to take you to dinner. Maybe we could go clubbing or something. I'd love to dance up-close to that sweet, sexy body of yours." He certainly had no qualms about laying it on thick right off the bat.

I heard a disgusted snort escape Russ. "Cami's not old enough to go clubbing. They won't let her in."

Ripper waved him off. "That's not an issue. I'm a friend of the bouncer at the club I want to go to. He'll let her in if she's with me."

"What club is that?" Russ asked.

"Racer's. What's it to you? Are you like her self-appointed watch dog or something?" He glared at Russ, his fists clenched, and I could tell he was starting to get angry.

"Cami's like a sister to me. I promised Hunter I'd keep an eye on her when he wasn't around."

I flipped his arm off my shoulder. "It's a job he takes way too seriously if you ask me," I said, unwilling to let Russ become Ripper's new target. "I'd be happy to go out with you. When?"

Ripper's focus was immediately directed back to me, like I wanted. "Right now is good if you're okay with it."

Dang. I hadn't planned on that response. I was hoping to accept and then figure out a reason to cancel later. I gave a quick laugh. "I can't go out to a club looking like this." I gestured to the conservative outfit I'd worn to class.

"No worries. I don't mind following you back to your place and letting you get ready. Besides, I brought you a present."

"You did?" I asked, wondering what he could possibly be talking about.

"Yeah." He winked at me. "Hang on. I'll go get it out of my car. Be right back." He turned and jogged into the parking lot. I could see his vehicle several spaces down.

"Cami, you can't go out with him. Hunter will take off all our heads," Russ said quickly.

"Well, then give me a plausible reason to deny him. I don't want to go with him, but I can't do anything that'll risk Hunter's cover, or put you in danger either."

Russ rubbed his hand over his head. "Man, this is so bad."

I looked down at the phone still in my hand and quickly pulled up Russ in my contacts. "Here—I'm texting you Hunter's number. As soon as we leave, call him and tell him what's happened. He can decide what's best. It's all I know to do right now." I sent the message and tucked my phone back in my pocket. Ripper was on his way back carrying a white, flat box in his hands.

"I don't like this at all, Cami. Hunter is going to explode."

"You're right. He will, but there's nothing we can do about it now."

Ripper joined us and handed me the package with a smile. "Open it."

I shifted my backpack off my shoulder and handed it to Russ. Accepting the gift, I moved next to the Camaro, setting it down on the hood. "I can't believe you brought me a present." I carefully slid the lid off, revealing carefully folded tissue paper.

"Like I said earlier, you made an impression."

I opened the paper and carefully lifted out the dress inside—if one could actually call such a small amount of material a dress. The tank dress scooped low in the front and even lower in the back. Made of black form-fitting spandex-type material, it was embellished with vertical stripes of gold sequins. I'd never owned anything even remotely this revealing in my life. My bath towel covered more than this dress.

"It's lovely," I choked out, my voice sounding way too high-pitched. I glanced over at Russ whose eyes were bugging out of his head. "What do you think, Russ?"

He swallowed hard. "I think Hunter will spank your butt if you step one foot in public wearing that."

Ripper laughed. "She'll look great. He should be proud he has such a pretty sister. Besides, he's dating my sister, so I say all is fair."

"Better bring a blanket to wrap up in," Russ said dryly. "You might catch your death exposing all that skin."

Ripper glared at him. "It's still summer weather."

Russ shrugged, not backing down. "Naked is naked."

"She's not going to be naked."

Russ folded his arms across his chest. "All

I'm saying, is *someone* is about to catch their death—one way or another."

An image of Hunter beating Ripper to a pulp crossed my mind. Russ was right. This was going to get bad quickly. I carefully folded the dress back into the box. "Thank you so much for this. Like I said, I'll need some time to get ready."

"I don't mind waiting. I'll follow you back to your place."

"Me too," Russ blurted out and Ripper turned to stare at him. "I, uh, forgot my notebook last night after we studied together."

I felt relieved to know I wouldn't be there alone with Ripper. "All right. Let's get going then. Russ, you can ride with me."

Ripper opened the car door for me, giving a wink as I slid past. "I can't wait to see you in that dress," he said in a low voice.

I smiled weakly, massive nerves flitting about in my stomach. He closed the door behind me, and I started the engine.

"This is *so* not good," Russ muttered.

I backed the car from the space. "Call Hunter—now."

CHAPTER THIRTEEN
Hunter-

I entered the club with Roberta hanging on my arm. She was excited and had been filling my head with nonstop chatter about dancing, but I only wanted to see Cami and make sure she stayed safe. I was so desperate to get here after Russ called, I thought I might die before my work shift was over. I quickly searched the room, initially skimming past the leggy redhead standing at the bar sipping a drink beside Ripper. My brain suddenly registered what I'd seen, and my head felt like it was going to explode as two emotions slammed into me simultaneously.

Lust and rage.

I'd never seen Cami dressed so provocatively before, and instantly I knew Ripper had bought her the dress. Her gorgeous curly hair was pulled away from her face and neck, piled loosely on her head. She wore big gold hoop earrings, and her makeup was done heavier than normal. The slinky outfit clung to her perfect body like a second skin. Dipping low enough in the front to show off the top of her cleavage, it scooped so low in the back it bordered being indecent, causing my temperature to raise even more. The hemline fell just past her tiny round butt, and I couldn't help wondering what she was wearing underneath it. If she bent over, or if the dress rode up even an inch, I'd have my answer. Her creamy legs were bare down to the fashionable black heels she wore. They were the most conservative things she had on, and I recognized them as something she'd worn previously.

My first thought was to storm across the room, throw her over my shoulder, and drag her out of here—case be damned.

I took a deep breath, knowing I needed to calm myself, but then Ripper *touched* her. His hand drifted across the bare skin of her back, skimming the lower part her dress before coming to rest on her bare thigh. He traced a finger against her leg, and she shifted away slightly. Everything in my vision went red. The blaring rhythm of the music matched the pounding aggression flooding through my system, and I could only process one thought: I was going to kill him.

Roberta stumbled as I yanked her forward, clamoring to regain her balance and gripping my arm tighter. I didn't slow down—even when I heard her let out a very unladylike curse, but I didn't care about her at the moment. All I could think of was the need to plant my fist squarely in Ripper's face.

"What the hell do you think you're doing?" I shouted, when I reached his side. I shoved his shoulder, and he fell back against the bar before standing to face me.

"Back it off, man," he yelled loudly above the music. His body was tense, ready to strike.

"I told you my sister was off limits! What part of that did you not understand?" I was struggling to keep myself in control, but losing the battle fast.

"Are you saying I'm not good enough for her? The street goes both ways, Hunter. You're dating my sister. That makes yours fair game."

I felt like I was going to grind my teeth into dust, I was clenching them so hard. He had a point, and I didn't know how to respond. I needed to get a grip.

"Did you buy her that dress?" I asked, folding my arms across my chest. Cami stood stock still, unspeaking, eyes darting back and forth between us, and I could tell she was scared by my reaction.

Ripper grinned and glanced at Cami, letting his gaze travel hotly over her. "I did. Doesn't she look fabulous?"

She looked incredible, but I wasn't about to admit it. Thankfully, Roberta stepped forward, picking her own fight.

"You made me cover up when I wore something this revealing to the club! You're always telling me to dress different—unless it suits *your* purpose!" She shoved her finger accusingly into his chest. "Then you go and buy something like this? Isn't that a bit of a double standard?" She wasn't faking. She was really angry.

"You're *my* sister," he replied with a shrug as if that explained everything.

"Yeah, well, she's *mine*," I replied, grabbing Cami by the arm. "Now if you don't mind, my sister and I need to have a private conversation." I pulled her away from the bar, but Ripper reached out and stopped me.

"Don't be upset with her, dude. I bought it for her. She was only trying to please me." He glanced between Cami and me.

"I'll be fine," Cami finally spoke up. "Let Hunter talk to me. If he doesn't let it out now, he'll be ranting about it all night. I'd rather get it over with."

Ripper slowly released me and sat back down, giving a slight nod. Roberta slipped up to the bar, and I heard her calling for a bartender as I led Cami away toward the hall that led to the restrooms. I was still fuming.

I threw open the door to the ladies room. "Everybody out!" I shouted at the women who were reapplying makeup at the counters. I must have sounded angry enough because no one even questioned me. They quickly grabbed their things and rushed out the door. I checked to make sure the few stalls were empty before I flipped the lock and turned to face Cami.

She was glowing, her eyes bright, clearly happy to see me, and the anger towards Ripper drained away when she smiled.

My eyes traveled over her and my hands naturally reached out to follow them, tracing her wickedly defined curves. "You look—"

"Like a tramp?" she asked with a laugh, blushing.

I shook my head. "No. You look rather amazing actually. It's kind of killing me. I can't hardly even see straight, let alone think coherently." My hands slid past the hem of her dress. "I'm dying to know what you're wearing underneath this thing."

She grinned; stepping forward to close what little space was between us and wrapped her arms around my neck. I noticed she had a small purse dangling from a strap on her wrist. I'd missed that before.

"I bet you are." She grinned and bit her plump bottom lip, not volunteering any more information. It didn't matter—I still groaned. I was strung tighter than a kite, and seeing her dressed like this had kicked my imagination well into overdrive.

I took a deep breath, attempting to think coherently. "Ripper's not going to leave you alone."

"I kind of figured that out. What should I do now?"

"If he wants to date you, then we need to try and stay together. Visit him at places and times where you know I'll be. He's dangerous, Cami. And he's not buying you gifts for his own health. He wants to peel you out of this dress as badly as I do. I have no idea how you'll be able to keep fending him off."

"I'll tell him the truth—that I'm a virgin, and I'm not ready to take that step. Maybe he'll lose interest then."

I shook my head. "I doubt it. He'll most likely see it as a challenge and try to wear down your defenses. And if he touches you, I won't be responsible for my actions."

"You're going to have to let him touch me, Hunter, at least in some capacity. Otherwise he'll be suspicious of why you're so overprotective of me."

I growled in frustration. "I can't do this! I'm ready to throw this whole dang case right now. It's not worth it. I just want to come home and be with the girl I love."

"Have you found out anything else?" she asked, lifting a hand to my cheek and stroking it softly. "I mean do you have anything on him?"

I nodded, nuzzling against her palm. I missed her caresses. "I've got him for grand theft auto. I helped him steal a car the other night. He has a whole garage hidden away in that massive warehouse of his. Some stuff they chop and sell for parts, but a lot are left intact and resold, mostly the more expensive models. They drive those to Las Vegas and sell them for cash on the black market. He has quite the setup going."

"Who is 'they'?"

"He has a couple of buddies that help him out, Seth and Nick. I'm sure you'll meet them soon enough. They're almost always with him."

"I hope not," she responded, pulling my head down toward hers. "I might fall apart if you don't kiss me right now."

There was no way I was going to deny her request. I held her tightly as my lips descended, kissing her swift and hard. Her body relaxed, softening against me, and I could feel every part of her beautiful shape. It felt like the warmth of her was burning into my skin, branding me with her very essence, and I loved it.

I broke away long enough to pick her up and set her on the counter, bending to kiss the space right behind her ear. "This dress and those heels make your legs look like they're miles long," I muttered against her neck.

"You like that?" she whispered running her hands along my back.

"Too much, I'm afraid." My breathing was increasing rapidly, right along with hers.

"Don't be afraid, I'll protect you."

I laughed in spite of everything, letting my hands continue to run around her body. "But who's going to protect you, Goody?"

"I don't need protection from you." Her hands traveled to my chest.

I snorted. "I beg to differ."

There was a loud banging on the door, and we instantly broke apart from each other.

"Cami? You okay?" Ripper's voice came through the door.

"I'm fine," Cami replied, her voice sounding agitated. "Just trying to get my boneheaded brother to see things my way."

"It's not going to happen," I replied loudly as I helped Cami slide off the counter.

"Hunter, lay off her why don't ya? She's a

big girl now. You need to loosen up."

Cami quickly opened the tiny bag strapped to her wrist and pulled out her lip-gloss, applying a fresh coat.

"She'll always be my little sister, so back off and let me handle this."

"Cami, let me in," Ripper said.

She gave me a quick glance and gestured to my mouth. I wiped it with my hand, removing some of her shiny lip-gloss that had transferred to me. She nodded and went to the door and opened it.

"Welcome to the lecture hall," she said, moving out of the way so he could step inside.

Ripper glanced between us. "You may want to take this outside or something. There's quite the line forming out there."

"No worries. We're finished," Cami said and she stormed out the door.

"Stay away from her," I warned Ripper. "She's too young for you."

"The age difference between her and me is barely wider than you and Roberta. Chill, okay? I promise I'll take good care of her."

I stepped toward him. "She's not used to guys like you. You're a fast player . . . she's . . . not experienced."

"Geez, Hunter. It's not like I'm gonna rape her or something. That's not my style."

I recognized my opening immediately and took it. "That's exactly my point. She was almost raped, and it was a very traumatic experience for her. She's very nervous about things that have to do with physical contact now."

He went completely quiet. "Shit, man. I had no idea. Did they catch the bastard?" Ripper asked seriously, clearly pondering this new information.

"He got his due punishment." I could feel my anger at Clay resurfacing as the mental images of him on top of her that night flashed through my mind.

"Which was what?"

"He was shot and killed."

Ripper's eyes widened. "By who?"

"By me," I said, lying about that part of the story.

"You killed him?" He was obviously shocked. "How'd you manage to get away with it?"

I shook my head and grabbed my shirt, pulling the neck over until he could plainly see the scar on my chest. "The guy shot me first. It was clearly a case of self-defense. We wrestled for the gun. I was the lucky one who got it in the end."

Ripper shook his head, and I could see the admiration in his eyes. "I had no idea, bro. That's crazy."

"Now you know—I'll do *anything* to protect Cami. *Anything*. I won't let anyone hurt her again."

He held up his hands in a surrendering gesture. "Dude, I get it. I won't harm her. She can control the ride."

Relief coursed through me, and I hoped he was sincere. If he was, then I'd successfully bought Cami some time and given her a plausible excuse for why she wouldn't get too close to him.

"I'm trusting you, man. Don't break it. My family means everything to me."

He nodded and clapped me on the shoulder. "I'll be careful with her."

I left the room, not bothering to see if he was following. There were several curious stares from the line of women waiting outside, but I didn't care what they were thinking. I was happy that, for the time being at least, things would be a little safer for Cami.

CHAPTER FOURTEEN
Hunter-

This one was going to be a piece of cake. I had the truck to myself this time, Ripper trusting me to go out on my own this go around. I did as he'd taught, driving through some of the classier parts of town looking for vehicles parked in illegal loading zones. Ripper explained that rich people were lazy. Either they don't care about parking tickets, or they think they're entitled to closer parking. No one would think anything of a tow truck picking up a car parked there.

We'd stolen several that weren't parked illegally too. It appeared the general public turned a blind eye to vehicles being towed. He had quite the racket going on here. Seth and Nick worked for different garages too, so the trucks were rotated. It seemed no one had a clue about what he was doing, either. No one but me, that was.

Now I was in on the action, growing closer to

the guys all the time. They were still pretty tight-lipped about anything to do with Manny, though. That made me a bit suspicious, like they were trying to hide something, which only made me more determined to wheedle it out of them. It was time to finish this and bust these guys. I was beyond tired of watching someone else manhandle my girl, and lately Roberta seemed to be really into kissing me whenever Cami was around. If I didn't know better, I'd think she was jealous of her.

I pulled in front of the bright-yellow Porsche resting halfway in the red fire zone and backed up to it. I dropped the yoke and slid it under the vehicle, clamping before lifting the hydraulic arm and driving away. I hadn't even stepped a foot out of the truck, and I'd stolen the car in less than a minute. It was almost too easy. Someone was going to walk out to the sidewalk and get a big shock when they found their car missing.

I drove back to Ripper's warehouse, being sure to take the streets that would have the least amount of traffic on them. I called him on the phone right before I got there, so they'd know to open the doors. Ripper was waiting, lifting the garage doors on the backside of the building as soon as I flashed my headlights in the prearranged signal. I drove into the lit space, and they closed the door to the well-camouflaged building behind me.

I noticed Cami immediately. She was sitting at an old desk with her schoolbooks spread out on the top, a pen stuck into her hair, busy typing away at the computer. She'd become a fairly permanent figure around here, something I was both happy and upset about. I loved being able to see her, but constantly worried about her safety. Ripper had kept his distance from her like he'd promised—not pushing her to do anything she didn't want to. It didn't stop him from kissing her, though, and I often had to watch the two of them snuggling together. He practically doted on her, always super attentive to anything she needed.

This past week of observing them had left me feeling murderous most of the time. I often had to leave the room when he kissed her, teasing and playing with her until she kissed him back. He was determined to bring her out of her shell, and it drove me insane. I knew she was only acting her role and doing it to protect me, but I suddenly understood how she felt about watching me with Roberta. This lie wasn't easy for either of us to live, and I often caught her staring at me longingly before she'd quickly glance away.

"Looks like you got a beauty," Ripper said approaching the vehicle as I got out, tearing my gaze away from Cami.

"Yeah, another sucker parked in a loading zone. When will people learn?" I shook my head, and Ripper laughed, coming to drape an arm around my neck.

"I knew you'd make a great addition to the team. Congrats on your first solo run."

I chuckled. "Thanks. It was almost anticlimactic, though."

"Why's that?" Ripper questioned.

"I don't know," I said with a shrug. "I guess I always imagined stealing cars as being much more of an undertaking."

"You've been watching too many old TV shows, dude." He laughed again. "We're high-tech around here with all the latest technology."

"Well, I hope the garage owners never catch on to what we're doing with their trucks. We'd be in a lot of hot water."

"Don't worry about it. If they haven't caught on by now, they aren't gonna. We've been at this for quite a while. It's down to a science by this point." He waved his hand. "Follow me. I have some cash for you. We made a bundle off those cars we stole last week. The parts we chopped also brought in more than I'd expected."

"Seth, Nick, and Roberta are back from Vegas?" I asked, as I followed him to the safe by the desk.

"Yeah, they got back about an hour ago. They made some good deals." He stopped to twirl out the combination. "They're in the kitchen now, grabbing something to eat."

"How you doing, Sis?" I asked, casually leaning against the top and crossing my arms.

She smiled and let out a deep sigh. "I'm overwhelmed. I can hardly keep up with all these class assignments. I think maybe I bit off more than I can chew."

I shook my head. "Not possible. Everyone knows you're the brains of the family."

She gave a little snort as she stared back at the computer. "Hardly."

"You know it's true. Is there anything I can help you with?"

"No. Thanks, though. I'll get through it eventually." She continued typing, and it annoyed me that we had to pretend we weren't thrilled to see each other.

Ripper stepped toward me holding a wad of cash. "Here you go. This is your cut."

My eyes widened in surprise. "Wow, that's a lot of money. I didn't think it'd be so much."

He smiled widely. "The guys we deal with are big money with mob connections. Plus, sometimes we throw in an extra incentive. We get some pretty good bonuses off that."

"Incentives?" My attention was immediately perked. Was Ripper dealing in other goods I needed to know about? "Like what?"

He chuckled. "You'll find out soon enough."

"Dude, tell me now if you're into the drug scene. I can't be a part of that. My brother is messed up bad because of that shit." I stared him down seriously.

He kept smiling and shook his head. "There's no drugs, bro. I promise. The incentives we give don't affect you or your part in all this."

"You know, you all could go to school and get an education like normal people." Cami gave us both a disapproving look. "Then you wouldn't have to be tied to this risky business."

Ripper slipped his arms around Cami's shoulders and kissed her cheek. I felt my insides crawl as I forced myself to remain still. "What's the matter, sweetheart?" Ripper teased. "Are you worried we're gonna get hurt?"

Cami locked eyes with me. "Of course I am. No girl wants to hear her brother and . . . the guy she's dating are messing around with the mob. It's too dangerous. There's got to be better ways to make money."

"You won't think so when I give you things like this." He reached into his pocket and pulled out a sparkling diamond tennis bracelet, laying it on the desk in front of her.

Cami sat unmoving for several seconds as she stared at it. It was amazing how little Ripper actually knew about her. She'd never been a girl whose head was turned by shows of wealth. She slowly reached out and traced her finger across the length of it. "Is it real?" Her voice was soft and she didn't look up.

"Yes," Ripper replied, lifting her arm so he could clasp it around her wrist. "Nothing but the best for my girl."

It took all my willpower not to protest his possessive words.

"I can't accept this," Cami said, finally looking up at him.

"Why not?" Ripper seemed confused.

"Because it's too much, too soon. What does a college girl like me need diamonds for?"

"You're over thinking this, Cami. Just accept it as a token of my affection for you."

I almost snorted. There was no doubt in my mind he was trying to bribe his way to better things. He expected something in return, and I knew exactly what that something was.

She glanced briefly from him to me, and I gave her a nearly imperceptible nod to go ahead, hating that she had to accept it to keep our cover. She looked at Ripper and gave him a tight smile. "Okay, thank you. This was very generous of you."

He bent and kissed her forehead. "Like I said, nothing's too good for my girl." She stood and he hugged her.

She responded loosely. "I've got to run to the restroom real quick," she said apologetically. "Too much soda." She gestured to the forty-four ounce drink on the table and left.

We both watched her walk out of the bay.

"Damn that chick is fine," he said appreciatively. "You weren't kidding about her being nervous. I sure wish I could get her to loosen up a little more."

"Still my sister, dude," I said, pocketing the money he'd given me. "Thanks for this," I added hoping it would distract him from further comments about Cami.

"No problem. I think I'll sell this car you got tonight as-is." He walked around it, surveying it closely. I'm going to move it into the shop next door, get these plates off it, and start taping it for a new paint color."

"Sounds good. I'll be over to help you in a bit. I'm going to find Roberta real quick and let her know I'm here. Here's the keys."

I tossed them to him as I headed across the room. The tow truck engine roared to life behind me, and I hit the button to open the garage door. I waited for him to clear it and then shut it again, making sure to press a button that would open the far bay door for him also.

He'd be busy for a while now, and I was determined to have a moment alone with Cami.

CHAPTER FIFTEEN
Cami-

I opened the door into the bay and felt a hand roughly close around my upper arm. I gasped as Hunter shoved me up against the wall, pinning me there with his body as his lips descended to mine. His mouth assaulted, laced with possessiveness and desperation as his tongue invaded, sweeping inside with delicious abandon. My knees shook, and I fisted his shirt in my hands, trying to pull him closer as I drowned in the sensations he was creating inside me.

This is dangerous! My brain shouted, reminding that Ripper could walk through the door any second and catch us. The thought quickly left as one of Hunter hands tangled in my hair, and the other drifted down my body. A soft moan escaped from me, and he growled in return, pressing harder.

"I can't take this anymore," he whispered harshly against my lips. "Seeing you in his arms—watching him touch you. It's driving me insane. I want to rip him apart." He claimed my mouth again, denying me any chance to reply, but I didn't care. I didn't want him to stop—I wanted him to continue his ravishing. My blood pounded in my ears, rushing with both fear and desire as I continued to clutch at him, desperate to keep this connection. Heat streaked through my veins and threatened to melt every part of me . . . I couldn't get enough.

"Cami, where are you?" Ripper's voice floated in from the hall, interrupting the moment, and Hunter released me abruptly, stepping away, his breathing rapid as he stared hotly.

"You are *mine*," he whispered, glancing once over me before he swallowed thickly, then fled the room through the far door that led outside.

My legs felt like gelatin as I quickly stumbled back to the desk and sat down at the computer, trying to slow my breaths.

"There you are," Ripper said, peeking inside with a puzzled look. "Didn't you hear me calling for you?"

I shook my head. "No, sorry. I think I'm coming down with a migraine or something. I don't feel very well." It wasn't really a lie. All of this pretending was starting to get to me.

Ripper's eyes narrowed for a moment, and he studied me as he walked over.

I felt my heart rate click a notch higher. Were my lips swollen? Could he tell I'd been kissing Hunter?

"You do look a bit flushed. Why don't you go

lie down in my room?" He said it casually enough, but there was no way I was going to cross that boundary. I needed to keep as much distance as possible between us. I felt sick every time he touched me.

"Actually, I think I may go home, if that's okay with you. I'll take some medicine and go to bed. I have a lot of homework due tomorrow, so I'll need to get up early and finish it."

Ripper rubbed a hand against my face. "Whatever you need, baby. It's okay with me. I'll probably be working on this car for a while anyway. Call me in the morning, okay?"

"I will," I promised, standing and grabbing my purse off the desk. Ripper turned my face toward his and placed a kiss against my lips. It was all I could do to not start weeping. I didn't want to kiss him. I only wanted Hunter. I hated all this faking, but it had to be done. I'd do anything required to keep Hunter safe.

Quickly, I gathered my books, and Ripper walked me outside. I couldn't help glancing to the bay next door where Hunter was bent over the dash of the new car. It looked like he was replacing the VIN plate. Ripper scavenged salvage yards to get bogus numbers off other vehicles that might match new models they brought in. He really had thought of everything, and I hated knowing as much as I did about this illegal business. Even though the police were involved, it still made me feel guilty and dirty, as if I were doing something I shouldn't be.

"Taking off already, Cami?" Hunter asked, looking at me casually as if nothing had happened between us.

"Yeah, I have a headache and a ton of homework," I hoped my voice wasn't shaking.

"Feel better," he replied before turning his attention back to the vehicle.

"Thanks," I mumbled as I continue to my car, wishing I could tell him goodbye properly. Ripper opened the door for me, and I slid inside, fumbling to get the keys into the ignition.

"Call me if you need anything."

"Okay, thanks." I started the car, and he shut the door so I could drive away. I made it through the alley and out to the stop sign on the street before my phone buzzed. I checked it, seeing a text from Hunter.

I love U.

I texted him right back. I love U 2. Then I started to cry.

The old theater felt the same—pretty but sad, as if it were unable to get past its own nightmarish history. I drug my hand across the yellowed wallpaper as I walked down the red-carpeted aisle toward the stage. I paused to stare at it before gingerly walking up the steps.

The heavy curtains suddenly parted, and I snapped my head around, wondering who was with me. A spotlight suddenly flooded out from the back wall, blinding me, and I lifted my arm to shield myself from it.

"Who's there?" I called out, my voice shaking. I could see the silhouette of someone sitting in the audience.

"Sing, Cami," a familiar voice said quietly.

Strains of music filled the air, but I couldn't sing. Something wasn't right. I had to get out of here.

I ran down the steps and sprinted up the aisle toward the giant doors, eager to escape the shadowed watcher. I reached the doors, frantically twisting the knob, but it wouldn't budge. Banging my fists against it, I started screaming.

"Help me, please! Someone help me!"

Something heavy hit me, knocking me to the floor, and I felt the breath whoosh out of my lungs. I opened my mouth to scream, but nothing came out, and I felt like I was suffocating.

Clay's face suddenly swam into focus as he pinned me to the ground. "What's the matter, Cami?" he asked, his expression a mask of concern. "Why do you need help?"

"Get off me!" I ordered as I twisted about beneath him.

"Why? What wrong?" he asked again. He dipped his head and began kissing my neck.

"Help me please!" I called out again in a panic, tears leaking from my eyes.

The thick doors burst open and Hunter rushed inside. Relief poured through me as he dragged Clay away, the two of them fighting desperately over Hunter's gun. I jumped at the sound of a shot firing. Clay fell to the ground, a pool of blood spreading beneath him.

"Cami?" Hunter swung around to face me, breathing heavily. "Cami? Are you okay?"

Relief flooded through me as he ran toward me. Suddenly, another shot rang through the air. Hunter stiffened, a surprised look on his face. Two more shots rang out, and he looked down at the blood pouring from his chest.

"I'm sorry, Cami," he said, and the same red fluid started running out his mouth. He fell to his knees, then hit the floor, revealing Ripper holding the smoking gun behind him.

"Hunter!" I screamed and jerked awake with a gasp. My chest was heaving and tears ran down my face.

With a trembling hand, I turned the clock on my nightstand. Three A.M. A disgusted sigh escaped as I flopped back onto my pillow, running a hand across my sweaty forehead. My temples throbbed, and I rubbed them, trying to ease the increasing headache.

"It wasn't real. It's okay. It wasn't real," I spoke aloud, trying to give myself a comforting pep talk. The nightmares were starting to come more frequently again. I wasn't sure what to do about them, but they were definitely tied to Hunter being on this case. I was more than ready for it to be over and done with. While I was happy to see him and spend time where he was, things were getting stressful, to say the least.

I did not like Ripper. Despite his good looks, every time he touched me, my skin crawled. It was getting harder and harder to keep acting interested. I knew exactly how Hunter felt, because I felt the same way about watching him with Roberta. She might be his contact, but she was totally into Hunter, that much was plain. I wondered if he was aware of it too, since it seemed impossible to miss.

I needed something to drink. I got up, put on my slippers, and grabbed my water bottle to fill at the fountain in the hall. Everything was blissfully quiet, though there was some light shining out from under a couple of doors. I wondered if anyone else was plagued with bad dreams too, or if they were simply having late night cramming sessions. I kind of wished I had another girlfriend here, someone I could share my concerns with whenever I needed. I'd been too busy with everything else going on to really make any friends.

I reentered my room and stared at my phone, tempted to call Hunter simply to hear his voice. I wanted to make sure he was okay, but I didn't know if he'd be with Roberta. I picked it up and dialed another number instead.

"Cami? Is everything okay?" Russ's sleepy voice answered.

"I'm fine. Sorry to bother you. I keep having nightmares, and I can't sleep."

"You aren't bothering me. I told you to call me whenever you needed. Talk to me."

"I keep dreaming about bad things happening to Hunter. I know he'll do his best to stay safe, but I still worry. These people are criminals, and he's with them all the time. I can't even go see him at night because he spends most of his time sleeping at Roberta's."

"That's rough, I'm sure," he replied sympathetically, still sounding kind of out of it. "How about I come get you? We'll find an all-night restaurant somewhere and have a milkshake or something."

"That sounds marvelous, but I don't want to drag you out on my account."

"No worries, really. I've been craving a shake for two days. I'll be there in fifteen minutes. Can you be ready?"

"Yeah, I'll meet you outside." I ended the call and glanced down at the t-shirt and shorts I'd fallen asleep in. They were good enough to wear to a diner, so I quickly rubbed the mascara out from under my eyes, ran a brush through my hair, and pulled it back into a ponytail. Grabbing my purse, I popped a breath mint into my mouth before heading to the lobby.

Staring out the glass doors, I waited until Russ pulled up in his new pickup, which had been a graduation present from his parents. He was quite proud of it. I hurried out the door and he leaned to open the passenger side for me.

"Hey, buddy," I said as I jumped inside.

"Hey yourself," he replied with a wink as he put the truck in gear and backed out of the parking space. "Sorry I was a little longer than fifteen minutes. I had to do my hair."

I snickered as I stared at the ball cap he was wearing. "Did you now?"

"No. That's code for I couldn't find my hat."

"Ah, I see. You are like the best friend in the whole universe right now. You know that, don't you?" I smiled widely at him.

"Yeah, that's me. I'm always out rescuing chicks from nightmares in the middle of the night." He laughed and I joined in. "Why didn't you call Hunter?"

I sighed and leaned my head against the back of the seat. "He's been under so much pressure lately I didn't want to worry him anymore. Plus he's all the way across town. I know he'd feel obligated to jump in his car and drive here to check on me. He's been spending the nights with Roberta, too, so I figured it would probably upset her if he went running off to me. I guess I didn't want to rock the boat any more than it already is."

He glanced at me with concern. "It must be tough for you to watch him with her all the time."

"You have no idea. She's stuck on him like glue—at least she is whenever I'm around. It drives me nuts."

"Does she know you're his real life girlfriend?"

I shook my head. "No. I think Hunter told her I'm someone he works with. He didn't want her to know for some reason."

"That makes sense. I think he wants to keep as much of his personal life to himself as he can. If things went badly, he wouldn't want anyone looking for you to get to him."

"Well, all I know is that it stinks not being able to tell people we're together. I swear I almost gag every time Ripper lays a hand on me. Between fending him off and watching Roberta and Hunter, I'm almost in a constant state of nausea. And that's not counting the mountains of homework I have to do."

"It's no wonder you aren't sleeping well. Your life's a complete mess. I'd be nervous too.

Sounds like this is a perfect time for you to go out and do something normal."

"I agree. Thank you."

"My pleasure," he replied as he pulled into the parking lot of a nearby Denny's. We went inside and a waitress greeted us and led us to a booth. There were a couple other tables with college kids there too.

"What can I get you to drink tonight?" she asked as she handed us menus.

"Actually, we don't need menus. We just want to get some shakes," Russ spoke up.

"Okay, that's fine." She pulled out her order pad. "What would you like?"

Russ gestured for me to go first.

"I'll take a strawberry," I said.

"And I'd like two shakes," he added. "One vanilla, one chocolate."

"No problem," she said with a smile. "I'll get those right out to you."

"Thirsty?" I asked with a grin after she left.

He shrugged and smiled. "Sometimes it's hard to choose."

"I've been a strawberry girl for as long as I can remember."

He shook his head and gave a sly grin. "I like strawberry too. Maybe I should've gotten three shakes."

I laughed. "You're going to be up the rest of the night on a sugar high."

"It's Saturday now. No classes. I can sleep all I want—if my roommate cooperates. Some of us weren't as lucky as others to get into private rooms."

"It's been nice, but lonely sometimes. You're welcome to come sleep in my room while I study if you want. It's the least I can do after you rescued me tonight."

"Thanks, but I think you'll be busy with other plans today."

"What do you mean?" I asked, confused.

"Is this seat taken?" a familiar voice interrupted.

I turned to see Hunter standing there with a grin, and I gave out a squeal of delight as I jumped up to hug him. "What are you doing here?" I asked, before quickly releasing him and glancing around. "Are you alone? Is it safe to hug you?"

He chuckled and pulled me back into his arms. "I'm alone, and please hug me all you want. Russ called me and told me you were having a hard night. I decided to come meet you."

We sat down in the booth, and the waitress came with our shakes.

"The chocolate shake was for you!" I said with a laugh, everything making sense now.

"Yeah, I told Russ to order one for me." He wrapped his arm around my shoulders and squeezed me to him.

"How long can you stay?" I asked, wishing we could get back to our real lives.

"I'm yours for the rest of the day." He leaned over and kissed the top of my head.

"How's that possible? What about the case?"

"Ripper is working at the station today, and Roberta has plans with some of her girlfriends.

I'll shoot them a text later and tell them I'm spending the day with Chris because he's having a bad day or something. It'll all work out. What do you say to taking a day trip out of the area together?"

I knew I was beaming. "I can't think of anything I'd love more!"

CHAPTER SIXTEEN
Cami-

I was home. I stared up the sidewalk toward my parent's house, excited to surprise them this way. Hunter—who insisted Russ come with us—spent most of the drive to Copper City reviewing the aspects of the case before we dropped Russ off at his house.

The police department was getting antsy that nothing new had turned up on Manny and was getting ready to go ahead and charge Ripper and his boys with Grand Theft Auto. Roberta would be granted immunity for her help and testimony against them. I was happy to know things would be ending soon. I wanted to get back to our regular lives.

"You ready to go in," Hunter asked, giving me a wink.

I reached over and grabbed his hand. "Have I told you how amazing you are? Thank you so much for doing this."

"I'd do anything to keep that beautiful smile

plastered to your face like it is right now." He leaned toward me, and I met him halfway, kissing him on the lips. He slid his fingers around to the back of my head and held me there, his tongue dipping deliciously inside my mouth.

I couldn't help the sigh that escaped, and he chuckled.

"You have no idea how good it feels to be able to do this out in the open and not worry about who's watching," I said.

He leaned his forehead against mine. "I have every idea. You've been so close, but so far away. I want this whole thing to be finished too. But let's not worry about that right now. I want you to enjoy some time with your parents."

He hopped out of the car, came around to my side, and helped me out, the same gentleman as always. I loved his impeccable manners. He held my hand as we walked up the sidewalk together. I tried the handle, but it was locked.

"I left my keys at the dorm." I rang the doorbell and giggled. "If they look out the window, they won't recognize the car. They'll have no idea who's here this early."

I heard a squeal from behind the door, and it was flung open. "Cami!" my mom practically shouted, dragging me into her arms. "What a surprise! I'm so happy to see you!" She suddenly held me back at arm's length. "Is everything okay?" A worried look crossed her face as she stared at me.

I laughed. "Everything is fine, Mom.

Hunter . . . uh, Dylan, thought it would be nice to take a day trip and come for a surprise visit."

She grabbed Hunter and hugged him too. "You have no idea how much this means to us, Dylan. We've been missing our girl something fierce."

He grinned and hugged her back. "It's my pleasure, ma'am."

She released him. "None of that ma'am crap now. It makes me feel too old. Call me Cecily. Get in here you two. Let me go get your dad. We'll all have breakfast together. It'll be perfect!"

We went into the living room while she scurried off down the hall.

"I think she's a little excited," Hunter said, still smiling.

I nodded. "She is. So am I! Thank you again for doing this. I needed the break."

He pulled me into his arms. "Anything for the girl I love." He glanced over to the sofa. "I have some pretty fond memories of this place too."

I blushed. "We did have some really hot make out sessions here, didn't we?"

"We did—all stuff I hope to repeat very soon."

"I'm game for that."

He kissed me again, holding me tightly as he tenderly explored my mouth. I wrapped my arms around him, feeling the electricity shoot between us, and I wished I could spend the rest of eternity like this—in his embrace.

A throat cleared behind us. "I see things haven't changed," my dad's voice interrupted and, we broke apart laughing.

"Hi, Daddy!" I launched myself into his arms, giving him a big hug, and he squeezed me back tightly.

"How's my girl?" he asked. "This is the best surprise to wake up to."

I released him. "It was Hunter's idea."

My dad chuckled and turned to him. "Dylan, thank you."

"It's my pleasure, sir," Hunter said, shaking his hand warmly.

"I see Cami still hasn't converted to using your real name. I thought for sure she would've by now."

Hunter smiled and glanced at me with a shrug. "Circumstances have made it a little difficult for her to make the switch."

"What do you mean?" my mom asked as she gestured for us to follow her into the kitchen.

"I'm working undercover and using the same alias again. I thought perhaps she'd told you about it." He glanced at me with a raised eyebrow.

I shook my head. "I didn't know if I was allowed to."

"So you've been all this time with no one to talk to?" He suddenly seemed upset.

"Russ has always been there if I needed anyone," I reminded him.

"Is Cami in danger?" my mom asked with a worried expression.

Hunter sighed heavily. "Unfortunately, yes. I've placed her in an extremely awkward situation. That's partly the reason we're here today. We needed to escape the intensity for a while."

I immediately noticed the alarmed look in my parent's eyes. Memories of what we'd been through with Clay were still too close to the surface.

"It's not all your fault." I rushed to defend him. "I'm as guilty as you are. I knew there was a risk of exposure if I met you. I could've said no, but I didn't." I went to the fridge and pulled out some eggs. "Why don't you and dad sit at the table while Mom and I make breakfast. You can fill them in on things." I looked at my mom. "If that's okay with you."

"Sure," she replied. "I miss being in the kitchen with my girl."

I let Hunter give them all the details while I helped prepare the food, only interjecting my opinion here and there when I felt the need to defend him. I didn't want my parents to be angry.

"Well, I can't say I like the idea of my daughter being in the middle of this, but it does make me feel better to know she has Chris, Russ, and you watching out for her," my dad spoke when Hunter was finished. "I'm glad to hear the department wants to wrap things up soon."

"Me too," Hunter replied. "I'm ready to get back to my normal life. I apologize again for allowing Cami to get dragged into this."

"We trust you, Dylan," my mom interjected. "You've already proven how devoted you are to keeping Cami safe. The bullet hole in your chest tells us all we needed to know about your character."

The room fell silent for several moments at the reference to what happened with Clay.

"Do you see his parents much?" I asked Mom. She knew exactly what I meant.

"I've run into them here and there around town. They're pretty withdrawn from society still. You know how small-town gossip is."

"It's not their fault. I don't want them being ostracized because of something Clay did."

"Personally, I think they blame themselves for not knowing he was . . . sick. They honestly thought the two of you were an item. They didn't see the warning signs, and now their son's dead because of it." She got some plates out of the cupboard and began setting the table while I started carrying the food over.

"Maybe I should go see them today. Do you think it would help?"

Hunter remained silent, but I didn't miss the pursed lips as he glanced out the sliding glass doors toward the pool. He wasn't happy with that suggestion.

"I don't know if it would be a good idea or not," my dad said. "I think they'd be uncomfortable if Dylan came with you, due to his role in the situation. He was here hunting their son."

"You're the victim, Cami," Hunter finally said. "You're not obligated to make anyone feel better. None of this mess was your doing. It's not your fault Clay was living in a make believe world, and it's not your fault his parents didn't notice what was happening with their own kid."

I sighed, wishing I could make him understand. "I realize that, but Clay was my best friend since I was five years old. He wasn't crazy the whole time, and I have lots of good memories of him. Despite how things ended, I still love him, and I miss having him in my life. Yes, it's been hard to forgive him for what he tried to do to me, but his family shouldn't have to suffer for his mistakes. Besides, I love them too. They were like second parents to me for most of my life."

I slid into the seat next to Hunter, dished my food, and started eating. The room was uncomfortably quiet.

"If you want to go see them, you should," Hunter finally said softly. "I just don't want to see you suffer through painful memories again."

I paused, staring at my plate, unable to make eye contact with anyone. "I still think of Clay every day," I confessed. "And I still have nightmares about that night. But I'm as guilty as his parents. I refused to see the changes in him until it was too late. He's dead because of me."

"He's dead because he tried to rape you, and he shot an officer of the law with the intent to kill." Hunter's voice quickly raised, a scowl crossing his face, and I had no doubt he was angry. "You're in no way responsible for his actions. You told him repeatedly he was only a friend to you. *He* refused to listen. *He* made the plan to kidnap you. Don't you try to take the blame for this!"

"Maybe we should talk about something

else," my mom suggested. "Let's not ruin the day arguing about a past that can't be changed. It won't help anyone."

Silence ensued again, and I pushed the eggs around my plate with the fork, suddenly not feeling very hungry.

"Honey," my dad said softly. "Would you be willing to go to some grief counseling? It might help you deal with things better."

"I'm not a head case, Dad," I spouted back.

"I'm not saying you are. I'm merely concerned you're still having nightmares, and you obviously miss Clay even though you're angry with him. Talking to someone might be beneficial. It can help you work through your feelings."

I shrugged. "I don't know. I don't want people to think I'm crazy."

"No one will think that, sweetie," my mom added. "They all know you went through a very traumatic event."

"This current situation hasn't been easy for us either," Hunter added. "Talking about it would probably help."

"Would you go with me?" I asked, looking over at him.

"Of course I would. It would help me too." He placed a hand over mine. "The department has counselors who deal specifically with post-traumatic stress. We can arrange something through them if you'd like. They have access to all the case details, and we could talk freely about things with them."

"I think that sounds like a good idea," my

dad said.

I put my fork down and looked at Hunter. "Can I talk to you privately outside for a moment."

He seemed surprised, but he put his fork down and stood. "Of course."

"Sorry, Mom and Dad. Go ahead and eat. I need to get something off my chest with Hun . . . Dylan." I really needed to put better effort into using his proper name. My brain didn't want to make the adjustment, though.

Hunter followed me out the sliding glass door, shutting it behind him. I walked to the far side of the pool and stood staring at the morning light reflecting off the water. He came up behind me and rubbed his hands against the upper part of my arms.

"What's the matter, Goody?"

It was time to face the music. I needed to tell him the truth, but I was terrified to do it at the same time. I was worried it would destroy everything between us, but I didn't know how I could go on like this anymore.

I trembled as I turned to stare him in the face. "I hate your job," I spoke boldly. "I want to be supportive of you and everything you love, but I honestly don't know how much more I can take." The floodgates were open now—I couldn't stop everything I'd been holding back. "It would be bad enough if you were a regular cop, sending you out to keep the peace, write traffic tickets—or whatever it is regular cops do—but I have to suffer in agony every moment you're undercover. I never know if someone is going to blow your alias, and I'm going to get a phone call saying you've been killed. I've been involved in your last two cases, and it's driving me insane. I have a hard time trusting anyone these days, and I'm constantly looking over my shoulder wondering if someone is trying to sneak up on me. Add trying to stay on top of my class schedule and having some sicko pawing me with his hands and lips all the time, and I'm seriously about to lose it! I mean it. I'm done."

Hunter's eyes were full of concern. "Why didn't you tell me this sooner?"

I gave a hard laugh. "Why? Because I know how much you love being a cop, and I don't want you to feel like you have to choose between your job and me. I don't want to lose you because I'm insecure."

He shook his head and ran a hand against my hair before bringing his palm to my cheek and stroking his thumb across my lips. My eyes watered at the affectionate gesture.

"Cami, baby, there's no choice. I'd always choose you, hands down, every time."

"Really?" I asked, unable to believe he'd quit his job for me.

He lifted his other hand so he was cupping my face. "I love you more than anything else. Don't you get it? I want to be with you forever." He gave a wry chuckle. "I planned on asking you to marry me, but this stupid job got in the way and messed everything up."

"You want to marry me?" I asked, swallowing hard.

He gave a small chuckle. "Is it so hard to

believe? I know you're young. We don't have to rush into anything. We can take all the time you need. I want you to live your life and fulfill your dreams like you want. I simply want to be part of it—if you'll have me."

"Hunter, I want you to be able to live your life and dreams too. I know how much you love being a cop." I didn't want him sacrificing things just to be with me.

"Honestly, I'd be happy flipping burgers if it meant I got to be with you."

I snorted. "Sure you would. I've seen the lifestyle you come from. You're used to having money."

He laughed and dropped his hand from my face to grab both of mine. "You know cops don't make that much, right? It's sad, but true. They're at the bottom of the job chain. Besides, I have plenty of money either way."

"What do you mean?"

"My parents are loaded. My sister and I received our trust funds when we turned twenty-one. It'll continue to pay large lump sums to us every five years until we're like sixty years old or something."

I was shocked. He'd never told me anything about his financial situation before. "Wow. That's nice of them."

"Yes, they wanted to be sure we were taken care of. The only stipulation on mine was that I keep a full-time job unless I'm incapacitated for some reason. My parents didn't want me sitting around being lazy. I've invested some of it, and I have a couple business ventures I've been mulling over in my head. I may be a police officer, but it doesn't mean I don't have other plans in mind for my future."

"Really?" I said again, shocked by everything he was revealing. "Like what?"

"Well, I could use my police skills to be a bounty hunter."

My eyes widened. "Isn't that still dangerous?"

He shrugged. "It could be, but most of the time people aren't expecting a bounty hunter to show up. Things go down relatively peacefully."

I sighed. "Danger appeals to you, doesn't it?"

"Seeing people who break the law brought to justice appeals to me, Cami. I like getting my man, figuratively speaking."

"Hmm. Still seems dangerous."

"I like cars too. How would you feel about being with a greasy mechanic? I'm good at it."

I shook my head. "I don't want you to change your life to suit me. That's not fair."

"What wouldn't be fair is losing you because of a job. I'd be crushed. Don't you remember Sheridan told you I was smitten with you? Well, it's true. I'd do anything to keep you by my side." He squeezed my hands tighter.

"It still doesn't seem fair," I grumbled.

"Then how about a compromise?"

"Like what?"

"I'll keep my job on the force, but as soon as this case is done, I'll ask to be assigned to patrol the school systems or something. I'll tell them I don't want to be involved in undercover work anymore."

"That sounds kind of boring for you."

"Are you kidding? What's better than working with kids? Besides, I really don't want to do the undercover thing anymore. It may have led me to you initially, but it's been pure hell staying away from you this go around. I'll finish this case and tell them I'm through. Deal?"

I studied him closely, noting the light shining in his eyes. He seemed truly sincere in what he was saying. "Deal," I replied, and he let out a breath I hadn't realize he'd been holding.

He pulled me into his embrace. "Don't ever leave me, Cami. You have no idea how much I need you."

CHAPTER SEVENTEEN
Cami-

"Thanks for breakfast, Mom," I said, giving her a hug before I helped to clear the table. "Sorry for all the drama. Things have been a little crazy lately."

"No need to apologize. I understand completely. We just want you both to be happy and safe."

"Well, I'm very happy—regardless of everything that's gone on, and Hunter is doing his best to look out for me. I do think I need to take care of some other things while I'm here, though."

"Like what?"

I sighed. "I think it's time for me to face some of the demons I have hiding in my closet."

"Take your time. You don't need to push anything," Hunter spoke up.

"No, I want to. I'm ready. I need to put some closure behind me. I think it will be healing for me."

"So what's your plan?" my dad asked, giving me a concerned look.

"I'm going to see Clay's parents and ask them if I can lay flowers on his grave."

"Would you like us to come with you?" my mom asked.

I shook my head. "No. Hunter can take me. I'll have him wait in the car while I go in." I looked at him apologetically. "I'm not ashamed to have you with me, but I don't want to make them feel any more uncomfortable."

He gave a small wave. "Don't worry, I understand. It's okay."

"There's a box of pictures and things he gave me in my room. I'd like them to have them. Memories are all they have of him now."

"I think that's a lovely idea, sweetheart," my mom said, hugging me tightly. "You have a good heart."

I didn't know how to answer. My heart didn't feel very good. There was still a lot of turmoil inside me when it came to Clay. "Do you care if Hunter and I get cleaned up? We brought extra clothes since we left in the middle of the night."

"That's fine. Dylan, feel free to use the guestroom and bathroom down here." Mom gestured down the hallway.

"Thanks," he replied. "I'll run and get our stuff out of the car."

An hour later, I balanced the box I was holding on my hip and lifted a trembling hand to knock at the door. I was incredibly nervous, which seemed strange since I knew this house almost as well as my own.

"Cami! What a surprise!" Kathy Bradley glanced at the box in my hand before looking out to where Hunter was sitting in the Camaro at the curb. "What brings you here?"

"Is it okay if I come in?" I asked, fidgeting restlessly with the box in my hand. My throat suddenly felt dry. It was odd to feel like a stranger with people I'd known my whole life.

"Of course you can." She opened the door wider, and I cast a glance back at Hunter before turning to step inside. "George, Cami's here."

Clay's dad appeared in the hallway, a surprised expression on his face. He looked as uncomfortable as I did. "Hi, Cami," he said.

They both stared at me expectantly.

"How've you been?" I grimaced at my choice of words—so much for making small talk. "Don't answer that," I quickly blurted out. "I simply wanted to come by and give you some things." I held the box out toward Kathy. "I thought you might like these pictures of Clay. There's a few things he gave me in there too."

His mom's eyes watered as she took it from me. "Cami, we're still so sorry about what happened. We don't know what we can do to make it up to you."

I raised a hand to stop her. "You have nothing to apologize for. What happened wasn't your fault. I'm not even sure it was Clay's fault. He was obviously sick. I'm sorry I didn't notice in time to get him some help before things got so far out of hand."

His parents stood there quietly not saying

anything. I fumbled trying to continue.

"I want you to know I don't blame you, and I want you to have these pictures so you can remember happier times with him. Regardless of what happened, he was still the best friend I ever had. I wish things hadn't gone down as they did. I still miss him."

Tears dripped down his mom's face and his dad sniffled. "Thank you, Cami. Your concern for our feelings means a lot."

"I also wanted to put some flowers on Clay's grave today, if it's all right with you."

His dad nodded. "I think Clayton would like that. Thank you for thinking of him."

A few awkward moments passed. I didn't know what else to say.

"Okay, I guess I should go then." I moved for the door. "Thanks for letting me drop by unannounced."

"Cami," Kathy called out and I stared at her. "You're always welcome here."

"Thank you," I said, my own eyes tearing before I turned and slipped out the door.

"How'd it go?" Hunter asked, firing up the engine as I slid into the seat beside him.

"It was . . . interesting . . . good, I think. I definitely caught them off guard."

"Well, hopefully it will help them in their path to healing also."

"I hope so too. They're good people." I stared at the house, my gaze wandering to where I'd often seen Clay standing at his bedroom window, smiling as he watched me walk up the sidewalk. The curtains were closed now, and I wondered if his room was still the same on the inside.

"Where would you like to go?" Hunter asked, interrupting my trip down memory lane.

"To the movie theater," I replied, turning to give him a tiny smile.

His eyebrows raised, and he gave me a concerned look. "Are you sure about that?"

I nodded fervently. "I need to do this."

He gave a big sigh. "Okay, if that's what you want. You know this wasn't exactly what I had in mind when I wanted you to have a day away from everything."

"I know, but it'll help me close the door on some things I've been keeping buried inside. I want to heal as well."

He reached over and took my hand. "I hope you know how proud I am of you. You're truly one of the strongest, sweetest people I've ever known."

I didn't reply, but continued to hold his hand as we drove through town. My thoughts wandered off again as we passed the high school. My last few days there had been rough, full of stares and whispers—even name calling in some cases. People had called me a nark, and a cop lover. I didn't say anything back to them. I may not have been a nark, but I did love a cop—fiercely. I'd never told Hunter about what I'd faced after he left me. It would have made him angry, and I didn't want to distress him. He was already upset about how things had gone before he'd been able to contact me again. It had become something we didn't really talk about. It was easier to pretend everything was normal.

We parked in the back of the theater. It was too early for it to be open yet, but I knew the staff would be inside getting things ready for the first movies of the day. I tried the door and it swung open. Hunter held my hand as we walked down to the office.

Jon was inside at his desk, and his face lit up in surprise when he saw us at the door. "Hey kids," he said warmly as he stood and came to give me a hug and shake Hunter's hand. "It's good to see you. What brings you here? I thought you were both living in Tucson now."

"We are," I said, shifting uncomfortably. "We came for the day. I visited with my parents and decided to confront some of the things that have been giving me nightmares since I left." I had never come back to work after Clay attacked me. I couldn't bear to be here. "I was wondering if you'd let me into the old theater?"

He pondered my request for a moment. "Are you sure?"

I nodded. "I think it will help."

"Alright then." He stepped out the door and began walking toward the staircase.

"Don't you need to get the keys?" I asked, knowing he always kept it locked to prevent it from being disturbed.

He shook his head. "No. I've changed a few things since everything happened. After they finished with the crime scene, I decided to keep the place opened. There's no reason to lock it where it can be abused again."

We climbed to the top of the stairs, and I walked to where the great wooden doors were flung wide open. It was strange to see them that way. I closed my eyes as I remembered screaming and pounding against them for help while I was trying to escape Clay.

"I'll leave you two alone. Take all the time you need."

"Thanks," Hunter said as Jon walked away. He took me by the arm. "You ready to go in?"

I couldn't speak, so I just nodded again. I was afraid of the images flashing to the surface in my mind. We walked to the doors and entered the space, and I let out a surprised gasp.

Nothing looked the same. The chairs were gone and all the carpeting was removed, leaving only the wooden floor behind. The wallpaper had been stripped away and the walls freshly painted. The stage was also gone, taken clear back to the far wall, and a giant, new digital screen was mounted there.

"Well, well," Hunter said, glancing around impressed. "Looks like Jon decided to open a new theater. Obviously it's still under construction, but it looks great."

I couldn't help the smile that crept to my face. "Nothing even looks the same." I turned around, taking it all in. "I love it! I'm so glad he decided to use this space. I was always so sad it was sitting here going to waste."

"This poor old room has had a tortured past, hasn't it?" Hunter agreed. "Maybe now it can be filled with happier memories."

"I hope so," I said, spinning around to look

at everything again. "I'm glad I came here. Maybe the nightmares will stop now—they're of a place that doesn't even exist anymore."

He wrapped his arms around me and held me close. "I hope you find the peace you're seeking."

"I will," I said determinedly, taking a moment to enjoy the safety of his arms. "Are you okay too? This was where you were shot after all. I guess I should've asked if you felt all right with coming here." I felt horrible, realizing I'd been so involved in my own trauma I'd failed to think of his.

"I'm fine, Goody. The only demons I have are regrets that I wasn't able to figure things out sooner. I wish I could've protected you better."

"Please don't feel badly. You did the best you could under the circumstances. Things would've been much worse if you hadn't intervened." I continued to hug him.

"I don't even want to think about it," he whispered, his grip on me tightening.

"Then don't. All's well that ends well, right?" I popped up to give him a quick kiss on the lips. "Let's go to the store and get some flowers now. I'm ready to visit the cemetery."

I stood by myself on the grass, looking at the small metal plaque that marked Clay's grave. Hunter stayed with the car, allowing me some time alone. I knew he had no desire to be here.

When I'd been here for Clay's funeral, I was

in complete shock, still unable to properly know what I was feeling. I hadn't cried a single tear—my emotions locked so tightly inside myself. Today I felt only sorrow over a lost friendship and regret for the relationship we could've had if things hadn't gotten weird. We'd planned to go to college and cross things off our bucket list together. I realized now, that even though we were making plans, we'd been seeing two different futures. Never in my wildest dreams could I have imagined an ending like this.

I stepped forward and placed the bundle of yellow roses next to the plaque with his name on it. "Yellow roses mean friendship, Clay," I spoke. "That's how I choose to remember you—as my friend. I want you to know I miss talking and laughing with you. I'm not sure why things had to happen the way they did, but if you want my forgiveness, you have it. I hope you're at peace now too."

It felt as if a giant burden was lifting from me, and I turned and walked away, knowing the door was closed. I'd never come to see him again.

CHAPTER EIGHTEEN
Hunter-

"I hope you don't mind spending a little alone time with me."

Cami smiled. "Are you kidding? This was the best idea ever! Besides, I've been starved for time with you." She flopped back onto the park grass—our impromptu picnic from Francesca's spread in between us. I'd been unable to resist the opportunity to recreate our first date. "I can't believe you got a whole strawberry pie too!"

I chuckled and leaned against the tree providing us a nice shady spot. "I know it's your favorite."

"But a whole one? There's no way we'll be able to eat it all."

I loved seeing the smile across her face. She hadn't been this relaxed in weeks. "Then give what's left to your parents, or better yet, take it home with you as a treat for later."

She sighed heavily, her smile slipping. "Do

we have to go back? I say we forget about everything and stay here forever. I've missed all this." She waved her arm in a broad arc.

"What? This park?" I teased, trying to get her smile to return.

She rolled to her side so she was facing me, propping her head with her hand. "No. Everything. Home, this town, us—how we were in this town—I miss all that."

"Shall I call Mr. Adams?" I joked. "We could see if he'll give us the keys to the darkroom, and we can go make out in it." I winked at her.

She giggled. "That was heaven! I had no idea what I was getting myself into back then, did I?"

"Do you regret it?" I asked before taking a sip of my shake.

She sat up and crawled over, climbing into my lap. She placed her palms on the sides of my face and stared deep into my eyes. "Not for even one second. I love you."

I'd never get tired of hearing those words from her. I set my shake in the grass and slid my hands around her hips. "Say it again." I stared at her beautiful mouth, thinking about all the things I liked about her lips.

"I love you," she said again, obliging me.

"I love you too. Now kiss me."

She grinned. "You're bossy today, aren't you?"

"Are you going to kiss me or not?" I arched an eyebrow, staring at her seriously.

She bit her bottom lip and appeared to ponder. "On our first date here I spent the whole time wishing you'd kiss me with those amazing lips of yours. You fought it, though, and wouldn't give in. In honor of that day, I think I'll decline your order and make you suffer like I had to."

"Wrong answer," I replied, moving quickly so she was pinned on the ground underneath me. I lifted her hands above her head and held her wrists with one of mine. "If I remember correctly, you wouldn't admit you liked me, and I had to do some tickling."

"Don't you dare tickle me again, Hunter!" She squirmed beneath me causing my body to react instantly. "If you'll remember, you didn't win that battle either."

"I did win the battle—just not on that day— but I'll win today." I grinned as I tickled her side.

She jerked and squealed. "Oh, I'm gonna kill you!"

"*Kiss.* You're gonna *kiss* me. Get your words right." I laughed as she tried to twist away. "Give it up, Goody."

"Fine! You win!" she gasped. "I'll do it!"

I stopped immediately, letting her catch her breath for a moment. "See? That wasn't so difficult, was it?" I grinned triumphantly.

"You're a . . . a . . . pig!" she countered.

I laughed. "I've been called way worse. Besides, pigs are thick skinned, so you're gonna have to try harder."

She groaned and rolled her eyes. "Just shut up and kiss me already."

"Gladly." I kept her hands pinned above her

as I lowered my mouth to hers. Sparks exploded the moment our lips touched. I'd intended the contact to be soft and subtle, but it quickly built into something hot and fiery. It amazed me how every time felt like the first time. I'd never known chemistry like this with any other girl, and I wasn't sure what it was, but Cami seemed capable of turning my insides out. She made intensely lustful thoughts tumble rapidly through my head every time she was near. All I could ever think of was claiming her, keeping her, making her mine in every way possible.

My lips traveled to her neck, and she moaned my name as I gently sucked at her skin. The scent of her hair was like an intoxicating drug—everything about her smelled amazing. I wanted to lick her—taste her everywhere. She turned her head to the side and arched her back. I slid my arm underneath her, crushing her tightly to me.

"I've missed holding you like this," I whispered in her ear. "I need to be able to touch you. This separation has been killing me." I nibbled at her skin again.

She sighed. "I know. I've missed you too."

The sound of children running and laughing close-by broke into my thoughts, and I quickly released her, rolling to my side, sad that it seemed like I always had to pull away from her. I propped my head and stared at her, running my fingers through her gorgeous red hair. "You're so beautiful." My gaze locked with hers. "I wish I could carry you off someplace the two of us could be alone together."

She linked her fingers with mine, and I lifted them to my lips, kissing them each tenderly. She sighed and closed her eyes. "Are you sure we can't run away together right now?"

"It's very tempting," I agreed. It would be so easy to pick up and leave everything behind.

She sighed again. "I can see the wheels turning in your head. Forget I even brought it up, Hunter. You're too dang trustworthy, and we both know it. There's no way you'd abandon this case before it's through. Your word is as good as gold."

I chuckled. "Why do you make it sound like that's a bad thing?"

She smiled. "I don't mean too. I'm just tired of being frustrated."

I laughed harder. "I give you my word—I promise to take care of any and all frustrations you may have."

She rolled her eyes and gave me a pointed look. "Your selflessness overwhelms me."

I lifted a shoulder casually, laughter still escaping me. "What can I say? I aim to please."

She huffed. "I give up!"

"Good that'll make things much easier."

She made a grumbling noise and shoved away from me, but she was still smiling.

"Oh no you don't!" I said as I grabbed her around the waist and hauled her back against me. "I'm not finished with you yet. I'm frustrated too, you know."

She lifted her head and glance around the park to where the kids were playing. "Really? Are you planning on educating the entire playground on the birds and the bees?"

"Okay, okay. I get that this might not be the most appropriate place for a make out. What if we drive to the spot on the hill overlooking the city? I seem to remember having quite a bit of fun with you the last time we were there." I gave her what I hoped was a smoky, suggestive stare.

She glanced up at the bright sky. "Sounds hot," she replied, having none of it.

"It wasn't before. I recall lots of wet clothing plastered to sexy curves." My gaze flitted briefly over her before returning to her face.

"It's called drowning, Hunter. If we'd kissed any longer in that rain storm we'd have been swept away."

"No, I'd classify drowning as what you did in the creek." The mood suddenly became somber. "I've never been so scared in my life. That's when I first knew my feelings for you ran a lot deeper than I'd allowed myself to believe."

"I thought I was going to die." She stared at me and stroked my face. "That's twice you've saved me now. I owe you my life."

I shook my head. "You don't owe me anything. All I've ever wanted from you was your love."

"You have it," she answered and lifted her head to my lips, kissing me again.

My phone vibrated in my pocket, and I slipped my hand down to pull it out, continuing to kiss her until she pulled away from me. I looked at the text with a sigh.

"Who is it?"

"Ripper. He wants to know where I am."

She gave an exasperated groan, collapsing back into the grass. "And reality comes to find us. Tell him to go away, that you're making out with your *sister*. See how he enjoys that."

"Honestly, I'd enjoy nothing more—but I'd prefer to be standing in front of him, so I could see his reaction."

She giggled. "Oh, please let me be there for that too! I can't wait for him to be hauled off to jail. He's seriously creepy."

I tapped a reply back into my phone and hit send.

"What did you tell him?" she asked, her curiosity getting the better of her.

"I told him the truth—said I was spending the day out of town with you and our friend, Russ."

My phone beeped again a few seconds later.

Keep Russ away from Cami. He's always around. I think he's into her.

I almost choked on my laugh.

"What?" Cami asked.

"He thinks Russ is into you. He wants me to keep him away."

She joined my laugh. "Russ would die if he heard this!"

Dude, U got it all wrong. Russ and Cami R just friends. Trust me, I replied.

What—is he like gay or something?

I laughed again.

No, but he's one of my best friends. He knows the bro code—no sisters.

Ripper responded right away. If U say so. U &

I don't follow that rule tho. When will u guys B back?

Later 2night.

K. Give me a shout. I've got plans 2 tell U about.

What kind of plans?

Car races—for pinks. Hit me up when U get here. I'll fill U in.

That sounded interesting. I wondered what was going on.

Will do, I answered.

"So what's Ripper so chatty about?" Cami asked, and I noted she sounded nervous again. It irritated me he had that kind of power over her. She'd gone from relaxed and happy to uptight in a matter of moments.

"Don't worry about him. He just wants to talk to me about some races."

"Races?" She looked confused.

"Yeah, that's all he said. He didn't go into any more detail."

"I've decided he's an adrenaline junky. Everything he does has to be risky."

"You could be right. It's a very real thing, and people can get addicted to the way it make them feel."

She didn't reply, instead twisting her hair around one of her fingers.

"Just hang in there a while longer, okay, Goody? The end is getting closer. I can feel it." I rested my hand on her thigh and squeezed lightly, hoping to reassure her.

"I hope you're right. I don't know how much more I can take."

Me neither, I thought.

CHAPTER NINETEEN
Hunter-

I glanced over at Cami, the glow from the dashboard softly lighting her features. She'd been asleep for the better part of the ride home. I was happy to see her relaxed again.

"I'd feel much safer if you kept your eyes on the road rather than on your girlfriend," Russ said sarcastically from the back seat. "Not much room back here for me to get tossed around like a hot potato if you decide to roll this sucker."

I stared at him through the rearview mirror. "Have I ever wrecked a car yet?"

"Eyes—road," he said again, gesturing with two fingers from his eyes toward the windshield, and I laughed.

"Wanna walk the rest of the way?"

"Whatever I need to do to live."

I chuckled again, shaking my head. "You're such a dick, man. I've missed you."

"Oh, I'm the dick—me—the innocent, helpless passenger in the backseat. That's kind of you. At least I'm not a whipped little bitch like you." He grinned and nodded toward Cami.

"Would you like to drive?" I asked, raising my eyebrows.

"Hell no, what do you think I am? A chauffer? That's what I have you for!" He leaned forward and punched me in the shoulder.

"Hey now! Hands to yourself or I'm gonna pull this car over right now and beat your ass."

"Do it," he replied with a grin. "That's a slam dunk case for police brutality if I ever saw one!"

"Because you've been such an expert witness for police brutality in your life," I bantered back.

"Yeah, well, there's always a first time," he came back with a grin.

"Jerk wad."

"Douchebag."

"Hey, dude! My girlfriend's in the car—chill! Be nice."

"Oh ho! You can dish it but you can't take it, can you—got to hide behind your little girlfriend." He laughed and batted his eyelashes, raising his voice. "It's okay sweetie. I'll protect you. Come to mommy."

"Man, what have you been smokin' today?" He was on one tonight.

"Nothing—I swear," he replied suddenly serious. "Drinking beer and smoking cigarettes is the worst thing I've done since I was in the hospital. I guess that's one good thing Clay did for me."

"Scared you straight?" I glanced back through the mirror.

He sighed heavily. "Pretty much, yeah. I don't ever want to go through that again."

"I don't blame you. I'm not gonna lie—I didn't think you'd make it. I've seen cases like yours out in the field. None of them survived. You were in bad shape." The memories of Russ foaming at the mouth as he seized in my arms would be something that haunted me forever.

He let out a puff of air. "I'm resilient like that. No way were you getting rid of me that easy," he replied, immediately lightening the mood again.

"Good, I'm glad. I'm sorry you got caught in the crossfire between Clay and me."

"It wasn't your fault. The guy was bonkers. And don't make it seem like I was the only one who suffered. I'm not the one with a bullet wound in my chest." He glanced at Cami. "All three of us suffered at his hands."

"Well, it's done and behind us. All we can do now is try to move on. Cami and I are going to look into some post-traumatic stress counseling through the department. You're welcome to join us if you'd like."

"Hmm . . . I'll think about it," he replied. "I don't know if I'm up to campfires and singing Kumbaya yet."

I gave a snort. "It's nothing like that. They'll only have us speak to the department psychiatrist."

"Well, in that case, I prefer the campfire. At least then I can roast marshmallows. That's got to be way better than chillin' with a head shrinker."

"I don't know . . . you've got a pretty big head. It could probably use some shrinking," I ribbed.

"Hey now! Be cool!" He slugged me in the shoulder again, and I flinched away, jerking the wheel slightly and causing the car to swerve.

Cami lurched awake, her hands flying to stabilize herself as she looked around wild-eyed. I quickly reached out to reassure her.

"It's okay, Goody. Everything's all right."

"What's happening?" she asked, still looking dazed.

"Hunter's trying to kill us," Russ said dryly. "Maybe I *should* drive."

I shot him a glare through the mirror. "If you'd quit distracting me, I'd drive just fine."

He let out a grunt as he leaned back into the seat. "Yeah, *I'm* the one who's been distracting you. I can't help it if I'm so damn pretty." I could easily see the eye roll he gave me.

"Apparently I missed something," Cami said, turning so she could glance between us.

"Just Russ being . . . Russ," I explained. "Go ahead and go back to sleep if you want."

"No, I'm okay. It looks like we're almost home anyway. I can't believe I fell asleep."

"I'm glad you did. I think you needed the rest."

She shook her head. "I wasted the time I had with you."

"There'll be more time—so much you'll be sick of me. This case will be wrapped soon if no new evidence is uncovered, and we won't have to worry anymore."

"I'll never be sick of you." She grabbed my hand.

"Please help me," Russ groaned. "I'm stuck in the car with two incurable romantics."

Cami and I both laughed. "You wait. One day it'll be your turn. You're gonna fall hard, and we'll get to tease you about all the mushy stuff you say and do."

"Not gonna happen," he replied.

"We'll see about that."

"Where are we going?" Cami asked when I turned off the freeway.

I sighed. "To Ripper's. He asked me to bring you by so he could see you before I took you home."

"Ugh! Do we have to? Can't we tell him I'm not feeling well or something? I don't want to ruin a perfectly good day."

"You want to call him and tell him that?" I asked. "I'll back your story if that's what you want."

She gave a groan. "No. Just take me there. I wouldn't put it past him to come to my dorm later if he doesn't see me. I don't want him there."

"Me neither. I'd tell you to go stay at my place, but I think you're safer around large groups of people. The dorm definitely has that. Plus, Russ isn't far from you and can get there quickly if needed."

Russ leaned forward. "Cami, you can call on me any time. I'll drop everything to help you."

"You've already proven that. And thanks, it means a lot. You're a good friend." Cami released my hand so she could reach back and pat Russ's knee. "Do you think it's safe to take Russ to Ripper's?" she asked me, concerned.

I shrugged. "I figure he's already met him and knows he's a friend of ours, so it would be a natural thing to do."

"Okay. I was worried after the comment he made today. I didn't want there to be any friction."

Russ perked right up. "What comment? He said something about me?"

I chuckled. "He's convinced you have a thing for Cami. He asked me to keep you away from her."

Russ burst into near-hysterical laughter. "You're kidding me, right?"

"No, not a bit."

"Man! That dude is seriously trippin'! He's freakin' crazy—not to mention blind. How the two of you have managed to pull off the brother/sister thing this long is beyond me. Anyone can tell you're a couple by watching you for a few seconds. It's ridiculous."

"People see what they want to see," I said. "He wants Cami, so all he can see is that. He can't see she doesn't want him. Plus, Cami's a dang good actress." I gave him a sharp glance through the mirror. "You need to make sure you don't slip up. We've got to keep this charade going a bit longer."

"Don't worry about me, bro. I got this. I won't let you down. I'll even act like I'm interested in Cami, if that's what you want."

"I don't think that'd be very wise," Cami

spoke. "The police think he killed his partner. I think the less angry you make him, the better."

"That's true. I guess I'll mind my manners then."

I turned down the street that led to my temporary home. "This is where I live now, in case you ever need to know or come by," I said pointing it out to him.

Russ craned his head to look out the small window. "Um . . . nice place. Does it come with the drugs or are those extra?"

I couldn't help laughing.

"I think I could probably get stoned from breathing the air in this neighborhood," he added.

"You're probably not too far from the truth," I agreed. "It's certainly not a very impressive part of town."

"The police department really rolled out the red carpet for you guys, didn't they? Nothing but the finest for their officers—they probably forked out a whole thirty bucks for the place."

"Yeah, well, that's part of the joy of being undercover I guess. You get to slum it like whoever you're blending with."

"You need a new beat. Have them send you to spy on Bill Gates or something—maybe some filthy-rich movie star. At least then you can dress nice and have some good digs while you're blending in."

Cami let out a snort of laughter. "You're hilarious, Russ!"

"Just telling it like it is. If I become a cop, I'll be asking for the fancy assignments."

"You'd want to be a policeman?" I asked, surprised.

"Oh, hell no! What do I look like? Stupid?"

I pursed my lips and shook my head. "Thanks, man. I appreciate the love and support."

He laughed heartily. "I'm messin' with ya, dude. Don't take it all personal. Honestly, you make being a cop look cool, but I don't know if it's really my scene."

"What is your scene then?" Cami asked.

He grinned. "I don't know that either. I'm treading water while I try to decide. I only enrolled in general studies so I'd have something to do here with the two of you."

"Keep trying new things," I encouraged. "You'll figure it out soon enough."

"Hopefully."

We fell into comfortable silence as we traveled the rest of the way to Ripper's. Being in this part of town always made me feel grateful for what my parents had done to raise Sheridan and me well. We'd taken so much of our lives for granted. We were the exception, not the rule. It made me sad there were so many people who struggled to survive. I couldn't imagine raising a family in a neighborhood like this. I'd be afraid to go to work and leave Cami and our children behind every day.

I smiled internally realizing whenever I thought of my future it was always by Cami's side. I had no doubt we'd marry someday and make gorgeous children together—who looked like their mother. I couldn't imagine anything better.

I turned into the alley behind the warehouse and parked by the door that led to the living quarter Ripper and Roberta had arranged inside, versus the garage area he'd want to keep secret from Russ.

"We're back," I stated flatly. "Time to resume our roles."

"Yay," Cami drawled out in a very under-enthusiastic voice. "Let's hurry and get this over with so we can go home."

"I agree." I secretly hoped Roberta was still gone with her friends. She was beginning to wear on my nerves as well. "For safety reasons, I think it's best if we tell everyone we went to see an old friend in the Phoenix area today. I don't want to direct attention to where you two are really from if we can keep from doing so. If there's too many questions about what we did, let me take the lead on the answers."

"Sounds good to me," Russ replied. "Now get out. My legs are killing me."

I did as he asked and leaned the seat forward so he could climb out behind me. Cami exited from her side and started walking toward the building.

The door swung open, and I saw Ripper silhouetted there. "Hey baby! You finally made it back!"

Cami smiled widely and walked right into his arms. "I'm sorry we were gone so long. Time got away from us. We had a nice day, though. How was work?"

Inside, I beamed with pride at the way she

directed the conversation back to him so he'd be talking about himself instead of asking about her day.

"Oh, it was about the same as usual. I did manage to acquire another car while I was on my shift. She's a beauty." He leaned down and pressed his lips against hers.

Barely suppressed rage filtered through my system, and I clenched my fists as I watched. My attention was diverted however when Roberta came bounding through the door, pushing Cami and Ripper out of the way.

"Hunter!" she squealed in delight. She ran up and launched herself on me, wrapping her arms around my neck and her legs around my waist. I couldn't even respond before her lips were plastered to mine. She made a great show of kissing me passionately, and I reluctantly gave in to the act, knowing she was thoroughly enjoying the performance.

"Hey, girl. I thought you were going out with the ladies tonight."

"I just got home. I left early. It was a bachelorette party for one of my friends, but after hanging out with them all day, I decided to call it a night. I was hoping maybe I'd see you. I texted your phone, but you didn't reply."

"Did you? I didn't hear it, but I've been driving so that's probably why."

"Well you're here now. That's all that matters."

Yay. Lucky me.

"I can't stay long. I've still got to take Cami and Russ home."

I think that was the first time anyone acknowledged Russ standing there. Roberta slid off me and extended a hand. "Hi, I'm Roberta," she said with a flirty smile.

"So I've heard. Hunter's told me a lot about you." He smiled back at her, obviously checking her skimpy shorts and tank top. "I don't think he did you justice, though."

Her smile widened, and I bit back a groan. I should've warned him not to feed the beast.

"I think I like you already," she replied, hooking her arm through his and leading him to Ripper.

"This is my friend, Russ, I've told you about," I introduced.

"Yeah, we've met before," Ripper said, the disdain clear in his voice. Neither of them attempted to shake hands with each other.

"So why'd you want to talk to me?" I asked, curious about his earlier message.

Ripper got an excited gleam in his eyes. "We're going to the races tomorrow night. We race for pinks—you know, ownership—in the final race. I usually race two cars." I wasn't expecting what he said next. "Since Manny isn't around anymore, I want you to be one of the drivers."

CHAPTER TWENTY
Cami-

"I'm scared," I kept my voice low as I glanced around, making sure no one else could hear me talking on the phone. Everyone's attention was gathered around the group of flashy vehicles parked around one end of the old abandoned runway in the middle of the desert.

"Don't be," Hunter replied. "I promise I'll drive as safely as possible. I've had driving courses with my *other* job, so I know what I'm doing. Everything will be okay. I promise."

I knew it wasn't wise for me to contact him on the phone with everyone milling around his vehicle. He couldn't talk freely, but I'd been mortified when Ripper had gone on to explain he wanted Hunter to race his Camaro—well, the department's Camaro. "What if you lose that car to someone else?"

He chuckled briefly. "I'm not going to lose it—I'll win this thing. I've got to go now. They're trying to get us organized."

"Please be careful," I whispered again.

"I will. See you when it's over." The line went dead, and I slipped my phone back into my pocket with a frustrated sigh.

"What's the matter, Cami?" Roberta's voice came from behind me, and I turned to face her. "Nervous for Ripper?" She gave a half smile. "You shouldn't be. His cars always win."

"I'm sure he knows what he's doing," I replied, not caring one bit about what might happen to Ripper. I chose to be honest with her. "It's Hunter I'm worried about. He's never been a drag racer."

Roberta stepped closer, speaking softly. "You don't have to keep up pretenses with me, Cami. I know this isn't any sisterly concern on your part. You're no more Hunter's sister than I am, but you seem awfully close to him. What is he to you? Your partner? And who's that Russ guy who was with you last night?"

"Russ is a friend of ours we took with us yesterday. He's not a . . . ," I hesitated, leery about saying the word out loud.

"Got it," Roberta said with a knowing look. I wondered if she realized I hadn't answered her first question. If she wanted to assume that meant I *was* a cop, then so be it. I'd never said it.

I decided to try and turn the focus back to her. "I'm sorry Manny disappeared. I hope we'll be able to figure out what happened to him."

She studied me with a hard look for a moment, and I wondered if perhaps I'd opened too difficult of a wound for her, but then her features softened. She shrugged and turned to watch the activity around the vehicle. "He wouldn't have run off without saying anything to anybody. Ripper and I always knew what was going on with him. All I know is he argued with my brother at the auto body shop over money from one of the deals they had going. I was tired of hearing them fight and told him I was going home, and he knew where to find me. I never saw him again." She glanced at me. "Ripper said they figured out their issue and he'd left, leaving Manny working on one of the cars in the garage with Seth. Seth said Manny had still been upset when he left."

"How'd you find out he was missing?" I asked trying to keep her talking.

"His car was left parked outside his parent's house, suggesting he'd gone home, but no one remembers seeing him. He was known to go off on his own now and again but never for more than a day. After two days had gone by with no contact from him, his mom filed a missing persons report. The only things anyone could find missing were his wallet, cell phone, and the clothes he'd been wearing."

"All things he'd keep on himself," I muttered, mostly to myself, but she still heard.

"Exactly. So unless he had some money stashed away somewhere, and he bailed on us, then something bad has happened to him. There's been no record of him showing up anywhere."

It definitely seemed suspicious and dangerous too. If Ripper had done this, then I didn't want Hunter anywhere around him. I wanted this case done.

"Hunter's been a huge support," Roberta continued, volunteering more information. "I'm glad he took the place of the other guy I was working with. He's always been there for me when I've needed him. He's got a good shoulder to cry on." She glanced at me with a devious grin. "And he's a hell of a good kisser too. I swear I'm addicted. I'm hoping maybe when all is said and done he'll continue to stick around."

It was all I could do to keep my face in what I hoped was a neutral expression. I couldn't even think of words to speak. I wanted to puke at the mere thought of losing Hunter to her. The rational side of my brain reminded me he was in no way interested. I didn't need to worry, but my heart was beating so loudly at her declaration that my pounding pulse was on the verge of drowning out the rest of my hearing. Hunter was mine! He belonged to me! She was clearly waiting for me to say something, but I didn't know what to answer. I was saved by a ringing sound from my pocket.

"Hey Russ, what's up?" I answered when I saw his icon pop up, relieved for the escape.

"Where are you?" he asked.

"Standing in the middle of nowhere at some abandoned airstrip, why?"

"Dang! I wasn't paying attention to the time while I was researching at the library. I wanted to come watch Hunter race."

"Well, I wish you were here instead of me. I'm a nervous wreck . . . okay, maybe that wasn't the best term for tonight." I ran my fingers self-consciously through my hair, turning away from Roberta who looked as calm, cool, and beautiful as ever. "I'm seriously freaking out here," I quickly whispered, slowly walking farther from Roberta. "And this girl—she just told me she wants to keep dating Hunter after the case is wrapped up. What do I say to that?"

Russ laughed loudly. "Tell her she's delusional! There's no way Hunter will even glance at her twice after this case is done. She's so not his type. She reminds him too much of Gabby. He hates it."

An image of Clay's co-conspirator popped instantly into my mind. "He said that?" I asked, feeling some of my insecurities slip away.

"He most certainly did. And you know *exactly* how much he loved Gabby."

I wasn't sure why I hadn't seen the resemblance between the two of them before now, but it made total sense. They were similar in build and appearance, very aggressive around men, always flaunting themselves. Gabby had always looked at me as if she knew something I didn't—which I guess she had—but now I realized Roberta treated me the same way. Immediately, I wondered what she might be hiding. Maybe she already knew I was Hunter's girlfriend, and she was just messing with me. I needed to keep my eye on her.

"How long do you think the races will last? Do I have time to get out there?" Russ added, breaking into my thoughts.

"I wouldn't even begin to know how to tell

you where we are. I'm not even sure I could find my way back at this point." I glanced at the desert terrain surrounding us. "I do know it took us about forty-five minutes to get out here, though.

He sighed, sounding disappointed. "Yea, it sounds like you're too far out anyway. Tell Hunter good luck and to call me if he ever does anything like this again."

"I will. Have a good night."

"Who you talking to, baby?" Ripper's voice caught me off guard so badly I jumped.

"Oh, for goodness sake! You scared me half to death, Ripper!" I placed a hand over my heart and tried to slow my breathing. "I was talking to Russ. He wanted to know if there was still time for him to catch the races tonight."

Ripper's smile was replaced with an immediate frown. "I don't like that guy."

"Really? Why?" I asked innocently, knowing the exact reason he felt that way. It secretly brought me pleasure to know it made him upset. Anything that made him uncomfortable was a bonus in my book.

"Because I think he's trying to put the moves on my girl." He reached out and drew me closer to him.

"And who's your girl?" I asked with a nervous giggle while trying to resist the urge to shove him away.

He smiled and brushed his lips against mine. "You know it's you. Now how about a big good luck kiss for your man?"

I was so thankful Ripper was a guy with

good breath, or this job would've been even worse. "Sure." I wrapped my arms around his neck and let him kiss me deeply—all the while trying to pretend it was Hunter instead. But Hunter was a better kisser than Ripper. There was no comparison.

Ripper pulled away with a smile, winking before he swaggered to where he'd left his car. I turned away and wiped my mouth with the back of my hand.

"Is it really that bad kissing my brother?" Roberta asked, arms folded as she stared at me.

I sighed. I'd forgotten she was there. "I'm sure he's fine for some girls. But he's not my type."

She gave me a little sneer. "I bet I know who is." Her gaze flickered to where Hunter was bent under the hood, looking at the engine of the red Camaro.

"What do you mean?" I feigned naivety.

She sauntered toward me. "I mean I think you have a thing for your partner."

I swallowed hard, again not sure how to reply.

She trailed a finger across my back as she walked past. "Don't worry, Red. Your secret's safe with me. He'll never know."

Roberta thronged her way to where Hunter was standing next to Seth and Nick and threw her arms around him, dragging his face to hers for a kiss. She hugged him when they broke apart, staring over his shoulder and giving me a taunting wave before she kissed him again.

I turned away unable to watch her flaunt it

anymore.

CHAPTER TWENTY-ONE
Hunter-

I'd beat every car pitted against me. Ripper had been right—he always won too. Since I'd come as part of his "group," I'd been lumped with him, but when everyone found out the Camaro didn't belong to him, they demanded we face off. It was more or less a formality, but Ripper wasn't happy with the development in the least. He raced to win vehicles. Nearly every year, his two cars—entered as a team—were the victors and each raced for pinks. Now, instead of having two cars to take home, he was getting none.

I searched the crowd for Cami's face as we got into our vehicles, but couldn't see her anywhere. I hadn't been able to talk to her all night because Roberta was constantly hanging on my arm, dragging me around and introducing me to people as if I was a prize she'd won. I was feeling frustrated.

We drove up to the start line and stopped.

"Hey!" Ripper shouted, gesturing at me through the window. I pushed the button to lower it. "You ready to lose that pretty car of yours?"

"I thought you said this was just a formality!" I hollered back.

"I changed my mind. Sorry! I gotta get something out of tonight!" He grinned and rolled his window up before I could say anything.

I looked his souped-up Dodge Dart over one last time before turning to face the strip in front of me. My knuckles tightened on the steering wheel. It was time to give this guy a taste of his own medicine.

Roberta's friend, Cherise, who I'd met at the club, stood in front of us on the midline in a half shirt and barely-there shorts. She grinned as she held a handkerchief in the air. I watched her fingers carefully, waiting for her to release it. The second she did, I hit the gas.

The cars peeled out, squealing loudly as we tore down the old cracked asphalt. I could see Ripper still beside me, neck and neck. I shifted gears, gunning the engine, and edged forward, speeding faster and faster as the digital odometer rapidly ticked higher.

Shifting again, I buried the gas pedal once more. I shot out far ahead of Ripper and couldn't help grinning. I might not be able to stake my claim on Cami yet, but I sure as hell was going to smoke him in this race.

The wheels of the Camaro ate up the road beneath me as the speedometer pushed past one hundred and twenty, and the car almost felt like it was floating when it hit the minor bumps in the road. One twenty-five and still climbing—I chuckled at Ripper's headlights in the rearview mirror. This race was mine.

I didn't expect the coyote when it ran out in front of me. I reacted naturally, hitting the brakes and jerking the wheel to avoid it. It was exactly the wrong thing to do. There was a jarring impact as Ripper's car clipped the back of mine, and suddenly my world was spinning around in circles as my car flipped through the air.

The sound of breaking glass and crunching metal screeched around me as I hit the ground with a crash, the hood smashing in towards me. Over and over I rolled—again and again—until I was certain the car would never stop. Dirt and gravel pelted me through the broken windows, as well as shards of glass. Instinctively, I lifted my arms to shield my face from all the debris. I gasped for breath as air bags burst to life around me, hitting me hard and filling the air with power. Everything seemed to be moving in slow motion, and I had no control of anything.

The car finally rolled to a stop, landing on its smashed-up hood, leaving me hanging from the seatbelt. I could feel all the blood rushing to my head. I had to get out of here! I fumbled for the latch and released myself, my head hitting the ground as I slumped out of my seat. There was enough crawl space in the busted window for me to slither my way out. I looked around, trying to orient myself to where I was, but my vision was too blurry. Dragging my hand across my eyes, I tried to refocus, only to discover there was blood dripping everywhere.

Damn. I was injured. There was a terrible ringing in my ears, and suddenly I was too weak to care. Cami's last words floated through my mind, "Please be careful."

Everything went black.

I heard screaming, somebody was touching me, pressing hard against the top of my head. Where was I?

"Hand me your shirt!" Cami's hysterical voice demanded, but I couldn't move to give it to her. My body felt like dead weight.

"I can't move," I muttered.

"Hunter! Hunter can you hear me?" she asked frantically. "Stay still, okay? Don't try to move. Help is on the way."

"What happened?" I asked, trying to figure out what was going on.

"I think he's trying to talk, but I can't understand what he's saying." That was another voice I recognized from somewhere. I searched my brain, trying to place it. Roberta.

"The helicopter is on its way. The dispatcher says they'll be here in about twenty-minutes. They're using my cell phone to track our location." Someone else blurted out—Nick maybe.

"What happened?" I asked again. Why did we need a helicopter? Was Cami safe?

All I could hear was shouts and talking all around me, but I couldn't even open my eyes. My body felt so heavy. Everything was heavy, even the warm air blowing on my skin felt too intense.

I drifted off into the void again.

Beating. Beating. Beating. Beat. Beat. Beat. Beat. Over and over again the sound drummed into my head growing louder and louder until it was unbearable. Wind rushed heavily across my face, and I gasped as stabbing pain rushed through my body.

"Somebody make it stop!" I hollered, trying to lift my hands to my ears, but it felt like they were strapped to my sides. I thrashed about, or tried to anyway.

"Mr. Wilder! Mr. Wilder!" An unfamiliar female voice shouted. "Please try to hold still. We're loading you into the helicopter. We'll have you settled in shortly."

I could feel myself being lifted. "Cami! Where's Cami?" I asked, fearing for her safety.

"What did he say?" a man's voice questioned.

"I can't understand him," the woman replied. "He's still not with it."

I was so frustrated. A sudden wave of nausea rolled through me, and I felt like I was going to throw up. I couldn't stop it.

"He's vomiting! Quick! Turn the board to the side!"

Spasm racked my body, and I couldn't get them to stop. Something hard and thin was poked into my mouth, and I could feel suction.

"I think he's done. Let's get him strapped back down. He's showing definite signs of a head injury," the female voice said. "Patch to the hospital, and let them know we're coming in with a Level One Trauma."

Soon the beating sound grew faster, roaring in my head, combined with a swaying motion that made me feel sick again. It was too many sensations to handle, and I gave into the creeping darkness once more.

The bright white lights above me were racing past—or was I racing past them? They made my head pound furiously, and I felt extremely dizzy. I closed my eyes in an attempt to stop it. More urgent voices surrounded me, but I couldn't concentrate enough to decipher what they were saying. Finally, I realized someone was calling my name, but I was too tired to answer. I chose instead to drift off back to sleep.

Slowly, I became aware of a constant, soft beeping sound, but couldn't place where it was coming from. Forcing my heavy eyelids open, I found myself lying in a dimly lit space, which I recognized immediately as a hospital room. Cami was slumped in a chair pulled close to the bed, her red hair spread out wildly, a stark contrast to the white blanket. She was breathing deeply as if she were asleep, but her hand was clutching mine. Chris was in a chair on the other side of the bed, asleep with his head resting on his hand. They both looked worn out.

There was a throbbing pain on the top of my head, and I reached my free hand to feel it, finding bandages wrapped there. I shifted slightly, checking out the rest of my sore body, but everything else seemed to be okay.

Cami woke with a start and stared at me with concern. "Hunter? Can you hear me?"

Chris opened his eyes and leaned forward.

"Of course I can hear you. I'm not deaf." I gave a sigh of exasperation. "What happened? How'd I get here?"

"You don't remember the accident?" Chris asked with a worried expression.

"Accident?" I tried recalling an accident, but there was nothing.

"What's the last thing you remember?" Cami questioned.

I paused for a moment, concentrating as I tried to sift through my mind. "There was a coyote . . . and I swerved," I replied, closing my eyes as memories of the race suddenly flooded back to me. "Did I win?"

Cami snorted, a look of disbelief etched on her face. "Seriously? You almost *died* and all you want to know is if you won? If I weren't so happy to see you, I'd knock you out myself right now. We've been terrified!"

I couldn't help laughing at her, even though my muscles hurt with the movement. "Well, did I?"

"No, I'm afraid Ripper spun right past you. You rolled off the runway. He skidded to the end. He only sustained some minor front end damage—nothing he won't be able to fix."

I grinned wider.

"What now?" Cami asked, not seeming very amused.

"We were racing for pinks. He won the Camaro. I hope he enjoys it!" I chuckled. "Fat lot of good it's gonna do him. I guess he can scrap it for parts."

Chris shook his head. "You're two for two now on assignments. You know that, right?"

"What do you mean?"

"I mean you got shot on your last undercover assignment, and now you've barely survived a car accident on this one. The department isn't going to be too happy about that. Not to mention you totaled the car they gave you."

"All the more reason for them to hear me out when I tell them I don't want to work undercover anymore."

He seemed surprise by my comment. "Really?"

I sighed, touching the bandages on my head. "I'm tired of being away from Cami. This wasn't what I signed on for, bro. She's not getting any rest either, because she's constantly worried about me. And I'm always worried about her getting tangled in these messes. I want out. Neither of us are cut out for this."

He stared at me for several moments before he nodded, signaling he understood, but he didn't say anything else. I was sure he wasn't too thrilled about it. He and I had bonded over our job. We worked well together.

I turned to Cami. "So what's the verdict? How bad off am I?"

"You're extremely lucky, actually. Other than some pretty good bumps and bruises, you managed to walk away with only a deep head laceration, which required seven stitches. You also have a pretty good concussion going on, but other than that, the CT scan looked fine."

"We've been waiting for you to wake up," Chris added. "You've been out of it for several hours. The doctor said they wanted to keep you a couple days for observation since you lost consciousness so many times—just as an added precaution. They plan on running another CT scan to make sure they didn't miss any bleeding."

"That doesn't sound very fun." I didn't want to stay here another minute, let alone days.

"Enjoy the rest, Hunter. You need it. I'll stay here to keep you company." Cami stroked the back of my hand with her fingers.

"You'll miss your classes. I don't want you to get behind."

"I don't care. You're more important than any grade. Besides, if I leave here, Ripper's going to be hounding me and following me around all the time. Is that really where you want me?"

"No," I replied quickly. I had no problem letting her win this argument. "Stay here. I don't want you anywhere near him—though I have to say I'm surprised he and Roberta aren't here."

"You're checked in here under your fake identity. The hospital is helping with your security by only allowing family members into your room—like your brother and your sister. I haven't told your parents what happened because I want to live a little while longer. Besides, I know your mom would be tearing this place down trying to get to you. We didn't want to blow your cover."

"So did the cops show up out there?" I asked.

Cami nodded. "Lots of them, but everyone had pretty much scattered."

"Was anyone cited?"

"There was no one left to cite but you. Your car was the only one there—everyone else left. Chris came to the scene for me."

Anger quickly boiled to the surface. "Are you telling me Ripper and his thugs left you out there *alone*?"

"I refused to go with them. I told them I was going to make sure your car was properly taken care of. It wasn't like the police weren't going to know how to find you. Ripper threatened to throw me in the car, but I told him if he did, I'd never speak to him again."

I attempted to drag a hand through my hair and was frustrated when I encounter the bandages again. I'd already forgotten about them. "I can't believe he left you behind." It made me furious that he'd run off and left her so he could cover his own butt.

"It actually worked out really good for us," Chris replied. "I was able to alert people about the undercover case going on and that Cami was part of it. The department is taking care of the vehicle. You'll be given a fake citation to help keep your cover."

"You can't be serious!" Cami frowned and

her face flushed a little. "After all he's been through, they're planning on sending him back in?"

"Only if he feels up to it." Chris glanced at me, clearly dropping the ball in my court.

"I'll be fine. I started this thing, I intend to finish it." I squeezed Cami's hand in an attempt to comfort her.

"This is so ridiculous!" She was angry, and I couldn't blame her.

"It'll all work out, Goody. I promise." I wanted to reassure her somehow.

"Like you promised me you wouldn't wreck the car tonight?" She had me there.

"I'm sorry, Cami. I really am. It was a natural reaction to swerve."

"Dude, next time—just kill the coyote," Chris said sarcastically.

"There better not be a next time." Cami shook her head, pursing her lips together so hard they almost turned white.

I had a lot of making up to do.

CHAPTER TWENTY-TWO
Cami-

"Hey, sleepyhead." I smiled at Hunter when he woke up again, placing the book I'd been reading on the rolling table beside his bed. "How are you feeling?"

He gave a groan. "Like I've been in a car accident."

I rolled my eyes slightly. "Go figure."

"I swear there's not a spot on my body that isn't screaming right now." He flexed his arms and then straightened them out, rotating them around as if he were trying to work out the stiffness.

"Well, considering the scrap of metal you crawled out of, I'd say you were pretty darn lucky."

He dropped his arms and stared at me. "Cami, I'm so sorry for putting you through all this. I can't imagine what it's been like."

I leaned forward and took his hand in mine. "Don't worry about me. You just concentrate on getting better."

He continued to study me. "You look beat. Have you had any sleep?"

"A little," I exaggerated. I couldn't tell him that every time my eyes closed I saw his car flying through the air, and it felt like the very breath was being sucked from me. When I saw him lying there with blood running from his head, I'd been certain he was dead, which led me to spend most of the night saying prayers of thanks on his behalf.

"What are you reading?" he asked me.

I laughed. "It's a romance novel one of the nurses had out at the desk. She said she was finished with it and offered it to help pass the time."

He raised his eyebrow and grinned. He looked so worn out. "Are you lacking romance in your life? I'd be happy to help you take care of that, you know."

"Take it easy there, big guy," I teased. "I think you better deal with your own issues for the moment."

He shrugged, his eyes twinkling with mischief. "Well, I do have this private room. The bed isn't too bad. It'd be a shame to waste all this alone time we're getting."

I chuckled again. "Now I *know* you're going to be fine."

He squeezed my hand. "You're right. I *will* be okay. Go home and get some rest—you look exhausted. You don't need to sit here."

I shook my head. "I'm not ready to let you out of my sight yet. Chris said he'd be back later. He also said the department was arranging an insurance loaner for the rest of your assignment."

He nodded. "Okay, thanks for telling me."

"I wish they'd pull you off this."

"Don't worry. I'm sure they're going to wrap things up soon."

"What are they waiting for?"

"I think they're waiting for Ripper to make another car run to Las Vegas. They've been in contact with the police there, and they're hoping to catch whoever is on the other end of this theft ring."

I sighed. "Well, I can't imagine it'll be too long before he makes another run again. He has a few cars ready to go, and we both know he doesn't like to leave them sitting around for very long."

"That's what I'm thinking. Since we haven't discovered anything else about Manny's disappearance, there's no reason for us to keep dragging things out."

"Good. The sooner we can be done with all this, the better. I want to get back to our lives."

He turned and stared at the ceiling for several moments.

"What are you thinking about?" I asked, curious about why he was suddenly so quiet.

"The future." He glanced back toward me. "I'm considering getting out of the police business altogether."

This surprised me. "Really? I hope it's not because of me. You love being a cop."

"I have enjoyed it, but there are things in

my life that are more important to me—like you. I don't want to do anything that will put my life with you at risk. I want to grow old with you, Cami. This accident is making me reconsider things. It can all end so quickly, I want to make every second count."

Love infused me, but I hated to see him give up the job he loved for me. "I want that too, but life can be taken from us at any moment in all sorts of ways. You quitting the police force doesn't guarantee us any more time together."

"I know, but I also don't want to put myself in more dangerous situations that could take me away sooner. There are other things I can do."

"Like what?"

"Well, medicine is interesting. I've had some first responder training and experience with emergency medical situations. Maybe I could be a firefighter paramedic or something like that."

I pondered this for a moment. "That might work. You'd still get your lights and sirens, and you'd rock the uniform."

He laughed. "What is it with women and guys in uniform?"

I shrugged. "I have no idea, but I like you in your dress blues. You look hot."

"Maybe I could get my own firefighter calendar," he joked, flexing his arms again. "I think I've got the muscles to pull it off. How would you like that?"

I smiled widely. "I think I just drooled a little. But I'd be the only one allowed to have a calendar. I don't want other women ogling you. Is a firefighter safer than being a cop, though?"

He sighed. "I guess there would still be danger, but if I was on the medical end of things, I'd be more in charge of taking care of people or other fire fighters versus fighting the actual fire. I mean, obviously, I'd have to do both, but I have several friends on the fire department. They actually spend more time working car accidents and medical calls than anything else."

"You're an adrenaline junky, aren't you?" I asked with a grin.

"There's no denying it. I'm definitely attracted to those types of jobs. I like the excitement and the idea that every day can be different than the one before." He gave me a sly look. "Of course my adrenaline gets pumping each time I lay eyes on you. Too bad I couldn't get paid to follow you around all the time." He winked.

I snorted. "Whatever."

His face grew serious. "I mean it Cami. I'd do anything to be with you. I love you." He groaned as he scooted aside, patting the space next to him. "Come lay by me. I want to hold you."

I glanced toward the door. "Will they get mad at me?"

"Who cares? The two of us went through something really traumatic together, and I want to be next to my girl."

Tears floated in my eyes. "I don't want to hurt you."

"You won't. It'll help me feel better."

I climbed onto the bed and curled up beside

him, lying in the crook of his arm. He wrapped it around me, holding me close, and it felt so good to be next to him. "I was really scared," I admitted softly.

"I know. So was I, but everything is gonna be okay now." He placed a kiss on the top of my head, and I wrapped my arm around his midsection. "I'm tired again. Shall we take a nap together?"

I nodded, my eyes already feeling heavy. I was drained. Hopefully sleeping in his arms would keep the bad dreams at bay.

"You've got to be kidding me," Hunter said as he stared at the Volkswagen Polo parked in the lot. He looked at Chris. "Seriously? This is what the department sent me?"

"Yep." He tossed Hunter the keys. "I'm thinking perhaps it's a subtle message that they don't want you driving over a hundred miles an hour."

"Ripper is going to laugh me off the premises when he sees this."

Chris shrugged. "It's supposed to be an insurance loaner. It has to look believable."

"I'm really going to miss that Camaro." He looked positively forlorn.

"Why can't you use your Camaro?" I asked. "Ripper thinks it's my car. No one would blink twice if I loaned it to you."

Hunter's face brightened immediately.

"No can do," Chris spoke up. "The department doesn't want to be financially responsible for his vehicle due to the nature of the case and the accident that's already happened. Plus, they don't want Ripper to trace the car back to him."

"I tried," I said with a shrug as Hunter's face fell again.

"Fine. I'll drive the girly car." He walked around to the passenger side and opened the door for me.

I gave him a skeptical glance. "Don't you think I'm the one who should be driving? You're the one with the concussion."

"I feel okay, and I passed all my cognitive tests."

"True, but the doctor still told you to take it easy for a couple days. Let me drive you home. You barely got out of the hospital."

He sighed heavily and handed me the keys. I gestured for him to get into the passenger seat, and he rolled his eyes as he did so.

Chris laughed, clearly enjoying this. "He's such a good patient."

I shut the car door. "I'm afraid our patient has no patience."

He grinned wider. "I think you're right. I'll follow the two of you back to the crack house," he said, using the nickname we'd given to the undercover house they were sharing.

"Okay. Sounds good."

"Thanks for your help with everything, Cami."

"No problem. Anything for my *brother*." I grinned as I walked around the car and got in.

"You two don't have to baby me," Hunter grumbled as I started the engine.

"We want to. Besides, it allows me the excuse of staying next to you without having anyone question my reasoning. Ripper's been calling and texting me a lot. He misses me."

"I bet he does," Hunter growled. "I don't look forward to seeing him all over you again. It's been nice to have you to myself for a change."

"Trust me, I don't want to go back to it anymore than you do. I don't like seeing Roberta all over you either."

He gave a frustrated grunt. "She drives me insane."

"She spoke to me at the race, you know. She's falling for you for real and thinks there might be an honest connection between the two of you. She's hoping the relationship will continue after the case is wrapped up."

He stared at me in amazement. "You're kidding!"

I shook my head. "Not a bit. She made it very plain that she was marking you as her territory."

"Well, she's either completely delusional, or I'm a better actor than I thought. That's insane."

I smiled. "Have you ever looked at yourself in a mirror? You could probably crook your finger at any woman in the world and she'd come running after you like a willing puppy dog."

He dropped the visor in front of him and stared in the mirror. "Really? Because all I see is a guy in desperate need of a shave, with a big bandage wrapped around his head. Hmmm . . . I've got a pretty good bruise going on." He lifted his hand to the discolored area around his cheekbone. "Yeah, I can definitely see why the ladies might go crazy."

I laughed. "Okay, so today might not be the best example, but I'd still follow you around if you crooked your finger at me."

He crooked his finger at me. "Promise?" He grinned.

"I promise."

"Well, good. You're the only one I want following me around anyway."

I glanced at him feeling a sudden burst of relief flow through me once more. "I love you. I'm so glad you're all right."

"I love you too, but I won't be all right until we're done with this case and I don't have to drive a car with hamsters in a wheel for an engine." He frowned as he stared at the dashboard.

I giggled. "I'm sorry you don't like it. It beats the alternative, though, which is walking."

He sighed heavily. "I guess. At least they got me a red one. Red's a good car color."

"It also gets the most speeding tickets," I reminded him.

"Not likely in this car. It has to actually be capable of going over the speed limit. Give me a Chevy any day of the week."

"Be patient. It won't be forever. You'll probably be driving yours again soon."

"One can only hope."

Ripper, Roberta, Seth, and Nick were all

waiting in front of the crack house when we arrived. Immediately I felt deflated. I'd hoped to spend some more time with Hunter by myself before they were involved again. "Yay. Looks like your fan club's here to celebrate your return," I said unenthusiastically as I placed the car in park.

Hunter didn't reply to my remark, instead quickly jumping out the door and striding toward Ripper. I sat there, dumbfounded as I watched him swing back and punch Ripper in the face.

Ripper was totally caught off guard, his head whipping to the left. Hunter punched him again in the stomach and then shoved him backward into the chain-link fence. Grabbing him by the shirt, Hunter slammed Ripper against the side of his car, parked in front of me. I jumped out and ran over as Chris and Roberta tried to push Nick and Seth away from the two of them.

"What the *hell* were you thinking, leaving Cami out on that airstrip by herself?" Hunter roared, banging Ripper's body against the car one more time for emphasis.

"Hunter stop!" I yelled, unable to believe I was actually defending Ripper.

He didn't take his eyes off Ripper. "Answer me, dammit!"

"I tried to take her. She refused to leave!"

"Then you should've stayed with her!"

"The police were on their way! We needed to get out of there!" Ripper argued back.

"You made the choice to go racing, bro. Take your lumps like a man! If you can't handle the heat, get out of the fire!" Hunter pushed away from him and pointed his finger in Ripper's face. "Don't you *ever* leave my sister behind! You gave me your word you'd take care of her. I consider this a serious breach of trust!"

Ripper wisely made no aggressive move toward Hunter. He wiped a small trickle of blood from the corner of his mouth. "I'm sorry. You're right. I shouldn't have left her."

"Don't apologize to me—apologize to her," Hunter said. He turned and briskly strode into the house without saying another word to anyone.

Ripper glanced at me. I could tell from his expression that his pride stung a little. "Cami—," he began, but I raised my hand to stop him.

"There's no need to apologize, but I think maybe it's best for all of you to go home until he cools off a bit. Let Chris and I get him settled. I'll call when it's safe to return to the lion's den." I gave a small smile, trying to diffuse the situation.

Ripper nodded and gave a slight gesture to the others to get into the vehicle. He walked around to the driver's side, pausing before he climbed in. "I really am sorry, Cami. It was a cowardly thing to do."

CHAPTER TWENTY-THREE
Cami-

"We need to do a Vegas run soon," Ripper said to everyone gathered in the garage, and my heart rate increased at the news. This was what we'd been waiting for. It meant the end of the case for Hunter and me. "We have six cars this go around which is more than usual, so I'll need everyone to drive, including Roberta and Cami. We'll come home in a rental van."

I glanced at Hunter. He didn't appear very happy with the news.

"Cami has school," he protested. He'd been extremely overprotective of me since he'd fought with Ripper. "She's already missed too much this week taking care of me while I was in the hospital."

"It's okay," I piped up quickly. "I've already turned in most of the work I missed. I only have one paper left, and I explained to my instructor what happened. He gave me an extension on the assignment." I smiled and glanced back at

Ripper. "I didn't even think about needing to rent a vehicle to get home."

"We always come home in a rental, unless we have an extra driver. It's cheaper than flying everyone, but we have time to plan still," Ripper stated, staring at me. "You tell me your schedule, and I'll try to work around it. I need to get with my contacts in Vegas and see what works for them." He came over and draped his arm around me. "I want you there. You and I are gonna paint the town."

Roberta gave a squeal and cuddled next to Hunter. "It's gonna be so much fun. Wait and see."

Hunter managed to muster a half grin and give her a small squeeze. He wasn't very happy at all.

"Party time, man!" Nick raised his beer and clanked it against Seth's. "Time for some drinking, gambling, and strip clubs."

"Sounds great to me!" Seth grinned, turning to Ripper. "Have I ever told you how much I love this job? Fast cars, fast cash, and even faster women! It's heaven!"

Ripper laughed and raised his own beer. "Here's to the fast life!" Everyone but Hunter and me chipped in their approval.

"I better get going. I need to visit the library in the morning before I go to class. I have to finish that paper as soon as I can." Even though I hated leaving Hunter, I was anxious to put as much distance as I could between Ripper and me. He'd been more aggressive with me ever since the fight. It was almost like he was trying to stake his claim on me, make our relationship more . . . encompassing. I wondered if he was trying to prove to Hunter that he really did care about me, but I didn't like it. I hurried to gather my books and slip my bag over my shoulder.

"I'll walk you out, baby," he replied, kissing my cheek.

"Night, Sis," Hunter said, turning casually away from me, but not before I saw the longing in his eyes.

"Goodnight," I replied, wishing I could run over and hug him.

Ripper led me out to where I'd parked and opened the door for me. He pulled me into his arms, running his hands down my back as he stared into my eyes. "I hate that you always have to leave. I wish you could stay here all the time." He bent to kiss me on the lips, and I forced myself to respond to him as best I could.

Kissing him was always incredible—incredible in the fact that while he was extremely good looking, I felt absolutely nothing. It seemed he should be able to tell. When I kissed Hunter, it was like the world was exploding around me with fireworks. It made me wonder if Ripper had ever been in love before or if girls were more of a plaything to him—someone to pass the time with. It was the only explanation for how my charade was passing his scrutiny.

I broke away as soon I could without making him suspicious. "See you later," I said with a small smile, turning to get in. My gaze fell on the back tire. "Oh no," I said with a grimace, pointing. "My tire." It was completely flat.

"Yep, that's not looking too good is it?" Ripper agreed. "Pop your trunk. I'll put the spare on for you. You do have a spare, don't you?"

"Uh." My brain scrambled for the appropriate answer. I had no idea if there was a spare, but I did know Hunter, and he believed in being prepared. "Yeah, I do." I hit the button on the key chain that would release the latch, hoping against hope I had made the right choice.

Ripper opened it and disappeared from view for a moment. "You have a little problem," he said, peering around to look at me gravely.

My heart raced a million miles a minute. I hadn't had any reason to check the trunk before now. What if Hunter's things were in there? Was there something that could blow his cover?

"What's that?" I asked, fear and trepidation speeding through my system.

"Your spare is flat too."

I felt relief course through me. "It is? Shoot. I must've forgotten to get it repaired after my last flat."

Ripper shook his head and let out a chuckle. "Women. I'll never understand your priorities."

"Sorry," I said, giving what I hoped was an embarrassed look. "I guess tires aren't that interesting."

"Everything okay out here?" Hunter's voice broke in, and I turned to see him standing outside the door.

"The car has a flat. Apparently, I forgot to get the spare fixed because it's flat too."

I saw a brief second of irritation pass over

Hunter's face, and I knew he was silently kicking himself.

"It's no worry," Ripper said, closing the trunk and coming to my side. "You can stay the night here, and I'll run both tires to the garage in the morning and get them fixed for you. I'd do it now, but I don't have the keys and it's all locked up."

I panicked, glancing to Hunter for help. I definitely didn't want to spend the night.

"Don't worry about it, Ripper," he said. "I'll take Cami home tonight. We can fix the car in the morning and drop it back to her. Let me go grab my keys." He turned to go inside.

"Hunter!" Ripper called after him. "It's okay, really. I want her to stay." He turned back to me. "What do you say, baby?"

"Uh, um," I faltered, glancing nervously toward Hunter. He looked as flustered as I did. I stared at Ripper. "I don't know if I'm very comfortable with that. I'm not sure I'm ready to take that step."

He gazed at me, brushing my hair away from my face. "Have I ever given you a reason not to trust me?"

I stared off to a spot across the old work yard. "Well, I can't think of—,"

"That's right. You can't think of anything, because there's nothing. I've been careful with you. Hunter told me what happened to you back home—how he had to save you from that guy. I'd never do that."

My eyes widened in shock. "He . . . told you?" I stammered, suddenly realizing why

Ripper kept letting me put on the brakes.

"Yes, and he showed me his scars and told me how he killed the guy who hurt you. Trust me—I'm not going to give your brother any reason to come after me. I've learned firsthand how protective he is of you." He rubbed his jaw and worked it out a little. "I'm still sore."

I glanced back at Hunter, knowing he'd fabricated the story a bit. I wasn't sure exactly what he'd told Ripper. He stared back, never flinching, but I could tell he wasn't pleased with this turn of events.

"Come on, Hunter. Tell her it's okay to stay," Ripper urged.

Hunter remained stoic, saying nothing.

Ripper turned my face back toward his. "I trust you, Cami, don't I? Why would I do anything to anger you? Look at all the secrets you know about me. You could take them to the cops—,"

"I'll stay," I piped up suddenly. He was hitting way to close to the truth.

"You will?" A triumphant smile lit his face.

"Yes, but only if you understand there'll be no . . . no . . . "

"I got it. You have my word." He pulled me in for another kiss, and I tried to respond as dread crept through me. There was no backing out now. I turned to Hunter, but he'd disappeared. Was he angry with me? My heart sank even more.

"Go ahead and put your things in my room," Ripper said, giving me a spank on the butt as he sent me back toward the door. "I'll get this tire taken off and ready to go to the shop first thing in the morning, so you won't be late for class."

"Thank you," I replied over my shoulder.

"Anything for you, sexy girl." He grinned, and I turned away so he wouldn't see my grimace.

I walked back through the door into the small alcove at the entry. Hunter was leaning against the wall—his head back against it.

"I don't like this," he said.

"Me neither, but he was hitting way too close to the truth."

"You don't have to explain yourself to me. I know why you did it, and it was the right thing." He sighed heavily lifting his head to stare at me. "But I still don't like it."

He reached out, took my books, and I followed him silently as he led the way to Ripper's room. He paused before the door, pushing it open and going inside to place my things on the large bed before turning to face me.

"What's Ripper doing outside?" he asked, coming closer.

"He's taking the tire off the car, so he can fix it in the morning."

He nodded and reached behind me, pushing the door closed and backing me up against it. "Tonight might actually kill me, Cami. The thought of you in the same bed with him . . . "

His lips met mine, and he pressed against me so close I could feel everything about him. Holding my face, his long fingers were practically digging into my scalp. I could feel his desperation seeping into me. He kissed me, deeply, frantically, as if he were trying to consume me in this one moment.

Heat flushed through my body. It was as if every part of me responded to his nearness. Where kissing Ripper made me feel dead inside, kissing Hunter made me feel as if every cell inside me was on fire—living, breathing, devouring everything in its path. Trails of goose bumps flooded my skin, and desire pooled inside of me. His hard muscles bunched and rippled under my touch as I slid my hands over his arms and down his back. I could hardly catch my breath as the kiss continued, snatching heated gasps when possible as both of us clamored to get more of each other.

He pushed away from me suddenly, taking several steps backward. "I need to get out of here before I lose my senses completely and someone catches us together."

I nodded. "I know, but I don't want you to leave me."

He was back beside me in a heartbeat. "Trust me, I don't want to leave you either, but we're risking everything here." He kissed me again, hard and brief before pulling me away from the door. "If you need anything, just call for me, okay? I'll be right on the other side of this wall."

"In bed with Roberta." I couldn't help my frown.

"Try not to dwell on it. We'll get through this." He turned the doorknob and stepped quickly into the hall, shutting it behind him.

My whole body was trembling, and I tried to calm myself with several deep breaths. I needed to get under control before Ripper showed up. I had no idea how I was going to make it through this night.

CHAPTER TWENTY-FOUR
Hunter-

I couldn't stop my fuming or internal grumbling as I turned down my side of the bed. I hated this case—hated everything about it, but I needed to see it through to the end even though it made me feel like a trapped prisoner in my own life.

I removed my shoes and my shirt, but left my pants on, as usual, before rearranging several pillows between Roberta and me. I tried sleeping on the floor when we realized we'd need to spend some of our nights together, but Ripper had a habit of walking in unannounced. It didn't look very realistic for his sister's boyfriend to be on the floor. We managed to convince him we'd had a fight the time he caught me there. After that, I'd moved to the bed. Better safe than sorry.

Roberta entered the room, wearing another one of her sexy lingerie nighties again. Her fresh, out-of-the-shower skin smelled wonderful as usual. Cami would die if she knew some of the things I'd seen Roberta wear to bed. There was no doubt in my mind she was into me. Her body language flaunted it often, special smiles, shy glances, biting her lip, stroking me at every opportunity.

"I know you told me you dressed like this before and you're doing it so things appear normal," I began, "but I can't help wondering why Ripper would know if you're dressing like this?"

She shrugged. "Sometimes I get a drink or something in the middle of the night—or even watch television, if I can't sleep. He's seen me dressed like this a lot."

"You don't put on a robe or something?" I didn't know why, but it seemed odd to me. Sheridan would never parade around me in such a manner.

She laughed. "No. Why should I? I've seen Ripper naked a billion times since we were kids. He's practically anti-clothes."

I snorted. "I would've shot my sister if she did that to me—if my parents didn't shoot her first."

"It's not a big deal. It's just skin." She leaned over to fluff some of the many black-and-hot-pink pillows she kept on her bed, giving me an ample view. I quickly glanced away, closing my eyes. I'd learned to feign sleep quickly around here, otherwise I was bound to see things I had no interest in seeing. Sure, she was a gorgeous girl. I'd have to be blind not to notice, but she wasn't *my* girl. Cami was the only one I had eyes for. It was hard for me to be convincing of my relationship with Roberta when Cami was here. I had to repeatedly remind myself not to watch and stare at her. From the moment I met her, she captivated my attention.

"So, it sounds like my brother is having fun with Cami. I think they're hitting it off well."

I forced myself to remain still. "What do you mean?"

"I swear I heard bed springs bouncing in there on the way back from the bathroom." She giggled as she slid into bed. "I think they're going at it."

Every instinct demanded I go bursting into that bedroom, but I knew Roberta was baiting me. I let out a shallow breath. "I doubt it."

"Why's that? You don't think your partner would do it with my brother?"

"I mean your brother is outside working on her car, so unless Cami is in there jumping on the bed, there was nothing for you to hear. Goodnight, Roberta." I rolled onto my side, away from her.

"She's not your partner, is she?"

My eyes instantly popped open, wary. "Of course she is." It wasn't really a lie. A girlfriend could be called a partner too. "Why?"

"Then are you in love with your *partner*?"

I grunted, my mind rapidly churning. I tried to stay relaxed as I kept my back to her so she couldn't read my face. "Why would you even say that?"

"I don't know. She seems young—really young actually, and she's sweet and pretty.

You're super protective of her too, always watching out for her, beating up my brother if he doesn't do what you think he should, running off with her and your friend Russ for the day."

"You and Ripper were both busy. There was no reason for me to be here," I replied, ignoring the rest of her statement. "I'm not allowed to have a day off with my friends? I did have a life of my own before I met you, you know."

"Is she your friend?" She continued to push the issue.

"One of my very best friends in the world." That was the absolute truth.

"Have you ever kissed her?"

"What's bringing all of this on?" I asked, frustrated I couldn't seem to shake her off this line of questioning. I rolled over to face her.

"If she were your partner, why would she actually be enrolled in classes at the university? That doesn't make any sense, and Ripper said she's a first-year student there. She spends all of her time here doing homework. I think she really is an eighteen-year-old college student. What I can't figure out is what she actually is to you. Ripper said you didn't want them together because you thought he was too old for Cami, but you're nearly the same age. So if that's the case, then what is she to you, and how did she end up involved in all of this?"

I sighed, running a hand through my hair in frustration. There was no way to deflect her. "She's my girlfriend, okay? You're right, and it's eating me alive to watch her with your brother."

I didn't miss how her expression fell, but she

quickly recovered. "How old is she?"

"She's eighteen."

She snorted in disgust. "You're such a hypocrite. Ripper's too old for her, but you aren't?"

"Look, it wasn't like that. Things were different for us."

"Different how?"

"We fell in love with each other when I was on another undercover assignment, posing as a high school student. I never meant to get involved with her—it just happened. I couldn't stop it."

"How old was she then?"

I grimaced. "Seventeen."

She gave a hard laugh. "You're a friggin' pedophile. I bet your department loved that."

"It nearly got me fired, but I keep trying to tell you it wasn't like that. It still isn't. We've never—"

She chortled in disbelief. "You're kidding me! You've never slept with her?"

"Listen," I said earnestly, wanting—no, needing—to make her understand. "I love her. I saved her life once when she nearly drowned, and I saved her from being raped. It formed a bond between us—a connection stronger than I could've ever imagined. Yes, she's young, but she's it for me. Don't you see? I *love* her. I snuck away to meet her one night, and Ripper followed me. I had to make up something on the spot. The department helped me follow it through. They wanted to keep my cover and keep her safe too. No one counted on Ripper falling for her as well. This whole thing keeps getting more and more complicated. I had to tell Ripper about the attempted rape to try and keep him off of her. This has been really hard on both of us.

"And before you go judging my choice, you might want to remember you're only a year older than she is, and you've done nothing but throw yourself at me since I got here. This isn't an age issue with you—it's a jealousy one."

She clenched her jaw and raised her chin. "You're awfully full of yourself, aren't you?"

I gave a sardonic laugh. "Have you met yourself? Come on. I'm not stupid, Roberta. I know you're into me." I could see she was starting to get upset. I needed to do something to calm her down and build a connection back between us. She could blow everything if she ran to Ripper in a bitter, angry, fit. I reached out and grabbed her hand. "You're a beautiful, sexy, young woman. I'm flattered you feel this way about me. If things were different in my life— who knows what might have happened between us, but they aren't. I can't change that." I hoped my words would be enough to appease her.

Her face softened and she sighed. "I'll get over it, I guess. You are turning your life upside down to help me."

"I want to find out the truth for you. I know you're lonely and missing Manny."

Her gaze fell to our clasped hands, her free hand fidgeting with the blanket, before she looked up with tears in her big eyes. "I want to know what happened to him."

I gripped her tighter. "I'll do everything in my power to find out for you if you promise to help me keep Cami safe. It's been hard to concentrate knowing she could be in danger."

She nodded, agreeing easily. "I'll help you."

"Thank you. It means a lot to me." My phone buzzed, reminding me I hadn't pulled it out of my pocket yet. I reached for it and saw I had a text from Chris.

Wassup?

How R U? I asked.

Relaxed. And U? Relaxed was our code word for everything being okay.

Uptight, I replied, letting him know something was up. Sis is spending the night here. R U sure U R OK?

There were a few moments of silence before the phone buzzed again.

Nah, feeling a little sick, actually. I need you to come get me. He was using our code to get me out of the house.

Where?

At the bar—Rusty's, down the street from the house. Too drunk to drive. He wanted me to meet him. I need my baby sis.

We'll be there shortly.

I couldn't help the relief that coursed through me. "Chris is calling for Cami and me to come meet him. I need to go. Are you going to be okay?"

Roberta nodded. "Be careful. Ripper's not going to be happy about this. He's been dying to have Cami stay here."

"I know, and I will be." I gave in to the

sudden impulsive urge to lean over and kiss her on the forehead. "Hang in there, Roberta. Everything will work out for the best—you'll see."

She gave me a half smile. "Go. Get your girl."

I grinned and hurried to put my shoes and shirt back on. "See you later," I said as I left the room. I paused before the closed door, lifting my hand to knock and then deciding better of it. I opened the door and stepped in.

"What the hell, man? You can't come barging in here like that when I'm with my girl!" Ripper shot me an annoyed glance over his shoulder.

"Really?" I laughed, relieved to find Cami fully dressed and sitting on the opposite side of the bed from Ripper who was taking his shoes off. "You do it to Roberta and me all the time." I silently praised Chris for his perfect timing.

"What do you need?" Ripper grumbled.

"Listen, dude. I'm sorry to interrupt whatever plans you had going here, but I heard from Chris. He's drunk—or high, or whatever—at the bar again. I need to go pick him up, but he's whining about wanting to see his baby sis, so I need to take Cami with me."

I didn't miss the look of sheer relief on Cami's face. Nor did I miss the one of pure irritation on Ripper's. Extreme satisfaction flooded through me. "Are you okay about coming with me?" I asked Cami. "You know how he is when he gets like this. You're the only one who can calm him down."

Cami sighed heavily, as if she were feeling

very put out. "I know. Yes, I'll come." She stood and went to grab her books. "I might as well bring these along if I'm going to be awake with him. Maybe I'll get a chance to work on my paper." She turned to Ripper. "Thanks for offering to let me stay. I'll come get my car tomorrow sometime."

He wasn't happy at all. "I'll walk you guys out. You seriously need to get that brother of yours into rehab or something."

I followed behind them, unable to keep a smile from creeping across my face. Ripper might not be aware that he and I were in the middle of a boxing match, but this round went to me.

CHAPTER TWENTY-FIVE
Hunter-

"So I got everything squared away with my contacts in Vegas." Ripper hopped into the tow truck as I was getting ready to pull away from the curb. "The cars are all ready to roll. I just need to reserve the van for our return trip and wait for Cami to get out of class on Friday morning. Then we can take off for a weekend of drinking and partying-it-up with our latest cash flow."

"Are you coming with me on this run?" I asked, starting the truck. I was surprised to see him here on his day off.

He grinned. "Yeah, I'm bored. Everything's done at the shop, and Cami has class all day today. She's practicing for some music concert."

Memories of listening to Cami sing on stage washed over me as I pulled onto the road. I missed hearing her perform. Her voice was honestly the most angelic sound I'd ever heard. "Don't even try to get her to ditch out on her music classes, dude. You'll lose every time. Singing is like breathing to her—essential."

"Is she any good at it?"

"The best. I see her performing on stage for a living someday. She's gifted."

"Hmmm. I may have to go see this concert after all."

I drummed my fingers against the steering wheel, feeling suddenly possessive of Cami's voice. I didn't want him to hear her sing. I knew he'd see how talented she was, and he'd want her even more. It was stupid, really. People everywhere were going to hear her sing, but somehow, when she opened her mouth, it felt like she was singing just for me. I liked it that way.

Ripper let out a snort. "Maybe I'll hop on stage and throw down with her a little—get some gangsta rap going on. She can sing the awesome chorus for me—you know, like Eminem and Rhianna or MGK and Ester Dean." He laughed.

"You sing?" I found it hard to believe.

"Yeah, but only to the stereo in my car." He slapped his leg as he laughed hilariously. "Cami and I need to come up with a Rapper name."

I rolled my eyes. "They don't sing those kinds of songs in college," I said, seeing an opportunity to deter him.

"What do they sing then?" he asked, leaning to search the radio.

"A bunch of these religious type songs—in Latin. You know—like monks or something."

"Really?" He raised his eyebrows as if he

were surprised. "I'm guessing I need to rethink attending this concert. That sounds brutal."

"It really is," I lied. Ripper was such a douche. He didn't give a crap about Cami. She was only a conquest to him—some reserved girl for him to conquer. It made me wonder what he'd do with her if this whole situation were real. Would he wear her defenses down until he got her to sleep with him and then discard her? The very thought made me want to deck him.

"I've got to say—I'm surprised you're so into Cami. She doesn't seem like your type at all."

He found a station he liked, and rap music filled the air. He leaned back and rolled the window down, beating out the rhythm of the song against the frame. "She isn't really. I usually like my women fast and loose." He laughed. "I mean, yeah, Cami's gorgeous, but honestly I first acted into her because it seemed to annoy you so badly."

I looked over at him, wondering where he was headed with this.

"I didn't know you that well. You were some guy who showed up with my sister one night, and she claimed you were her new fling, so I decided to case things out a bit. I was surprised when I saw you meeting with this beautiful girl, and you seemed all nervous. I thought for a second you were hiding something—cheating on Roberta. It was clear you didn't want me talking to Cami."

My knuckles were turning white against the steering wheel. "So you're dating my sister to piss me off?"

"Hell no! Once I got talking to her, I really liked her. She's different—special."

"And she better stay that way," I warned.

He lifted his hands in a surrendering gesture. "You don't have to worry about me. You've shown me the lengths you'll go to protect her. So where we headed?" he asked, changing the subject.

"Ironically, one of the hotels called us out. They want us to haul off a car that's been in a tow away zone for the last twenty-four hours."

Ripper grinned. "Can we keep it?"

I laughed. "I seriously doubt that's what they have in mind."

"It would be nice for us, though, wouldn't it?" He lightly punched me in the shoulder as he chuckled at his own joke.

"It sure would."

When we pulled up at the location, we found a nice BMW waiting for us.

"Damn. I really wish we could keep it now. I could make some dough on the resale of this thing."

"Watching you around cars is like watching a kid in a candy shop. I swear you'd date one if you could," I joked.

He chuckled. "A car would be the perfect girlfriend, don't you think?" He made a gesture with his hands. "She's got the perfect curves, puts out whenever you want, and waits patiently until you're ready to use her again. And this beauty?" he added pointing to the vehicle we were picking up. "Let's just say I'd ride her hard."

"Wow. Pipe down, bro," I replied, giving him a concerned look. "I was only kidding." I liked cars, but he was really taking it to the extreme. "If you want, I can call the mental hospital. Maybe they have a ward for 'special' car guys, and you can get the help you need."

He laughed. "You're such a pal. Let's get this thing and go."

It didn't take us long to hook the vehicle up and head out again toward the impound yard. My thoughts were wandering aimlessly about how much longer this case was going to drag on when, suddenly, I heard a siren click on behind us. I glanced in the rearview mirror to find a squad car tailing closely behind us.

"Please pull to the right and stay in your vehicle," a voice came over the loudspeaker.

"What the hell?" Ripper asked as he glanced behind us. "We aren't doing anything wrong. Are you speeding?"

"No. Just play it cool, dude," I replied as I pulled over. "Maybe we have a taillight out or something." My heart was racing. What if it was an officer I knew? He could blow my cover. I dug my phone out of my pocket, quickly checking to see if I'd missed a message from Chris. There was nothing. Surely I'd be informed if something were going down right now.

The door to the squad car opened, and an officer stepped out. "Turn off the vehicle, and step out with your hands up please."

My eyes widened as I turned to look at Ripper. "Do what he says, man. This is a legit haul. He's got nothing on us, so don't give anything away."

He nodded, and we both opened the doors and stepped out with our hands raised. That was when I saw the second officer standing on the passenger side of the squad car. He had his hand on his holster. What was going on? If these two idiots blew my case, I was going to be pissed.

"Walk over, place your hands against the wall, and spread your legs."

"Did we do something wrong?" Ripper called out.

The officers pulled their weapons. "Do it now!" The one on the loudspeaker shouted.

"Don't resist, man, go," I urged Ripper as I walked around the vehicle. He followed me to the wall, and we leaned against it.

The cops approached, and I couldn't help wanting to laugh. So this was what it felt like to be on the other side of the gun.

"Do either of you have any weapons on you?"

"No," we replied simultaneously.

"We're going to pat you both down real quick." One kept his weapon trained on us while the other patted us down. He recited the Miranda rights while he handcuffed Ripper before doing the same to me.

"Can you please tell us what's going on?" I asked, trying to remain calm through my irritation.

"The vehicle you're hauling was reported stolen yesterday. Do you know anything about that?"

I couldn't help my laugh of irony as I glanced at his badge. "Look, Officer . . . Hartly, all I can tell you is we picked this vehicle up in a tow away zone. We have a legitimate haul order. My papers are in the truck. You're welcome to contact the hotel that called us out and my boss to verify the order. As far as whatever was going on with the car before that, I have no idea. I'm just following the instructions I was given to pick up the car and take it to an impound yard."

"Let me see your identification please."

We clumsily dug our wallets from our pockets, handing them to him. He pulled our driver's licenses and studied them. "Jack Rivera and Hunter Wilder? Is that correct?"

"Yes, it is," I replied.

Stay here while we verify your story." Officer Hartly stepped away, leaving us with other cop—Officer Mayhue, according to his badge. Hartly went to the truck and got out my clipboard, carefully looking over the information before carrying it to the squad car and getting inside. I could hear him talking on the radio as he called in the information he had.

"Dispatch, this is Unit Seven, calling in a vehicle check—possibly matching a 10-29. License number 9, 8, 7, Henry, Adam, Lincoln. Driver's license, Adam 00908853 to first name, Hunter, spelling, Henry, Union, Nora, Tom, Edward, Robert, last name, Wilder, spelling, William, Ida, Lincoln, David, Edward, Robert."

"10-4 Unit Seven, standby," the radio unit crackled. He was telling dispatch to run a stolen vehicle check and see if I had any warrants.

"This is so friggin' bogus," Ripper mumbled, shaking his head.

"If you haven't done anything wrong, then you have nothing to worry about. Do you?" Officer Mayhue stated.

"Look, man, we didn't try to run, we didn't resist arrest, and we've completely cooperated with you. That should tell you something." The anger showed on Ripper's face. "You pigs go around all the time acting like you own the damn place."

"Hey, buddy. Take it easy. It's all going to be okay," I reminded him. There was no reason for him to be antagonizing this guy.

"Better listen to your friend here," Officer Mayhue warned. I was thankful when Ripper held his tongue.

"Unit 7," the radio crackled again. "10-21 dispatch for a Code 1."

Hartly looked surprised. "10-4. Standby." He pulled out a cell phone, and I pretended I had no idea dispatch had told him to call them for a confidential message. He was going to feel stupid when he found out who I really was.

Several minutes went by as we stood there waiting. I rocked back and forth on my heels, observing the cars driving by and the people staring at us. This wasn't going to be very good publicity for our boss, Charlie, at the garage. The name was plastered in large letters down the side of the truck. I hoped people wouldn't think something shady was going on and spread bad rumors about the business. There were several honest hard workers there.

Finally, Officer Hartly exited the vehicle and came back over. "Let them go, Jeff," he said to the other cop. "Their story checks out."

"I told you it would," Ripper said, giving them both a hard stare. He rubbed his wrists when they released the handcuffs, handing us back our identification.

"The vehicle is stolen," Officer Hartly said. "It looks like someone took it for a joy ride and abandoned it."

"So what do I need to do with it?" I asked, rubbing the circulation back into my wrists.

He nodded toward the squad car. "Come over here, and I'll give you the address for the police impound yard they want you to take it to."

"I'll wait in the truck," Ripper grumbled, heading for the cab while I followed Officer Hartly.

"Nice to meet you, Officer Wilcock," he said as soon as we were out of earshot. "I hope we didn't cause any problems with your investigation. Is there anything we can do to assist you?"

I shook my head. "No thanks. I think I've got it under control."

"If you ever need any help, please feel free to give us a call." He handed me a card. "This is the impound lot where they'd like you to bring the vehicle. They want to dust it before returning it to the owner."

"All right. Thank you. I'll get it right over."

"Good luck with your case. Sorry for the

inconvenience."

"No worries. Have a good day."

I turned and headed back to the tow truck, breathing a sigh of relief. That was a close one.

"I can't believe I almost got busted for someone else's job." Ripper shook his head in disgust.

"We'll need to lay low for a while," I said.

"Why's that?"

"They just found a stolen car on the back of a tow truck—if they put two and two together . . . , "

"I got it," Ripper grumbled giving a deep sigh of irritation. "It's a good thing we're getting rid of our stock soon."

I agreed wholeheartedly, even though it wasn't for the same reason.

CHAPTER TWENTY-SIX
Hunter-

There was a knock on my bedroom door, and instantly I was awake, wondering what was going on. Chris never bothered me in the middle of the night. "What is it?" I called out.

He poked his head inside. "Get dressed. We've got to go. There's a break in the case."

I immediately sat up and reached for the clothes I had on earlier, hurrying to get dressed. "What's happened?" I asked, feeling suddenly nervous for Cami's safety.

"They found a body. Chief called and says they wonder if it might be our missing person. They want us to talk with the investigator on the scene. There's something he wants to show us."

My pulse picked up. This could be what we've been waiting for. I hurried and put my shoes on, making sure to grab my real ID and badge from where I kept them hidden in the room. I slipped the card into my wallet, and headed out the door.

Sabino Canyon was located in the Santa Catalina Mountains outside of Tucson. It was a place many locals and tourists frequented to enjoy hiking, nature, tram rides, and playing in the waterfalls, so I was a little skeptical of this being a body dump. It seemed an odd place to hide someone, given the high traffic of the area.

We pulled into the well-lit parking area bustling with activity. Several police vehicles, forensics trucks, and park ranger units were in the lot. Brightly glowing flood lamps, on huge stands, pointed down the hill, and yellow police tape marked off a large area and disappeared from view down the path.

"Have there been any missing hikers reported?" I asked. That would be my first guess if I found a body here.

"I haven't heard of any. I'm thinking there must be something special with this victim, though, if they're having us come see it."

"Well, let's go find out what it is then."

A young officer came up and asked to see our badges before leading us a significant way down the marked trail. He directed us off the path to a cordoned area.

"Can I help you?" a tall, thin man with thick, black-rimmed glasses questioned.

"I'm Officer Napier, and this is Officer Wilder," Chris introduced us. "We were contacted tonight by Chief Robson and told you might have found a missing person who matched the description of a case we've been working on. He said you found something that might help us." We both flashed our badges again so he could validate them.

"I'm the forensics team leader, Officer Grady. Nice to meet you. Hikers discovered the body about thirty minutes prior to sunset after they chased their small kids who'd run off the trail and into the brush. It's mostly skeletal remains at this point, and judging from the marks on the bones, it looks as if more than a few animals have snacked on it." He pointed to where he'd been working. "There are also fragments of what appear to be a white t-shirt, jeans, and motorcycle boots, which I'm told match the description on your missing persons report."

Certain areas had been marked off with police tape to keep anyone who wasn't part of the investigations unit out of the area, but the floodlights lit things up pretty clearly for us, and we could see everything he was describing to us.

"From the position of the body, I'd say it was probably pushed off the edge of the ledge up there by the road," Officer Grady continued. "There's no marks disturbing the ground around the area other than those of the hikers, so I'm sure there's no evidence of the person who disposed of the body left here. If there was, it's probably long been washed away by the rain. This body's been here for a while."

"So you feel fairly confident this was not where the death occurred?" Chris asked.

"Judging by the fracture on the skull, my first assumption would be blunt force trauma.

We won't know until we collect everything and run more tests, though."

"You haven't found any identification on the body then?" I asked, assuming this was the case since we'd been asked to come have a look.

Officer Grady smiled. "Only the teeth. As soon as we get a match on DNA or dental records, we'll let you know if this is your guy. This is what I wanted to show you, though. It wasn't found on the body, however. It was several feet away wedged near the base of a rock. It could be some random trash that's blown there, but we wanted to see if it meant anything to either of you, first." He reached for a plastic evidence bag lying on the table and handed it over.

Chris and I both stared at the faded, weathered business card that read Charlie's Garage and Towing. Goose bumps trailed over me.

"Our missing person worked for this garage," Chris stated.

The investigator's eyebrows shot up. "I guess this isn't trash then, is it?"

"Can we keep this discovery under wraps until we know for sure? If it's our guy, it could affect an ongoing undercover operation we have in the works. We don't want anyone alerted to the discovery."

"We'll try to see it's kept quiet for the time being then."

"Thanks a bunch. We appreciate it." Chris reached out to shake the man's hand. "We'll wait for your call."

The two of us turned and started back up the steep hill. "So what do you think? Where do we go from here?"

"We wait for a positive ID. If it is Manny, which it certainly looks like it will be, then we should be able to get a warrant that'll allow you to search for evidence."

"I wonder if we have enough probability to get a warrant right now?" I questioned.

"It doesn't hurt to ask, I suppose. Let's go see what the chief thinks."

"I'd start in the garage. The group spends most of their time there. With all the tools they have, I'm sure there's an object that could cause blunt force trauma. I could easily begin checking for trace amounts of blood with a UV light.

"Actually, maybe you should be the one to check," I added, suddenly thinking of an opportunity to do a thorough search. "Ripper wants to take all these cars up to Las Vegas this weekend after Cami is out of school, and I happen to know where he keeps the spare key for the garage. You could take a whole forensics team in if we can score a warrant in time."

"You may be on to something there." Chris smiled, seeming pleased with the idea. "Hopefully we'll have a positive ID on our John Doe by then too. How long will you be gone?"

"At least Friday and Saturday. Knowing the way these guys like to party, I imagine they wouldn't come back until Sunday. If not, I bet I could persuade them to stay and play for a little while longer."

Chris clapped me on the shoulder. "I think this could work out. If we find anything, we can have an arrest warrant ready when you come back."

"And then this stupid case will be wrapped up, Cami will be safe, and the two of us can finally move forward with our lives. It can't happen soon enough for me."

"Hang in there for one more weekend, bro. One way or another, we can probably get you your arrest—whether for grand theft auto or murder."

"I don't care which one they bring him in on, I just want him put away for a long, long time. I don't need him getting out on a technicality and coming after Cami and me."

"Too bad we can't falsify records of you being busted too. If he thought you were both in jail somewhere, maybe it wouldn't be an option for him. But with Roberta knowing the truth and you being the lead officer on the case, I can't see how we can protect your true identities."

I sighed. "Me neither. That's why I want this done by the book." I got into the passenger seat of the car and stared at him when he slid in beside me.

He gave me a puzzled look. "What is it?"

"I'm gonna leave the force." Surprisingly, the words were much easier to say than I'd imagined.

He turned away, slipped the key into the ignition, and pulled out of the space. "You love this job," he stated.

"I do, but I love Cami more. She's had too

many bad things happen to her recently. I won't be responsible for putting her through more. Being separated from her and knowing she's out there worrying is killing me. I can't live a double life like this anymore. I want to be with her all the time—to know she's safe and happy." I hoped I was explaining my feelings adequately.

"You told me in the beginning she was the one for you. You meant for the long haul, didn't you?"

"You know that's what I meant. I love her, Chris. I want to marry her."

"Have you asked her to?" He glanced at me before turning back to the road.

"Not yet, but I plan to as soon as this case is over."

"Do you think that's wise? She's still really young, Dylan."

"Have you met her?" I laughed. "She might be young, but she's a smart girl. She's always known exactly what she wants, and she goes for it. She makes things happen, and she doesn't let fear keep her from doing what she thinks is right."

"I'm not saying you're wrong to ask her. I simply want you to make sure now is the best time. You're operating on high emotions right now. In your relationship with her, you've often fallen into the role of protector. You need to make sure that isn't what's driving your feelings here."

I gave a sarcastic chuckle. "You think the danger is heightening the relationship?"

"It's happened to others before. They're

brought together under traumatic circumstances and get together only to have the relationship fall apart later when all the emotional baggage dissipates."

"I fell in love with her long before I knew she was in danger. This is real, Chris. I've dated plenty of other girls. None of them ever made me feel like this. I want to spend the rest of my life with her, and I want it to be a long one. That's why I'm quitting the force. Being in this car accident has made me reconsider a lot of things that are important to me."

He nodded. "I understand. I totally support you in your decision to leave and to marry Cami. I only wanted to make sure you were considering everything and not rushing into any decisions you might regret later."

"I'll never regret anything that has to do with her. She's the most important thing to me. As long as I have her, the chips can fall wherever they want. We can deal with anything as long as we're together."

Chris smiled. "That's exactly how I feel about your sister."

"I know you do. It's the kind of relationship I want to have with Cami. She fits in with us, and she has a humble, beautiful, personality."

"Not to mention she's gorgeous," he said with a knowing grin.

"She is, isn't she?" I shook my head and smiled to myself. "I swear, she can be in a pair of baggy sweats and an old t-shirt—her hair all piled on top of her head in those messy buns of hers—and to me, she still looks like she just stepped off some fashion runway. I can't stop staring at her. I feel so lucky she chose to be with me."

Chris laughed. "You're not so bad yourself. I think she probably feels the same way about you."

I shook my head. "I doubt it. I'm nothing special."

"You forget—I've known you for a while now. I've seen the girls line up around the block to get a piece of you."

I snorted. "Whatever."

He raised his eyebrows. "Name one time in the last ten years you didn't have a girlfriend, had at least one or two girls chasing after you, or you weren't casually hooking up with someone."

I paused, quickly thinking back. I'd never really paid attention to it before, but girls had always surrounded me. Maybe that's why I'd taken them for granted before now. "I didn't have a girlfriend while I was in the police academy," I finally stated.

He rolled his eyes. "It wasn't because you didn't have willing women. I personally know of at least three cadets who asked me what your situation was."

"Really? How come you didn't tell me?" This was news to me.

"Because you were concentrating on something besides girls and partying. The whole family was excited to see the change happening inside you. You went from being a playboy to a young man who was truly dedicated to something. I didn't want to distract you from it. That's why I question your decision to leave the force. It seems like becoming a police officer was what gave you the direction you needed in your life."

"It did help me grow a lot and approach things more maturely. I'd like to think I've changed enough that I wouldn't revert to my old lifestyle, though. Besides, it's not like I don't have another plan in mind."

"You do?" He seemed surprised.

"What? Did you think I planned on quitting and living off my trust fund while I flipped burgers part-time?"

"No. I guess I thought maybe you were considering going back to school and playing football or basketball again so you could be near Cami."

"I'll be going back to school, but not so I can do that."

"What then?"

"I'm considering becoming a paramedic. One of the things I really like about police work is helping people. I'd still be able to in a career field like that. I've handled emergency medical situations in the past well too. It seems like the natural change for me, and it would still allow me to work in emergency service."

He nodded as I spoke, agreeing with me. "I think it's a career field you'd enjoy. You can handle extreme situations well, and you're an empathic person when it comes to dealing with others."

"I may combine it with fire science too. I

figured I'd have a better chance of finding a job if I were trained as a firefighter paramedic."

"I'm sure you're right, though the job has dangers of its own."

"I know, but I'm much less likely to be shot on the job, and there's practically zero chance of being called to do undercover firefighter work."

He laughed heartily. "That's true, though it would be funny if you were."

"So you support my decisions?" I asked, knowing his opinion meant a lot to me.

"I do. I can see this isn't some rash choice you're making—you've put a lot of thought into it. I think you'd be an amazing fire fighter paramedic."

"Good. You can help me break the news to Mom and Dad then."

"I wouldn't worry about them. I think they'll readily agree with your choice, especially when they hear about your accident. They've been worried about you being in dangerous situations too."

"You seriously didn't tell them about the accident?" I asked, surprised.

He shook his head. "No. You were okay, and I didn't want them freaking out and possibly blowing your cover."

"Did you tell Sheridan?"

He winced. "No."

"You know they're going to kill you when they find out, right?"

"That's what I'm afraid of."

I slugged him lightly in the shoulder. "It was nice knowing ya, buddy. I'll be sure to send flowers to your funeral."

"I was hoping you'd help me keep the secret," he said wryly.

"And miss all the fireworks? Now why would I do that?" I laughed.

"Thanks for having my back, man." He pursed his lips together, and I laughed harder.

"You know I always have your back."

He smiled. "I know."

CHAPTER TWENTY-SEVEN
Cami-

All the lights and sounds almost put me on sensory overload. There was so much to look at and see, I couldn't possibly begin to take it all in.

"What do you think?" Ripper asked as he casually draped his arm around my shoulders. Hunter walked along the other side of me, holding Roberta's hand, following Seth and Nick who were ahead of us.

"It's incredible. The pictures I've seen don't do it justice. There's just so much—everything."

"I can't believe you've never been to Las Vegas before," Ripper said. "Hunter's been here before, why weren't you with him?"

I flashed a look in Hunter's direction, not knowing what to answer.

"I came here later on with Chris," he piped up, rescuing me. "Our foster parents were never big on traveling. They didn't have the money for stuff like that."

"Then how did you and Cami get lucky enough to end up with not one, but two, Camaros?"

"It's called hard work, dude. My boss helped me get mine, and Cami won hers along with a scholarship to the U of A in a competitive academics program the school district held. She's one smart cookie, aren't you, Sis?" He winked at me.

Ripper looked impressed. "So were you like valedictorian or something?"

I laughed. "Something like that," I answered, amazed at how Hunter could make things up off the top of his head. He made things sound so natural even I could believe the lies, and I knew the truth.

"Since when do you go for smart girls, Ripper?" Nick asked with a snort.

"Yeah, Cami might be too good for you," Seth added with a chuckle.

"Are you saying I only date dumb girls, and that I'm stupid too?" Ripper asked incredulously.

"Well, if you aren't smart enough to figure it out yourself . . . ," Roberta let her sentence dangle, and I couldn't help but laugh even harder.

Ripper gave a disgusted grunt. "For your information, I don't choose the girls I go with based on how smart they are or aren't. I like them for their good looks."

"Oh, so you're just shallow then?" Roberta asked. "That sounds so much better."

We all laughed again, and Ripper got a sour look on his face. "I was trying to tell Cami how hot she is, thank you very much."

Hunter visibly stiffened beside me, and Ripper noticed. "What's your problem Wilder? You don't like me talking about your sister that way?"

"Hunter doesn't like anyone talking about me, period." I rushed to smooth things over. "He's a little overprotective, in case you haven't noticed," I teased, reaching over to poke Hunter playfully in the ribs as I tried to diffuse the tension between them.

"Oh, I've noticed," he grumbled. "You need to chill, man. I'm not going to do anything to hurt her."

"Good," Hunter replied. "Let's keep it like that."

"Contrary to popular belief, apparently, I'm not actually stupid." He lightly punched Seth and Nick in their backs with his free hand. "And for those who think I am, maybe you should remember who's paying your bills. Either that, or I can hire on some new people."

Seth held his hands up in surrender. "No need for threats, man. I was just messing around with you."

"Me too," Nick spoke up hurriedly.

"Great. Now that's taken care of, what do you guys want to do first? We have tonight and all day tomorrow to play around. The delivery is arranged for tomorrow night."

"How's it going to go exactly?" Hunter asked. "This is my first time on this end of things, so I'm out of the loop."

I knew he was trying to get more

information, so he could give it to the police who were going to help us here in Vegas.

"Don't worry, it's not hard. Roberta and I will go have a meeting with them sometime prior to the exchange, and they'll tell us where to meet them. When it's time to make the drop, we exchange keys and give them the cars, they give us the cash, and we all go home happy."

Roberta grunted and Hunter cast a glance at her. "What's the matter?"

"Nothing," she replied with a wave of her hand. "Forget it. Where are we going? I'm ready to party."

"I think Cami should choose, since she's never been here," Ripper said with a smile, giving me a cuddle.

"Don't let me pick. I have no idea what there is to do besides hearing about the fountains outside the Bellagio and the pirate show at Treasure Island."

"Let's do that then. We can take the timed walk down the strip and catch all the free attractions," Ripper suggested.

"Are you serious?" Seth moaned loudly, his shoulders slumping. "I want to gamble and party."

"Cami and Roberta aren't old enough yet," Hunter reminded them.

"Roberta is. She has a fake ID she uses here all the time," Nick added.

Hunter shrugged. "Well, Cami doesn't, so unless you know somewhere she can score one, bars and casinos aren't an option. I'm not going to risk either of us getting arrested trying to sneak her into places she's not supposed to be."

There was more grumbling from both Seth and Nick.

"Don't let me stop you from having a good time," I said wishing they'd all go somewhere and leave us alone. "I'm more than happy to walk the strip by myself. I can catch up with you later at the hotel."

Hunter snorted and rolled his eyes at me.

"It's not safe for a pretty girl to be out walking alone on the strip," Ripper said. "You might get picked up and taken somewhere you'd never want to be."

"Like where?" I asked, not following.

"It doesn't matter," Hunter spoke up. "You guys can go wherever you like. I have no problem staying with Cami and showing her the sights. We can catch up with you later. Feel free to go hit the clubs and have some fun."

Ripper pulled me closer. "Nah, that's okay. I promised Cami I was going to paint the town with her tonight. I can't ditch out on my girl when it's her first time in Vegas." He placed a light kiss on the top of my forehead.

"It's okay, really," I said with a smile, eager to be rid of them. "I don't mind at all. After Hunter's accident, I made up my mind to spend more one-on-one time with him and Chris. There's nothing like a near-death experience to make a person reevaluate their priorities. Family comes first."

"You're a good sister," Hunter said with an appreciative look. He gripped my hand. "Don't ever doubt it."

"Come on, Ripper. Let's go party," Seth whined. "She'll be okay."

Ripper sighed heavily as he looked at me. "Are you sure?"

I nodded. "I'm actually really tired after our trip. That was a long drive. I think if Hunter's okay with it, maybe we can catch a show where we can sit down. I'd love to watch any of the musical performances here."

He laughed. "I keep forgetting I'm dating an artsy girl." He turned his attention to Hunter. "You sure, man?"

Hunter nodded. "I'm good with it."

"I want to stay with Hunter and Cami," Roberta spoke up.

"Really?" Hunter seemed surprised.

She nodded. "I don't need to go clubbing. I've already got the hottest guy on the strip."

I had to force myself to remain passive. I knew it was all part of the act, but I also had no doubt she was truly into Hunter. She didn't want to leave the two of us together.

Ripper's phone started vibrating, and he pulled it out, looking at the screen before he answered it. "Hey Ernesto, what's up?" He paused for a moment. "Yeah, we're here. The cars are all ready for tomorrow." He paused again. "Yes, she's here this time too." He glanced toward Roberta. "Okay, no problem. We'll meet you there."

"What's going on?" Hunter asked, instantly on the alert.

"Nothing, man. The guys we do business with want to meet with Roberta and me for some drinks and get things set for tomorrow."

"Where at?"

"Down the strip at Mandalay Bay."

"I'll come with you," Hunter volunteered immediately. "Cami can wait for us in her room."

Ripper clapped him on the shoulder. "Go have fun with Cami. This is a private meeting they request sometimes. They don't even let Seth and Nick come."

"Yeah, they think their high roller parties are too good for us."

"Why does Roberta need to go?" Hunter asked.

"They like her. I had her with me the first time we met. They consider her part of the team."

"Are you okay with that?" Hunter asked her. "I don't want you doing anything dangerous."

She nodded and gave a little laugh. "I'll be fine. Haven't you figured out that danger is my middle name?"

He appeared to ponder this for a second. "I thought your middle name was sexy?"

She giggled. "I have lots of middle names. Stick around, and I'll show you plenty more."

"Deal. I plan on being around for a while." Hunter pulled her into his arms right in the middle of the sidewalk and gave her a big kiss. She wrapped her arms around his neck and hugged him close as she kissed him back.

"Get a room," a pedestrian said as they passed, and everyone around us laughed.

"We have one," Roberta said as she broke

away staring at Hunter with stars in her eyes.

He smiled back, and I had to look away. It hurt my heart too much to watch.

"My turn," Ripper whispered in my ear before turning my face to his. His lips touched mine, and I lifted my hand to stroke his cheek as I quickly pulled away. "Have a good time tonight."

"I will, but not as good as if you were there. I'll call you when we're done."

"Okay," I nodded, noticing that Hunter was now watching the two of us the way I'd been watching him a minute ago.

"Let's go," Ripper said to the others. "Seth and Nick, you can play in the casino while you're waiting for us."

"All right!" Seth exclaimed, rubbing his hands together. "Party time!"

They said their goodbyes and headed down the sidewalk together.

"So it's just you and me," Hunter said as we watched them walk away.

"Looks that way. Sorry you got stuck with the underage girl?" I teased.

He smiled. "There's nowhere else I'd rather be. Now *I* get to paint the town red with you, which is how it should be anyway."

We turned back toward the Venetian, which was where we were staying.

"So what do you want to do?" I asked, wishing I could slip my hand into his. I kept them clasped in front of me instead.

"I'm going to take you to dinner at a nice Italian restaurant, and we're going to see if there are any shows that appeal to you—if the concierge can get us tickets."

"Sounds great. Too bad the Venetian doesn't show The Phantom of the Opera anymore. I would've loved to see it here."

Hunter's eyebrows shot up. "Honestly, that surprises me. I wasn't sure if you'd care for that musical anymore after what happened with Clay."

I shook my head. "I'm not going to let Clay ruin it for me. It's still my favorite."

He draped his arm around me. "You're stronger than you look, you know that?"

"Are you saying I look wimpy?" I teased back.

He laughed. "No. I tend to think of you as my fragile girl who needs protecting. You often surprise me with how strong you are."

"I think it's a love thing. I always feel like I need to protect you too."

We stepped on the moving sidewalk that would take us up to the second floor shops of the Venetian. Hunter kept his arm around my shoulders until we stepped off, and then he pulled me into a secluded corner. He kissed me quickly, before stepping away and looking around.

"I'm sorry. That probably wasn't the wisest thing to do," he apologized.

"Why? I don't mind, and it's not like anyone here knows who we are."

"Yeah, but you're here with Ripper. We may frequently run into other people at the hotel. It would be obvious if you were seen being romantic with two different guys and me with two different girls. Plus, there are security cameras all over these places. You never know who's watching. We need to be careful in public."

I glanced around, suddenly feeling paranoid. "You're right. Let's go to your room and find a show to see."

"Sure thing, Sis," he said good-naturedly.

I groaned. "Can I just say—I can't wait until I'm not your sister anymore?"

He laughed. "Me neither, Goody. Me neither." He glanced at me as he slid his hands into his pockets, and I wondered if he were having trouble keeping them to himself too. "So, I have a request for you."

"What's that?"

"I know it's your first night in Vegas, but would you mind if we didn't stay out late? I was thinking if you happened to fall asleep early in my room while you're waiting for Ripper to get back, then I could tell him I didn't want to wake you up because you weren't feeling well. It would keep you from having to sleep in his room tonight."

"That sounds like a great plan to me. I'd much rather be with you."

"I worry about you having nightmares while you're with him. I don't know if you might talk in your sleep."

"My nightmares have been less frequent since you took me home, but I can understand why you'd be concerned."

"I know being with him puts you under stress. I want you to feel safe."

"What will be our excuse for tomorrow night?" I asked. "You know Ripper wants me to stay with him. It's been hard to keep coming up with reasons to put him off."

"We'll think of something, and if we don't, tell him it makes you uncomfortable. What's the worst that'll happen? He'll dump you for not putting out? That's more than fine by me."

I laughed. "Me too. It's funny really. He's been a nice enough guy, but knowing what he's capable of makes me feel sick to be around him. I don't like it when he touches me."

"I don't like it either," Hunter growled, a frown creasing his face. "In fact, I feel the extreme need to punch him every time he gets near you. Hang on a second." He reached into his pocket and pulled out his phone. "It's Chris. He says for me to call him."

"I hope everything's okay," I replied while Hunter pushed the card into the key slot and opened the door. I sat on the bed, watching expectantly while he dialed the number.

"Hey Chris, what's up? Yeah, I can talk. It's just me and Cami here at the moment." He paused and then nodded as if he were agreeing with whatever Chris was saying. "How does that affect the deal going down here tomorrow?" He waited again. "Ripper and Roberta have gone to meet a guy named Ernesto at Mandalay, but he wouldn't let any of us go with them. He said it was private. Okay, I got it. Send me the information when you have it. I'll take care of things on this end. Thanks, Chris."

"What's happening?" I asked, feeling like I

was about to die of curiosity.

"Chris said the body was positively identified as Manny. Their forensics search turned up blood evidence on Ripper's toolbox in the garage. It's a match. We've got him on suspicion of murder and grand theft auto."

My heart pounded, with both relief and nerves—relief that everything was nearly over, and nerves from knowing I really had been spending time with a killer. "What happens now?"

"Tucson PD is setting up a joint effort with Las Vegas PD. They're going to tap into my phone signal and bust everyone at the car exchange tomorrow. Ripper will be extradited back to Arizona for the murder charges. Chris is going to send me information on the detectives who will be in charge of things here." He smiled. "Hopefully, in the next twenty-four hours all of this will be over with."

I stood up and wrapped my arms around his neck. "It can't happen soon enough for me. Please promise me you'll be careful."

"We both need to be careful. Both of us will be there. Remember not to resist, and do whatever they tell you. They may not know who is who in the beginning, and it could cause things to get a little rough."

At this point, I didn't care if a cop face-planted me into the dirt and cuffed me to a pole. All I could think of was one more day, and then it would all be done.

CHAPTER TWENTY-EIGHT
Cami-

"Cami! Cami!" Hunter's urgent voice penetrated my sleepy mind as he shook me violently.

"What is it?" I asked, sitting up immediately.

"Get your shoes on. We've got to go right now!" He was frantically throwing on his shoes, tying the laces.

I quickly did what he asked, wondering how we'd gone from a nice relaxed evening to this.

"What's happening?" I grabbed my purse as he shoved his wallet back into his pocket.

"Turn off your cell phone," he ordered me as he shut his down. "We've been made. Apparently, there's a dirty cop here in Vegas. He intercepted Chris's report and blew our cover to Ripper and Ernesto. Ernesto's thugs are on the way here right now. Roberta managed to text me a warning. She said they don't know my real name, only that an undercover officer had infiltrated, but they know it's me." He grabbed my hand and pulled me toward the door as I pushed the button to shut down my phone. "We've got to get lost here and find a safe place until we can get help. I can't trust the police, because I don't know who the leak is."

My heart was racing, and I wondered if I was stuck in another bad nightmare. "Please tell me I'm dreaming," I muttered.

"I wish I could." He opened the door and peered out into the empty hallway. "Let's go."

We ran down the hallway toward the circular sitting area, which had several halls branching off from it. Hunter paused for a moment, glancing between the hall of elevators and the bridge that led to another section of the hotel. "This way," he said, guiding me toward the bridge.

The elevators dinged open behind us, but we didn't pause to look and see who it was. A guard sat halfway down the breezeway, and he stood, staring at us curiously as we hurried toward him.

"That's them!" I heard an unfamiliar voice behind us.

"Help," Hunter said to the security guard. "Those guys behind us tried to rob my girlfriend."

Immediately, the security guard reached for his Taser and called for extra reinforcements. Hunter didn't stop running, dragging me through the maze of opulent halls as I tried desperately to match his long stride.

"Keep running!" he ordered. "The guard won't be able to hold them all off!"

Busting through a set of doors that marked an emergency stairwell, we clamored down them as quickly as we could. My breath was coming in short, fast bursts, and I noticed his was too. We hit the door at the bottom, continuing down the corridor. Ahead, I could see the exit that led out onto the street, and we made our way toward it, surging through.

He glanced around quickly.

"Which way?" I asked, nervously checking behind us.

"We need to get away from the most cameras. They can track us that way," He huffed. "I think we need to stay off the strip." We started running again down the sidewalk, weaving our way through the throngs of people, rudely bumping and jostling them. Several shouted as we passed by, but I was too scared to worry about apologies.

When we hit the corner, Hunter pulled me down the side street, never breaking his pace. I could feel my strength waning. I didn't know how much longer I'd be able to keep this pace. My lungs felt like they were on fire. "Hunter, I've got to catch my breath," I pleaded.

He paused for a second to glance around. "This way. I have an idea."

I numbly followed, concentrating only on staying next to him. He dragged me through a glass door into a very gaudily decorated foyer, which boasted several giant white, feathery plumes beside crazy-looking costumes of every kind imaginable. Music drifted from a small dimly lit chapel with a few rows of small white pews, and I suddenly realized it was one of those quaint wedding chapels Las Vegas was so famous for.

"Can I help you?" a smiling lady in a white business suit asked from behind a glass counter. She was wearing a tag proclaiming her name, Marie Sanchez.

"Yes," Hunter gasped, flashing his amazing smile. "We want to get married."

She gave us a curious look, obviously wondering why we were panting. "Are you okay?"

He nodded. "I've been trying to get her to say yes for ages. She finally did. We ran all the way here. I'm not taking any chances on her changing her mind."

I offered the woman a smile, it was the best I could do at the moment.

She clasped her hands in front of her. "Well, you came to the right place. We offer several packages you can choose from. I'll grab the catalog—"

"We want that one," Hunter said, pointing to a photo of a man and woman dressed like Elvis and Priscilla Presley. It was awful. He grabbed me around the shoulder and yanked me up against him. "We want it all—wigs, clothes, everything. Give us the works. We've always been huge fans of the King, haven't we, baby?"

I tried to keep my false grin plastered to my face. "Yep," I panted out the lie.

"All right then. Follow me to the dressing rooms." She led us around the corner and down a small hallway. "Here's the bride's room, and this one right here is for the groom. I'll bring your wedding attire to you."

"Sounds perfect," Hunter replied, leaning to kiss my forehead.

"I'll need your names and to see your identification. Also, if I could get a credit card from you, so I can print the paper work, that would be great."

"Dylan Wilcock and Camilla Wimberley," Hunter supplied, reaching into his pocket for his wallet as I reached into my small purse for my driver's license. Hunter pulled out several cards, sorting through them before he found what he was looking for and handed them to her. I gave her mine as well. "We'd like to purchase the costumes also, instead of renting them, if that's an option—so we can remember this day."

"Of course it's possible!" she replied, sounding very happy at the news. "I'll be right back with them. I think I can appropriately guess your sizes." She hurried off down the hall.

"Now what do we do?" I asked.

"We are going to get into these costumes. No one will look for us as Elvis and Priscilla and people won't blink twice at seeing someone dressed like them here. After we're dressed, I'll pay for the costumes, and we'll tell her we changed our mind. Then we'll take a taxi to another hotel and check in under my real name and let Chris know what's going on."

"Sounds good." I was glad he had some sort of plan. I was exhausted.

"Are you going to be okay?" he asked, running his hands over my shoulders as he stared at me with concern.

"I'll be fine. I'm just happy we got out of there. I take back every bad thought I ever had about Roberta. She really came through for us."

Hunter nodded. "She did."

"Here you go," Marie said, reappearing with two garment bags draped across her arm. "This one's for you dear," she handed the top one to me, "and this one is yours. I'll be right outside the doors here, filling out the paperwork if either of you need any help."

"Thank you," I said politely, glancing one more time at Hunter before I stepped into the small dressing room. I pulled the white dress out of the bag. It had a high neck and lace-covered sleeves. The rest of the dress fell in loose folds to the floor and had a massive train. It was quite simple—the high waist giving it a maternal appearance—almost like something a bride would wear to cover a pregnancy.

The veil had a crown and boasted yards of voluminous tulle, and there was a black wig in the package too. I sighed heavily. This was definitely not my idea of proper wedding attire, but it should suit our purpose as a disguise. Hunter was right—no one would think twice about seeing someone imitating Elvis and Priscilla Presley in Las Vegas.

Dressing quickly, I threw my belongings into the provided plastic bag, eager to get out of here and to a safer place. Chris would be able to send the help we needed, but I was afraid to trust anyone else at this point. It was a totally helpless feeling.

Surveying myself in the large mirror, I dug into my purse for my eyeliner and applied it liberally to get into character. It was more than I'd ever worn in my life, but it would definitely complete the Priscilla look I'd seen in pictures and hopefully hide my true identity even more. Sighing heavily, I grabbed my things and made my way out of the room.

Marie was waiting for me there, smiling. "Here's your ID, dear. Mr. Wilcock is waiting for you in the chapel."

I slid it into my purse. "Thank you," I said.

"And I need you to sign this piece of paper."

"Okay." I quickly did as she asked before following her to the chapel.

Hunter was standing there in a black brocade dinner suit and wig that matched Elvis's famous hairdo. I had to bite my lip so I wouldn't laugh.

He didn't look amused, though. "Come here," he ordered abruptly with a serious look. He held his hand out to me and pulled me close. "There are men outside the building looking for us," he whispered into my ear. "Just follow my lead."

Fear shot through me as I nodded. Hunter led me to the altar where a man in a suit was waiting. He smiled happily at us, and I gave him a faltering smile in return. It was then I noticed the Elvis song, *Love Me Tender*, playing softly in the background. Another man I hadn't noticed before stepped up to the side of us and began capturing pictures with his camera.

"Welcome, friends," the minister began. "We're so happy to have you with us tonight.

Would you like the long ceremony or the short one?"

I heard the bell on the door jingle softly from the other room.

"The short one, please. We're anxious to have this done." Hunter leaned down and placed a kiss on my cheek. "Don't turn around," he warned quietly.

"Are you here for the Wilcock wedding?" I heard Marie ask whoever had entered.

"We are gathered here this evening to unite the two of you in love, which is the greatest of all things. So let us proceed. Dylan Wilcock, do you take Camilla Noelle as your lawfully wedded wife?"

"I do," Hunter replied. My hands were trembling as my ears strained to catch more of the conversation behind us.

"No, I'm actually looking for a girl and someone by the name of Wilder who ran off together. We're trying to stop the wedding," an unfamiliar male voice spoke. "Do you have any other couples here?"

My heart was pounding so loud I was sure the man could hear it.

"Camilla?" the minister's voice interrupted me, the camera still flashing in my face.

"What?" I asked, confused. He raised his eyebrows and looked toward Hunter in question. "Oh, I mean, yeah. I do. Sorry, I'm a little nervous."

"No, I'm afraid not," Marie responded. "This is the only couple here."

The minister shot an anxious glance down

the aisle behind us, and I was sure he was worried about us being angry over the loud talking behind us.

Hunter cleared his throat calling the minister back to attention.

He sputtered and smiled as he quickly searched for his place. "Then by the power vested in me by the state of Nevada, I now pronounce you man and wife. You may now kiss the bride."

Hunter grabbed me, his lips crushing mine. "Just keep kissing me," he whispered as the photographer continued clicking away.

I did as he asked, shaking, hoping the monstrous veil was hiding us enough from whoever was observing. I heard the door chime again, and I hoped it was the man leaving the building.

"Congratulations!" Marie said from behind us.

We gingerly turned, scanning the room. It was empty. I couldn't help my sigh of relief.

"The limo you asked for, Mr. Wilcock, is at the curb waiting to take you to your hotel. Why don't you come here and get a few more pictures under the arch."

We did as she asked, both of us pausing to give nervous glances toward the door. The photographer snapped a few more photos.

"We'll send the proofs to the email address you gave me, Mr. Wilcock. Congratulations again!" She handed him a large white envelope and the bags with our belongings. "Here's your receipts and certificate. Thank for your business."

"Thank you," Hunter smiled and shook their hands before turning and kissing me again. "Keep your head down when we go outside, like you're watching where you're stepping."

I nodded and followed him. Maria helped our escape by throwing rice at us as we ran across the sidewalk, giving us a plausible excuse to duck. I slid into the open door the driver was holding, and Hunter slid in beside me."

"We did it," I said.

"Don't count your blessings yet," Hunter said warily. "We need to make sure no one follows us."

I sighed heavily, leaning my head back against the seat. "Will this thing ever be over?"

"Soon, Goody. Real soon. Hang in there."

"Where to, Mr. Wilcock?" the driver asked as he slid into the front of the vehicle.

"Well," Hunter replied with a sigh. "This was kind of a spur of the moment decision, so I don't actually have a reservation anywhere. How about one of the nice resorts—somewhere else, though? We'd like a place a bit more peaceful than the strip."

"I'd recommend Green Valley Ranch Resort and Spa," the driver said. "It's out of the way, but still close enough to the attractions you might want to see."

"That sounds perfect," Hunter agreed. "Let's see if we can get a room there."

"Would you like me to call ahead and find out for you, sir?"

"That would be wonderful. Thank you."

The privacy window closed, and Hunter turned to look out the darkened glass as we pulled away from the curb. I did the same, and we watched the traffic patterns of all the vehicles around us. It didn't appear anyone was following us.

We arrived at the prettily lit resort, the glow highlighting its very beautiful Mediterranean style structure and sculpted grounds. The driver opened the door for us. "They're waiting for you inside. There are rooms available as well as a special honeymoon package."

"Thanks so much for your help. How much do I owe you?"

The man quoted his price, and I noticed Hunter tipped him generously too as he handed him the cash.

"Have a wonderful evening," he spoke again.

Hunter ushered me quickly into the fancy building. We were safe—for the moment.

CHAPTER TWENTY-NINE

Cami-

Hunter tossed the pre-paid phone down on the nightstand next to the king bed in our room. The only light on was a dim lamp, which cast his face in shadow as he ran a hand through his hair.

I was still wearing the wedding dress, but I'd pulled off my wig and veil. Tossing them next to Hunter's Elvis wig and our honeymoon goody basket in the chair, I sat on the edge of the bed. Hunter sank down beside me and loosened his tie, pulling it off and opening the top button of his collar.

"So what's the verdict?" I asked, concerned.

"Chris says to lay low where we are. He isn't going to share our location with anybody, just to be safe. The department there is going to try and get in touch with the Vegas PD superiors and let them know the case has been compromised due to a leak in their staff."

"Ripper and his gang are going to be long

gone."

Hunter nodded and sighed. "You're most likely correct."

"Maybe we should catch a flight and go home."

"Chris is afraid they might be watching the airport for us. He said to hang tight. He'll be here to get us in the morning."

I could tell he felt defeated. "I'm sorry."

"Sorry for what? You aren't responsible for any of this. Who knows—you may have even saved my life tonight."

"How so?"

"If I'd gone with them, I would've been there when they found out who I was. The chance of escaping would have been practically none."

The mere thought of him coming to harm made me feel nauseated. "I'm glad you were with me."

"Me too." He lifted his hand and stroked my chin. "I love you," he said softly. "I'm so sorry about this evening. That definitely wasn't the way I imagined us getting married."

I laughed. "Don't worry about it. People will get a big laugh out of our sham wedding story someday."

Surprise flickered in his eyes. "Cami, you do realize we actually got married—for real."

"Wha—what?" I stammered. "No."

He gave a wry laugh. "Yes, we did. I gave them my real name to protect us from anyone looking for someone with my alias. We signed the license—there were witnesses. We just got married."

I closed my eyes, my mind frantically replaying everything that had happened this evening. I'd been so absorbed in the guy at the door, that I'd missed my own wedding. "Please tell me we didn't tie the knot dressed in Elvis and Priscilla costumes." I was mortified. I stared up at him, searching for another answer in his eyes, but there wasn't one.

He took my face in his hands. "Listen, you were clearly married under duress. Vegas weddings happen all the time—and so do Vegas annulments and divorces. We can easily end this."

My lips trembled and unshed tears suddenly blurred my vision. "Is that what you want to do?"

He studied my features carefully. "Goody, I was going to officially ask you to marry me after this assignment was done. You know how much I want to be with you. It's all I want."

I swallowed thickly, my heart full of love for him. "Then I don't want an annulment. This may not have been our ideal wedding, but we can have another one with our family."

"Are you sure?" His thumbs stroked my cheeks.

I nodded. "I'm sure. I love you."

"I love you too, Mrs. Wilcock."

He smiled softly, leaning forward until his lips gently touched mine, and I closed my eyes as the realization rushed through me. Hunter . . . Dylan, was really my husband! He was mine, and he wanted it to stay that way! Joy rushed through me. He pulled me closer, lifting me so I was on his lap, and I slid my arms around his neck, kissing him deeply.

His tongue slipped into my mouth, tangling with mine, and I pressed harder against him. A small moan of pleasure escaped his mouth, and I loved knowing I was the one responsible for it.

"Stand up," he ordered gently, and I did as he requested. He turned me so I was facing away from him, looking at both of us in the large wall mirror. He gently lifted my hair, draping it over my shoulder, before skimming his fingers across my skin. He stared at me through the glass, his eyes locking with mine. "So beautiful, my wife."

Goose bumps flared at his words. I couldn't help the smile that crept onto my face. "Say it again," I responded.

He leaned closer, his mouth very close to my ear as his hands slid down my arms. "My wife," he whispered again, his fingertips gripping me as he emphasized the words. His lips touched my neck as he placed a tender kiss there before replacing it with his tongue, trailing it lightly on the surface. Watching his actions in the mirror was like seeing a long-wished-for dream coming true before my eyes.

His hands released me, and there was a tug on the zipper of my dress a moment before the air brushed against my skin. He straightened, removing his jacket and tossing it toward the chair, then started on the buttons of his shirt.

Suddenly I was very nervous. "Wait," I interrupted, turning and placing my hand on his to stop him.

"What's the matter?" he asked, immediately looking concerned. "If you're not ready still, I'll wait. It'll be hard, but I'll do it."

I smiled, butterflies whipping about madly in my stomach. "Thank you for being concerned about me. I'm well . . . a little . . . unprepared for this."

I could see the disappointment in his eyes. "That's totally understandable. We can wait." He didn't understand my meaning.

"You're so sweet, but you don't understand. I *want* to. I'm just nervous."

I reached for the top button of his shirt and began unfastening, my hands shaking so badly I felt like a bumbling idiot. His stare never left me, heating my skin. There was nothing to stop us this time—it was really going to happen. Hunter had wanted it to be something special between us. How could we get more special than our honeymoon?

One button open—I moved onto the next one, but Hunter reached up and grabbed my hands.

"You're shaking." He lifted them to his mouth and kissed the back of each one. "You don't need to be afraid. I promise I'll be as gentle as possible."

I blushed, unable to help it. It was so strange to be openly talking about this. "I'm not afraid of you. I'm excited."

He grinned and cocked an eyebrow at me. "Excited is good."

"Yes, it is," I replied, turning my hands so I could kiss his in the same fashion before I gingerly continued my previous task—even undoing the buttons at his wrists. When I was finished, I pushed the shirt from his shoulders, and he let it slide the rest of the way down his arms until it fell to the floor. His eyes never left me, watching as I placed my palms flat against his chest and trailed my fingers down the ridges of his stomach. His abs tightened even more, and I heard his breath catch.

Pulling the gown away from my shoulders, he paused to kiss each one. "Your skin is so beautiful. It feels like silk. I love rubbing my lips against it."

I gave a light laugh. "I can barely think when your lips are anywhere near me."

He chuckled. "That's good to know for the future."

"Planning future ambushes already?" I teased.

"Absolutely. I promise there'll be lots of them." His gaze traveled from my head to my toes. He laughed when he got to the bottom. "Nice shoes," he commented with a wink.

I glanced down at my tennis shoes. "It's the latest fashion for brides on the run. Didn't you know?"

He pulled me closer, kissing the top of head. "I'm so sorry we didn't have time to get you the right shoes—or anything for that matter."

"I'm not. If it wasn't for the crazy circumstances, we wouldn't be here right now." I ran my fingers lightly up and down his back, resting my head on his chest. "I don't want to be anywhere else but here—with you."

He reached down and scooped me off my feet. "I neglected to carry my bride over the threshold," he said. "Can I make it up by carrying you to bed?"

"I'll think about it," I replied with a grin.

"Think fast. It's only gonna take me two seconds to get there."

"Oh all right. I guess," I relented, unable to wipe the smile from my face.

He carried me around to the side and then paused.

"What's the matter?"

"I didn't think this through very well. Reach down there and pull back the covers."

I giggled and did as he requested, and he carefully laid me down on the sheets before going around to the other side and climbing in, scooting quickly over. He ran his fingers through my hair, spreading it out beside me.

"One of my biggest fantasies has been imagining your red hair spread out on the pillow while you're lying in my bed."

"Really?" I found that interesting.

He nodded. "The color is so striking. I've been imagining what it would be like to wake up and see it every morning."

"Let me help your imagination—it will most likely be a massive tangled mess."

"Good." He grinned.

"Why good?"

"Because if it isn't, then it means I haven't been doing my job properly."

My mouth formed an "oh" as his meaning sunk in, but there wasn't any chance for sound to come out. His lips covered mine, followed by the rest of his strong body as he kissed me deeply, passionately.

Sparks quickly lit between us and, what had previously begun as slow and gentle, suddenly escalated into something much more frantic and needy. Every part of me felt as if it were on fire, my skin made molten by his touch. The rest of our clothing disappeared in a blur of sensuality, small gasps, fevered breaths, touching, and more kissing. I thought I might explode.

"Say my name, Cami. Say it now," Hunter commanded his face a mask of love, need, and concentration.

"Dylan, please!" I called out, unsure of what I was asking him for. My world suddenly burst into bright colors, and I clung to him, nails digging into his skin as I held on for dear life. My heart was pounding out of my chest and my emotions swirled out of control as I realized how truly desperately I was in love with him. He was my world, my life, my everything—and staring into his eyes, I saw those same emotions mirrored back at me. He was part of me now, and I a part of him, two halves that made a whole.

I noticed the slight sheen of perspiration on his brow and he smiled at me. "You called me Dylan," he stated, slightly out of breath.

I bit my lip and nodded as I stared into his warm chocolate eyes. "Is that okay? I mean it is your name."

"It was perfect," he replied. "Everything about it—about you—was absolutely perfect."

Tears welled in my eyes and slid softly over the rims.

"What's the matter?" he asked, reaching with his thumb to wipe them carefully away.

I shook my head. "Nothing. Absolutely nothing. I'm just happy I could please you too."

He chuckled and rolled to the side of me before gathering me in his arms. "Goody, don't you ever worry about pleasing me. You please me all the time—more than you'll ever know."

I snuggled against him, loving the feel of our bodies pressed so intimately together. "This seems like a dream. I can't believe I really belong to you now."

"Well, then I guess I'll have to keep proving it to you, repeatedly."

I sighed against his chest. "Sounds fun."

He chuckled. "Yeah, it sure does." He squeezed me tighter. "I love you, Camilla Noelle Wilcock."

My heart felt like it would burst, I was so content and happy. "I love you too, Dylan."

CHAPTER THIRTY
Hunter-

The tiny crack in between the hotel curtains gave enough light that I could silently observe the beauty of my pretty wife while she slept. Nothing could've prepared me for how I felt at waking and seeing her there. I'd never known real love until I met Cami. The rest of my life seemed somewhat hollow by comparison, and I knew I'd do anything for her.

Memories of her tangled in my arms flitted through my mind, causing my body to respond instantly to the enticement. I couldn't allow myself to be greedy enough to wake her, though, especially knowing how long into the night I'd kept her busy. There had been some time spent sleeping or comfortably dozing, but most of it was spent exploring and re-exploring one another.

The pre-paid phone started vibrating on the nightstand, and I quickly answered it. "Just a minute," I whispered. Carefully, I slipped from the bed, determined not to disturb Cami and let her rest as long as she could. "Sorry," I apologized to Chris after closing the bathroom door. "Cami's still sleeping. I didn't want to wake her. She's worn out."

"Is she okay?" Chris asked, sounding concerned.

I chuckled. "Yeah, she's fine. I, uh, kept her pretty busy last night is all."

There was moment of silence. "This information surprises me, since I'm normally the guy you're telling to butt out and mind his own business."

I grinned. "True, but there's something else you need to know. I neglected to mention it when we spoke earlier."

"Really? What's that?"

"Cami and I got married last night."

I heard him choke. "You're kidding me!"

"Not even a little." I couldn't stop grinning. It was nice to share the news with someone who'd be happy for us.

"You realize your parents and sister are going to kill you, right? Her parents too, most likely."

"Probably, but before anyone goes all crazy on us, they need to hear the story of how it came about. It certainly wasn't planned, and it definitely saved us from being caught."

"So, regardless of how it happened, I'm assuming neither of you want to put an end to this arrangement?"

"None whatsoever. I'm never letting this girl go. I love her too much."

"Well, in that case, I'm very happy for you, bro. Congratulations!"

"Thank you. What's the news this morning? I'm slightly anxious to get this bride of mine to a safer location."

"I can help you with that. I'm here in Las Vegas now with a couple of other officers who are going to help escort you safely home. We've already booked your flights, and we'll pick you up from your hotel at ten this morning to go to the airport."

"What's happening with the case and Ripper? Any news there?"

"Vegas PD is working on their end to plug their leak, and Seth and Nick have already been caught. Apparently, Ripper didn't inform them of what had taken place. The police apprehended them when they returned to the Venetian last night. The cars had already been dropped or moved. They're no longer in the parking garage. According to the valet service, all the tags were turned in, and the vehicle reclaimed by their owners."

"It sounds like they successfully made the switch then."

"That's what we're thinking."

"Which means Ripper got paid, and he has Seth's and Nick's money as well."

"Yes. We've had officers from Vegas PD running through the security tapes, but we haven't found any footage of him yet. We don't know where he's headed for sure, but we have officers staking out the Tucson location."

I snorted. "There's no way in hell he's going

to return there. He knows that's the first place we'll be looking for him."

"We figured as much but decided to watch just in case. His car is still there. We thought perhaps he might return for it."

"I doubt it. He can steal another one easily enough, and he should have plenty of money stashed away somewhere. He could easily leave and start again anywhere. I'm thinking he'll lay low for a while. Try targeting Roberta. She's the one who tipped me off. If she's with him, or knows where he is, I'm sure she'd tell us. After all, it was her involvement that led us to him in the first place. She wants to bring him down for killing Manny."

"Has she tried to contact you again?" Chris asked.

"I have no idea. Cami and I turned our cell phones off immediately after she texted. I didn't want anyone to trace us with the signal."

"Maybe you should check your phone—try texting her, and see if she answers."

"I don't want to do that while I'm here with Cami. If the mob is involved, they could get to us easily. Once I know she's safe, then I'll check."

"Time is of the essence, Dylan. The longer we wait, the better chance he has of getting away."

"So come get us now, then. I want him arrested too, but I won't risk Cami getting caught in the crossfire again." I hated to put things off when I knew they needed answers, but I was adamant about keeping Cami protected. She was my wife now. My first duty would always be to her.

"How long do you need to get ready?" Chris asked.

"Give us an hour."

"I'll be there in thirty minutes."

"Fine, we'll meet you in the lobby in an hour."

Chris laughed. "Boy, you sure are stubborn this morning."

"Give me a break. It's my first morning with my wife. I'd like to wake her nicely instead of starting our marriage by dragging her off to a new hiding place."

Chris sighed. "Take your cell phone to the lobby and ask for an envelope. Leave it for me at the front desk. I'll be by to get it in a few minutes. The guys and I will try to contact Roberta from a different location and see what we can find out. We'll come get you when it's time to go to the airport unless something new develops."

I grinned. "Thanks, man."

"You owe me big time," Chris replied. "Now go drop off the phone and enjoy your wife."

I quietly slipped out of the bathroom—pausing briefly to make sure Cami was still resting peacefully. She was so beautiful. Smiling, I carefully grasped the bag with my clothes in it from yesterday, trying not to rustle it too much as I carried it back to the bathroom. I quickly dressed and grabbed the key card so I could go down to the lobby.

"Good morning. Can I help you?" the smiling

receptionist spoke.

"Yes. Do you have an envelope that can hold this cell phone? My brother-in-law accidentally left it in my pocket yesterday. He's coming here for it in a couple of minutes."

"Sure. No problem." She sifted through a drawer before handing me an envelope and a pen. "Write his name on there for me. I'll have him show his ID when he claims it."

I smiled as I wrote his name down. "Ask to see his badge too."

She looked puzzled. "His badge."

"Yeah." I grinned, as I tucked the phone inside. "He's a cop."

"Oh, I see. Is there a reason I need to see his badge?" she asked, still appearing confused.

"No. I just like to hassle him." I winked at her and she laughed.

"Got it."

"Thanks for your help." I turned away and headed back toward my room.

"Anytime," she called after me.

I quietly slipped back inside and quickly undressed again before sliding into bed beside Cami. She gave a little moan and rolled toward me, stretching out her arm and draping it across my waist. She stiffened and opened her eyes, blinking rapidly.

"Hey gorgeous," I whispered.

She gave a half smile and relaxed. "Mmm. So I wasn't dreaming then. I was worried I'd wake up and find out this had all been some crazy thing my mind concocted."

"Nope. It's real." I ran my hand through her

wild curls. "I hope that's okay with you."

"It's better than okay," she muttered with a yawn, cuddling even closer. "I love you."

I'd never get tired of hearing her say those words. "I love you too."

"Do you think we can stay in bed all day together?" She ran her hand lightly over me, causing every nerve to snap to attention.

"As much as I would love that, Chris will be here at ten. He has tickets to fly us home."

She poked her bottom lip out slightly in a pout. "Well, that stinks."

"Tell you what—you let me get you somewhere safe, and I promise to spend a whole day in bed with you."

She giggled. "Gee, I really had to twist your arm, didn't I?"

I laughed and kissed her forehead. "But as for right now, we're operating on limited time this morning. I'm sorry."

"Well, then I guess we better hurry and get with it. Huh?" She smiled as she pushed herself up so she could reach my lips, draping herself across the top of me.

I couldn't stop grinning. What a fantastic way to start the day.

Cami and I were ready and waiting in the lobby when the car carrying Chris and the two other plainclothes officers pulled up. They quickly hopped out and helped us get our wedding attire loaded into the trunk before we all climbed back in and headed toward the airport.

"Cami, this is Officer Vincent and Officer Johnson," I introduced. "Officer Johnson was initially supposed to be the undercover guy on this case."

"Nice to meet you," he said with a nod toward her.

"I'm sorry to hear about your appendix. I hope you're feeling better now," she said politely.

"I'm doing much better, thank you." He smiled in a friendly fashion at her.

"Cami is my wife," I added springing the news on them.

Vincent and Johnson both laughed. "We already heard the news. Congratulations. I don't think I've ever seen ole Napier that surprised before," Johnson spoke up.

I eyed Chris. "Who else have you told?"

He raised his hands. "No one. I swear. They were in the room when I was talking to you this morning."

"Well, don't spread it around to anyone else. That's the last thing I need is for our parents to hear it through the grapevine. It wouldn't be pretty."

"No it wouldn't," Chris agreed. "I've already been imagining the talking down your mom is going to give you. She won't be very happy about missing the wedding."

"We'll have another one for all our family and friends," Cami said. "It's true, things didn't go the way we planned, but we still want to be able to celebrate with everyone who's close to us."

"I'm sure they'll appreciate that," Chris agreed smiling as he glanced at me.

"Any news with the phone?" I asked.

"Yes. You had a text from Roberta asking if you were okay. I responded as you and told her you were fine and in a safe place. I asked if she was okay and if she knew where Ripper was."

"Did she reply?"

He nodded. "She said she was with him, driving back to Arizona in a rental car. Ripper apparently has some money stashed somewhere, which he needs to get so they can leave. She said she would text more later, when they stopped. I told her you would be flying back to Tucson today, so if there was a delay in the response, it was because you were in the air."

"Sounds good. Is there any other news?"

"Not really, other than Seth and Nick both backed up Roberta's story about how Ripper and Manny fought on the night Manny disappeared. They've also confessed to the car thefts and have agreed to testify against Ripper in exchange for a lighter sentence. They'll be extradited back to Arizona and face charges there."

"Perfect. Now if we can just catch Ripper, we can put all of this behind us."

"What will happen to Roberta?" Cami asked.

"She was given immunity in the beginning for coming forward voluntarily and agreeing to testify against her brother. She wants him put away as bad as we do," Chris explained.

"I hope she's okay while she's with Ripper."

I glanced over at her. "I was under the impression you didn't care for her much."

She shrugged. "I don't really—but only because I was sure she was after you. I don't want anything bad to happen to her."

"Don't worry. I'm sure she'll be fine," I replied, trying to reassure her. "Ripper has no reason to suspect her."

"I hope you're right. It sounds like he's a very bad person."

CHAPTER THIRTY-ONE
Hunter-

"Hi, Mom." I smiled widely and silently prayed for strength from above when she opened the door.

"What a surprise!" she exclaimed, stepping aside to allow Chris, Cami, and me to enter. "I wasn't expecting to see the three of you anytime soon. Does this mean your case is finally finished?" She stepped next to me and grabbed my face in her hands, turning it carefully from side to side. "What are these bruises and scratches from?" she demanded with a frown before turning to face Chris with her hands on her hips. "Have you dragged my boy into trouble again?"

Chris swallowed hard, and I wondered if he realized he'd reached to loosen his tie or if it was a reflex from knowing my mom was about to hang him.

"Is dad here?" I asked, trying to deter her.

She glanced at me briefly before turning

back to Chris. "He's at the office. Now what's going on?"

"Why don't we go sit down first, and I'll explain everything," Chris suggested. "Cami and Dylan are exhausted. They've been through a lot."

She pursed her lips together and led us down the hall to the arched entryway of the sitting room. She gestured to one of the large leather sofas and sat across from us. "What's going on?" she said again. "How did you get hurt?"

"I'm fine, Mom, really. I was in a minor car accident. That's all. As you can see, I got a few scratches and bruises. Nothing to worry about." I cast a sidelong look in Cami's direction, and she rolled her eyes.

"Actually, Mrs. Wilcock, Dylan was in quite a terrible car accident. He was drag racing against the suspect in the case he's working on, and he rolled his vehicle several time at an extremely high rate of speed. It was quite terrifying," Cami said calmly. "We wanted to call you, but the police department asked us to wait, in hopes of keeping the case from being compromised. Thankfully, Dylan was okay and only required a few stitches to a cut on his head. He was unconscious for a while, though."

I groaned out loud, knowing we were in for it now.

"Thank you, Cami," my mother said evenly. "You have no idea how refreshing it is to be spoken to like an adult. These two," she gestured between Chris and me, "seem to think

I'm a fragile flower incapable of handling any kind of bad news."

My eyes widened in shock. I couldn't believe what I was hearing.

"And you!" She jabbed a finger in Chris's direction. "You should've known better! You can still have the decency to pick up the phone and let us know what's going on!"

"Would you really have sat here waiting for news?" I asked, trying to defend Chris.

"It doesn't matter. We're your parents. We have a right to know what's going on, whether it's serious or not."

I sighed. "You're right, Mom. I'm sorry we didn't let you know." There was no point in arguing with her. She always won.

"And shame on you for being reckless in a vehicle! You know how dangerous that is!"

"Mom! I've been trained to drive at a high rate of speed. It's not like I have no idea what I'm doing."

"I know what training you've had, and they're called *defensive driving* courses for a reason. It means you aren't supposed to go out and *actuar como un idiota*!"

I knew she was really angry when she reverted to using Spanish to tell me I was acting like an idiot. "You're right. I should've let you know," I repeated. "It won't happen again. There's more I need to tell you, though."

She let out a huff and looked at me pointedly. "What now?"

"We've been infiltrating a car theft ring. The case led us to Las Vegas this weekend, and we were really close to making a bust, but my cover was blown before the deal went down. Thankfully, my contact managed to tip me off, and Cami and I were able to run before they came for us."

"Cami was with you?" She looked positively horrified.

I waved her off before she could continue. "Yes. It's more of me being an *idiota*, but I'll get to that later." I took a breath and plunged ahead. "We were spotted before we could make a clean getaway and ended up running into a wedding chapel to hide while they searched for us. We put on some costumes they had for people who are into themed weddings. Anyway, the men searching for us were right outside the door, so we posed as a couple getting married before escaping in a limo that took us to safety." I reached over and squeezed Cami's hand.

Silence. Her expression didn't change, and I winced. This was even worse than when she was speaking Spanish. She took a deep breath and stood, walking toward the archway before turning around suddenly. "Are you trying to tell me you got *legally* married?"

I nodded. "That's what I'm telling you."

"In costumes—in some shady wedding chapel—in the middle of the unholiest place on earth?"

"Yep."

She made a sign of the cross and rolled her eyes heavenward. "*Perdonarlo, Padre,*" she whispered before crossing the room with her arms outstretched. "Welcome, Cami darling, to the family!" Cami stood and my mother hugged her close. "You poor dear. I know I've taught my son better than to get married in some sham of a chapel. You should've been married in a big church and had your union blessed by a proper priest." My mother glared down to where I was sitting.

I gave an exasperated laugh. "What? It's not like I planned for this to happen. I hadn't even properly asked her to marry me yet!"

"Well, then you better do it now. This girl deserves to have everything she's dreamed about."

She and Cami broke apart and Cami laughed. "It's okay, Mrs. Wilcock. It might not have been the ideal situation, but I'm very happy about it all the same."

My mom smiled at Cami as if she was the most wonderful thing she'd ever seen. "Aren't you just precious." She patted Cami on the cheek and hugged her again. She stared hard at me again. "I hope you gave her a decent honeymoon."

I stood and pulled Cami into my arms. "Mom, it was the best I could do on short notice—a nice room at a five-star resort."

"It was perfect," Cami said, leaning her head against my chest. "The best night of my life."

I kissed the top of her head, knowing she was blushing without even looking at her.

"What are your plans now then? Will you take her on a real honeymoon?"

I sighed. "That's why we're here, actually. The guy we're trying to catch is back in the area. He knows where Cami lives, so it's not safe for her to go there. I was hoping she could stay here in my room while we get things wrapped up. I need to know she's somewhere protected."

"Of course she can stay. I'm assuming you will as well?"

"It depends on how long this thing drags on, and when I'm needed. As of right now, we're waiting to be contacted by our informant." I glanced at my watch. "I honestly thought we would've heard something from her by now."

"I hope she's all right," Cami added.

"Me too. Let's go get you settled in. You need some sleep. You hardly got any last night."

She blushed to her roots. "Yeah, well neither did you," she responded brazenly.

I smiled. "I'm aware of that—trust me—I'm not complaining one bit." I grabbed her by the hand and started walking toward the door.

"You might want to get ahold of your parents too, Cami," my mom called after us. "Feel free to use the house phone if you need."

"Actually, we talked about that on the plane. We're going to wait and tell them in person. It'll be easier to explain," I responded.

"I doubt it. You're here right now, and I'm still not quite sure how it all happened."

"I'll give you the play by play later on," I promised her.

"Dylan, what costumes were you wearing?"

I stopped dead in my tracks, a huge grin crossing my face. "Elvis and Priscilla."

She raised her hands to the heavens,

speaking Spanish so rapidly even I could hardly understand her. I started laughing as I led Cami out into the hall, and I could hear Chris laughing too.

"I like your mom," Cami said with a smile.

"She's great, isn't she?" I released her hand and hugged her against me. "I'm glad you like her."

"It's nice of her to let me stay unannounced."

"Are you kidding? You're her daughter-in-law now. She'll treat you as if you were royalty or something. Family is everything to her."

"It seems so strange to belong to your family. I guess I never really thought about how it would be once I got married." She started laughing. "It's a good thing my dad decided to like you, or your life would be a mess."

"Yeah. It took me getting shot and crawling on my knees to beg for forgiveness before he was willing to have anything to do with me." I chuckled at the memory. "They aren't going to hate me now, are they?"

She sighed. "I hope not. They've both known we were serious, but I don't think they ever imagined me married at eighteen."

"Well, they're going to have to get used to it. I'm not going anywhere."

She wrapped her arms around my waist, squeezing me tightly. "You better not!"

Arriving at my room, I waited for her to go in before following after and closing the door. I made sure to lock it this time. Cami didn't miss the sound, turning to glance at me.

"I thought you had to leave."

I shook my head. "I'm to keep watch over you until I'm needed again. Those are my official orders. Chris will call me when he hears anything. Until then, there's just a bunch of waiting around."

"Hmmm. What to do?" She cast her gaze around the room. "I guess you can play your video games or watch television while you wait. Keep it down—I'm going to take a nap."

She nonchalantly headed for the bed.

"Oh, no you don't." I grabbed her arm and yanked her up against me. "Nice try, but there's no way I'm letting you get away that easily."

She stared at me innocently. "Did you want to do something else?"

I chuckled as I began backing her toward the bed. "You know very well what I want to do."

"I honestly have no idea what you're talking about." She was trying to hide her smile—unsuccessfully.

"Really? Well, that *is* disturbing. I guess all the hard work and effort I put into your training last night will have to be repeated again."

She snorted. "Sorry. It must not have been very memorable. Maybe you're a bad teacher." She bit her lip, and I was sure she was trying to anticipate what I'd do next.

"Did you hit your head this morning?" I asked, running my fingers through her hair as I prodded her scalp, continuing to inch her backward.

"No. Why?" Her nose wrinkled in confusion.

"I was wondering how you got amnesia,

because there's no way you forgot how great last night was."

She started laughing. "Someone is a little full of themselves. I didn't realize how cocky you were."

I grinned. "Not cocky—confident. There's a difference. I'd show you the difference, but I'm not sure you'd remember."

She rolled her eyes and opened her mouth to respond, but that's when the back of her knees hit the bed.

"We're here," I said softly. "So what's it going to be—bedtime or video games?"

She paused as if considering it. I released her and turned to walk away, but she grabbed a fistful of my shirt and pulled me back. "Bedtime—definitely."

I wrapped my arms around her, and lowered my face to hers. "So you do remember?"

She giggled. "Yeah, the haze suddenly cleared."

I kissed her mouth gently. "Well, let me remind you again anyway."

CHAPTER THIRTY-TWO
Hunter-

"Which one's the right place?" I asked Chris. "There's another one down the street."

"I don't know. She said the storage unit on Oracle Road. This was the first one I looked up."

"We need to text her back."

"She isn't going to answer, Dylan. She was lucky to get the text out to us while Ripper was sleeping."

"I guess we'll stake out both of them then. Which one do you want?"

"I guess I'll take this one," he replied.

"You know what? I have a much better idea. Call dispatch and tell them we need a search warrant. You said it was unit thirty-two, right?"

"Yeah, that's what Roberta texted."

"I'm going to flash my badge and tell the owners the warrant is on the way. They can call to verify if they need. If we open the right one, it's going to have the money in it, correct?"

Chris shrugged. "If he left it in plain sight."

"Well, he's got to have something in there that'll prove it belongs to him."

"And if he makes an appearance while you're in there?"

I lifted the police radio in my hand. "You'll warn me, and I'll arrest him. Besides, all the other guys should be in place soon. It's not like we don't have back up."

"Be careful. I don't want to be the one telling your mom and Cami you got shot again."

"I will be. Besides, I'm wearing my bulletproof vest this time, and I know you've still got my back, bro." I punched him in the shoulder and climbed out of the car.

There was a thin, dark-haired young man sitting behind a counter in the office reading a magazine. He looked up when I walked in, his stare immediately going to the weapon in my shoulder holster. "Can I help you?"

"Yes," I replied, slipping my badge off my belt and laying it on the counter. "I'm Officer Wilcock. We received a tip that a murder suspect we're trying to apprehend may be coming to retrieve belongings at a storage unit he rents. We aren't sure if it was at this location or the one down the road. My dispatcher is sending a search warrant. You're also welcome to call the station yourself to verify this. I'm wondering if perhaps you could check your records and tell me who unit number thirty-two is registered to."

"Sure. No problem," he said, quickly going to his computer and tapping in a few things. "I'm showing it register to a Juanita Valdez. Does that sound familiar?"

I shook my head. "No, it doesn't." I got on the secure radio channel Chris and I had. "This unit is registered to a Juanita Valdez. Does that ring any bells?"

"No, I don't recognize that name from any of the information we were given," Chris radioed back. "I'd check it anyway. He could have it registered under a false name, or it could be a friend's storage unit he keeps things in."

"Copy," I replied, turning my attention back to the man at the counter. "Would it be possible for you to open this for me? I just want to look inside. I won't disturb any of the contents. Like I said, we'll have a warrant sent to cover any legal issues you might have on your end."

"I'm happy to help." He walked over to a thin cupboard and unlocked it, opening the door to reveal many sets of numbered keys hanging on small hooks. He grabbed the one marked thirty-two and locked the cupboard again. "Follow me."

He led me outside, across the yard, to a corner unit located behind another row and opened the lock. "It's all yours," he said, stepping back and gesturing for me to open it.

Reaching down, I grabbed the handle and opened the door. I started laughing. "This is definitely not the right locker. Not unless our suspect has taken up knitting, crocheting, and doll making." The place resembled a crime scene for the miniature, with bags of different doll-body parts stacked everywhere, along with massive skeins of thread and yarn. It really was a bit creepy looking. "Thanks for your willingness to help us out." I handed him a card. "But if you see anything suspicious, please feel free to notify us in case we don't have our facts correct."

He took the card and stared at it for a moment. "I'll be sure to do that. Sorry it wasn't what you were looking for."

"Don't be. It helps us get one step closer. I'll have a couple of officers keep an eye on this place today anyway."

"Okay, thank you. Good luck." He extended his hand, and I shook it before heading back to the car.

"Any luck?" Chris asked as I slid in beside him.

"Nope. It was full of doll-making supplies. Let's go over to the other place. I told the manager here that we'd still have a couple of officers stake the place out today, in case we missed something."

"I agree. That's a good idea."

In the span of a few minutes, I found myself standing outside the second storage unit of the day, this one being registered to a Margaret Rivera. Things were suddenly looking up. I slid the door open and found the space full of tools and car parts.

"This is the one we're looking for," I said to the middle-aged attendant, Laura, standing beside me. I radioed the information to the guys setting up around the perimeter.

"Everyone has access to these during regular business hours. At night, after we're closed, they can get access if they have one of the twenty-four hour security cards, but they have to pay an extra fee for those."

I closed the door, not wanting to touch anything inside in case it might be evidence. "Do your security cameras monitor the yard all the time?"

"They do."

"Would it be possible to check the footage for the last twelve hours perhaps—to see if he's already been here? I don't want to waste time sitting here if we missed him already."

"Sure. Come back inside."

I radioed what I was doing to Chris and the team. He was parked beside a building across the street in the alleyway to avoid any vehicles on the road alerting Ripper.

Laura helped me arrange the security video on fast forward so we could get through it quickly. She sat beside me silently as we watched it together. We were several hours into the tape when my radio went off.

"He's here," Chris stated. "Driving in through the front gate right now. I don't recognize the vehicle, but Roberta is in the passenger seat."

"10-4," I replied, ducking low behind the counter as I watched the car pass by. I turned to glance at the current security feed when he drove past my line of sight. "Laura, I want you to leave. Walk out the gate and turn to the right. An officer will meet you there and guide you to a safer location." I had no idea if Ripper was armed, and I didn't want any civilians caught in the crossfire.

She nodded, brushing her salt-and-pepper hair away from her face with a trembling hand before she reached for her purse. "Can I call my husband when I'm out there?" she asked.

"Of course. Hopefully we'll get this taken care of quickly. You may want to call your boss as well. We'll mostly likely send a crime scene unit here to collect evidence from the storage unit as well, and we'll need to shut the place down for the day.

"Okay. I'll let him know." She hurried off to the door.

"I'm sending the attendant out. Don't let any other civilians enter the premises."

"Copy," Chris replied. "Two of us are coming in to back you up. Squad cars are on the way."

"10-4. I can see the vehicle on the security camera. He's stopping in front of the unit, and they're both getting out of the vehicle. I'm heading out into the yard now. Please go to radio silence while the suspect is approached."

As soon as Laura was safely through the gates, I left the building and made a dash across the lot to the next row of storage units. Pulling my weapon from the holster, I peered around the corner to assess the situation.

Ripper had the door open. He was out of sight, but Roberta was standing near the opening watching whatever he was doing. Waiting a few seconds, I hoped to catch her attention and signal her away, but she never glanced my direction. Silently, I began my approach, creeping closer along the far side of the vehicle.

Ripper was inside the small space, rummaging through the drawers of a metal tool chest, and pulling out several plastic bags containing thick wads of cash in each. There had to be an incredible sum of money there. If he managed to get away, he'd be set.

I raised my weapon over the hood of the vehicle, leveling it in Ripper's direction. "Hands in the air!" I hollered.

He froze for a second before slowly lifting his hands as directed. "You going to shoot me, Hunter?" he asked, glancing my way. Roberta stood frozen beside him.

"Not if you do everything I tell you. I'd really like this to go down smoothly."

He stared hard at me. "I trusted you, man."

"I know."

"I pulled you into my inner circle—let you date my sister. You were just using her. We didn't mean anything to you, did we?"

I hadn't expected a reaction like this from him. He seemed genuinely depressed about my betrayal. "Look, I'm sorry, but I had a job to do, and now it's time to finish that job. If you hadn't been breaking the law, then this wouldn't be an issue. There'd be no reason to arrest you."

"And what about Cami? What was her role in all this? Was she a cop too?"

Apparently, Roberta hadn't filled him in on the details—obviously because it would've shown her involvement if she said too much. This little tidbit of information gave me some hope. The less he knew about her the better.

"Cami was an innocent bystander who got

caught in the middle of things because I was careless. She never intended to deceive you. The department factored a cover for her when you refused to let things go. Making her disappear would've raised your suspicions."

"You had it all planned out, didn't you?" He glared hard at me.

"Sorry, bro. It had to be done. Now both of you step outside, and put your hands against the wall nice and easy."

Roberta came forward and did as directed, but Ripper stayed put, glancing back down at the money.

"Don't even think about it, man. It's not worth getting shot over."

"I don't believe you'd shoot me," he said, locking eyes with me.

"Even if I wouldn't, I can't vouch for the other guns trained on you at the moment."

Ripper moved forward, looking both ways down the alley, seeing Chris and Officer Johnson for the first time—their weapons raised.

"There's no escaping this time, Jack," I spoke, calling him by his given name.

I saw the resignation on his face. He stepped forward and placed his hands against the wall. I let out a sigh of relief. Regardless of who he was, I didn't want to shoot him. I hurried over and holstered my gun as Chris and Johnson moved in closer, a squad car with lights flashing pulled up behind them, and two more officers jumped out.

I quickly patted Ripper down, removing a gun tucked into the waistband of his pants.

Once I was sure he didn't have any other weapons on him, I pulled his hands behind him and snapped them into the cuffs. "Jack Rivera, you have the right to remain silent. Anything you say can, and will, be used against you in a court of law. You have the right to an attorney. If you cannot afford an attorney, one will be appointed for you. You are being placed under arrest for multiple counts of grand theft and suspicion of the murder of Manny Perez."

"What?" he shouted, yanking away and looking frantically around. "What are you talking about? Manny hasn't been seen in months!"

"We found his body where it was dumped in Sabino Canyon," I told him flatly, and Roberta let out a sob.

"You killed him!" she yelled, leaving the wall and pounding him in the chest. "I knew you did it! I knew it!"

"What the hell is going on?" Ripper shouted, unable to deflect Roberta's attack.

I grabbed her from behind and wrapped my arms tightly around her arms as the other officers rushed forward. "It's okay," I said as she squirmed. "It's all over now. Let them take him."

She turned into my chest and wept, clutching onto me like she was drowning.

"Take him away," I said to Chris. "Call a different car for Roberta."

He nodded and grabbed Ripper by the arm, dragging him to the vehicle.

"This is bullshit!" Ripper shouted. "Bullshit! I swear I'm gonna sue everyone in this damn department! Do you hear me?"

Chris had to physically push him into the vehicle. I could still see him thrashing and yelling inside, but couldn't understand what he was saying.

"Roberta," I said gently. "I'm going to place you in handcuffs too. I know you were offered immunity for your testimony, but we need to arrest you so Ripper doesn't think you were involved in setting him up. Okay?"

She nodded and stepped away from me, holding her hands out in front of her. Chris handed me his cuffs, and I placed them on her.

"There's a crime scene unit coming to collect the evidence in the storage unit," he informed me.

"Good. All the stuff in there is most likely stolen," I replied. "They should probably look for blood evidence on anything, just in case too."

A second squad car pulled in behind the first, and I led Roberta down to it and opened the door for her.

"Hunter." She paused staring at me with a funny look. "It's strange, but I don't think I was ever told your real name."

"Dylan," I responded, wishing I could withhold it, but it would come out in the court proceedings.

"Dylan," she tested the name out. "I know you're with Cami, but is there any chance after all this is over that you and I—"

I held up a hand to stop her. "Roberta," I paused, not knowing how to deliver the news gently. It had been obvious she was growing too attached to me. I decided to lay it out there for her. "Cami and I got married while we were in Vegas."

"Married?" Her mouth dropped open in shock. "I . . . I can't believe it." Tears welled in her eyes. "You really didn't feel anything for me, did you?" she asked, mirroring Ripper's question.

"Friendship," I replied, trying to soften the blow. "It was all I could feel. Cami—she's it for me. I'm sorry for the heartache you've been through, but you're a beautiful girl, and I have no doubt you'll find love again. Give it time."

She smiled wanly. "You don't have to say anymore. I get it." She slid into the vehicle without any further issue and stared straight ahead as I closed the door.

"Add another victim to the trail of broken hearts you've left in your wake," Chris said with a chuckle.

"That was never my intention. I tried to keep her at arm's length."

"I know, buddy." He clapped me on the shoulder and gave a sigh. "The things we have to do in the name of the job."

"Yeah, well this was my last job," I replied as we both watched the squad cars drive away.

"You're sure you're serious about that?" He gave me a concerned look.

"Dead serious." I started walking back toward the storage unit. "I'm done."

CHAPTER THIRTY-THREE
Cami-

"I can't wait for all the court stuff to be finished with this case. I'm so ready to be out of there for good," Dylan said as he straightened his tie in the mirror. He turned and saw me staring at him in appreciation from the doorway and grinned. He was so hot in his official police uniform. "How do I look?"

"Honestly?" I asked, going to him and running my hands up his chest. "This may be one thing I'm really going to miss about your job."

He laughed and cupped my face in his hands. "Maybe I can keep it . . . you know, as a costume for later. Have you ever had any cop fantasies?"

"I'm having one right now," I teased, and he groaned out loud.

"That's not very fair of you. You know I have to leave now for this blasted court hearing."

"I'll still be here when you get back."

He bent and lightly kissed my lips. "Have I told you how much I enjoy you living in my apartment?"

I smiled. "Only about a thousand times in the last two days. And I *am* your wife—it would be a little weird for me to be anywhere else."

He reached around and pinched my butt. "You know what I mean." He sighed heavily. "Kiss me again. I've got to get going."

I slid my arms around his neck and gave him a big, long kiss. He didn't seem too eager for it to end, and neither did I. The longer we kissed, the more frantic it got. He walked me backwards—neither of us breaking apart as we moved—until we ran into the wall.

He released me then, bracing his hands on the wall beside me. "Dammit, Cami. I've got to leave."

"Are you sure?" I asked innocently. I had no problem keeping him here with me.

He laughed and pecked me briefly on the lips before stepping away. "No, I'm not sure. I want to stay right here. You don't play fair at all."

I smiled. "Sorry. I like being in your arms."

"Likewise," he replied.

"Come on. I'll walk you to the door," I said as I moved past him.

"Okay. Let me grab my gun real quick."

I raised an eyebrow and snickered at him.

He shot me an exasperated look. "Don't even go there."

I made the motion of zipping my lips and throwing away the key, and he shook his head.

Following me to the front of the apartment,

he paused for a few seconds as I opened the door, and kissed me again. "Hopefully this won't take too long. Keep that fantasy playing, and I'll be back as soon as I can."

"Sounds great to me. Good luck."

He smiled. "Thanks."

I watched him run down the steps and out to the Camaro. He glanced up and waved at me again before sliding in and driving off. I closed the door and leaned against it.

I was so happy. Everything was finally starting to work out for us. Yes, my parents had been shocked, but they'd taken the news well. So had Dylan's dad. Both our mothers were now in a frenzy trying to plan the perfect wedding so we could celebrate with family and friends. As far as I was concerned, all was perfect as it stood right now. Dylan was my husband, the case was done, and we were living together. It was all I ever wanted.

I walked to where several unpacked boxes of my belongings still sat untouched. We'd gotten a little distracted putting things away. I opened the top one and was reaching inside when the doorbell rang. I wondered if Dylan had forgotten something, or if Russ was here to help. I opened the door and was shocked to find Roberta standing there. She was dressed nicely and had a big trendy bag hanging from her shoulder.

"Uh, hi, Roberta." I leaned out and glanced around, but no one else was with her. "Dylan just left for Ripper's hearing. I thought you'd be there too."

She shook her head. "Ripper doesn't know

I'm not in jail still. No one has told him I was the one who turned him in. Is it okay if I come in?"

I hesitated. We weren't really friends, even though we'd spent a lot of time together. She'd made it clear she was interested in Dylan.

"Honestly, Roberta, due to your involvement in an ongoing case, I don't think it would be wise for me to let you in. I wouldn't want to compromise things, and Dylan could be accused of not doing things by the book."

Roberta shifted anxiously. "Oh. I didn't think about that. I definitely wouldn't want to get Hunter in trouble." She gave a nervous laugh. "Sorry . . . Dylan. I have a hard time calling him that after calling him Hunter for so long."

I smiled. "Trust me. I understand completely. I've only recently made the switch myself. I still slip up once in a while too."

She nodded and looked around absently. "Hun . . . Dylan told me you two got married. Congratulations."

"Thanks," I replied, wondering why she was still standing here. "Did he tell you where we lived? I didn't know any of you were aware of this address."

"Uh, no. I ran into that friend of yours—Rud? He told me."

"You mean Russ?" I was one hundred percent positive Russ would never—under any circumstances—give our address out to Roberta. Something wasn't right.

"Yeah, Russ. Sorry. I'm so bad with names."

"No worries! Let me call him real quick, and

he can come over. That way we have someone who can vouch for us, in case we need it."

"You don't need to call. I won't be here much longer. I just wanted to give you something," she said in a rush. "I was hoping Hunter would be here so I could give it to you together, but you can tell him I brought it by. Tell him it's a wedding present—my way of saying thank you to both of you. I have it down in the trunk. Can you help me with it? It's kind of heavy."

I was shocked. "You didn't have to get us anything. He was simply doing his job."

"He might have been, but you weren't. Besides, he really helped me out with everything."

"I'm not sure what the protocol is for something like this, Roberta. I know the department has rules, though. Would you mind coming back later, when he's home? I'd feel more comfortable with that. I'd hate to do something wrong."

She fidgeted again and glanced around, almost as if she were waiting for someone.

"Is there anything else you need?" I asked, feeling exasperated. She didn't seem to want to leave.

"Yeah, can I borrow your phone real quick? Mine was taken as evidence, and I don't know when I'll be able to get it back."

"Sure." I reached into my pocket and handed it out to her. She took with a shaky hand and dropped it. I bent to retrieve it, but when I stood, I found a gun pointed at my chest. I raised my hands immediately to signal submission, dropping the phone as I did so. It shattered on the ground. "What's going on, Roberta?"

"You and I are going for a little ride, that's what's going on." She tilted her head toward the parking lot.

"Look, if you want to steal the Camaro, Dylan has it. I don't have a car."

"I don't want your damn car. That was Ripper's deal. I never wanted to be involved in the first place. Get walking."

Leaving the door open and the remnants of the phone on the ground, I prayed Dylan would realize I was in trouble and be able to find me somehow, but that could be hours from now. Who knew what would happen between now and then? My mind moved franticly, trying to seize onto an idea that would help me get out of my current predicament.

"Why are you doing this? You're in the clear. They caught your brother, and you've gotten immunity for your testimony. You're jeopardizing everything." I needed to keep her talking.

She didn't say anything, but pulled a set of keys from her pocket and tossed them to me.

"What do you want me to do?"

"You're driving. It's the yellow and black mustang in the lot over there."

Immediately, I recognized it as new. "I thought you said stealing cars wasn't your thing."

"It isn't," she sneered. "But unlike Ripper, I actually invested my money into interest-bearing accounts. I siphoned off the interest into other accounts. I gave the police what Ripper gave me. But the rest is mine. I *earned* every penny of that money."

I wasn't going to argue with her reasoning. She wasn't exactly making sense right now.

She went to the passenger side and opened the door. "Slide across," she ordered.

I got in and clumsily slid over the center into the driver's seat, buckling out of habit.

"Start it and put it in drive."

"Are you going to tell me what's going on? None of this makes any sense. I don't understand why you would do something like this when everything was working out for you." I pulled from the space and slowly made my way out of the parking lot, turning onto the highway in the direction she indicated. Roberta kept the gun low and trained right on me.

"Pull into the left lane and stay in it until I say otherwise."

I did as she asked, my heart beating rapidly.

"Ripper didn't kill Manny. I did.".

I turned to stare at her, open mouthed, trying to make sense of what she'd just confessed.

"Why would you frame your brother for that?" I couldn't believe it.

She gave a sardonic laugh. "My brother—and Manny for that matter—were the worst kind of scum. You know those private meetings they had with buyers? Well, they took me along to sweeten the deals."

I had a sick feeling. "I don't understand what

you mean."

"I mean the whole crazy overprotective brother act was just that—an act. They made me into a whore—all so they could get more money! I kept hoping Manny would get jealous and do something about it, but he never did. He sat by and let those vile men use me however they wanted, same as Ripper."

"That's terrible, Roberta!" I honestly felt disgusted for her. "Why didn't you leave?"

"I was going to, but then Manny and I had an argument one night in the garage after everyone had gone. I got really angry and shoved him hard. He tripped over a car part lying on the floor behind him and fell back and smashed his head against one of Ripper's tool boxes." She got quieter. "I knew immediately he was dead—there was blood everywhere."

"But it was an accident!" I protested. "Why didn't you tell someone?"

"Because I suddenly realized I could frame my brother for the whole thing and get rid of him too. He deserves to rot in jail!"

"Yes, he does, but there's still time for you to come forward and tell your part of the story. It doesn't have to end like this!" I pleaded, hoping to make her see reason.

"I got away with it once. I can do it again," she replied calmly. "Hunter will be devastated when he loses his wife. Who better to comfort him than someone who's been through the same thing?"

"You want Dylan," I said flatly, everything suddenly made sense.

"Yes, I do. And as you can see, I always get what I want."

I said nothing—gripping the steering wheel so tightly I could hardly feel my fingers. No one in the surrounding cars was paying any attention to us, that I could tell. I had to do something now. There was no way I was going to let her get to Dylan.

In a split second, I'd made my decision. I cranked the wheel hard and fast to the right, causing the car behind us in the next lane to T-bone Roberta's side of the vehicle. Her head crashed into the window shattering it, and my head whipped in the same direction, but the seatbelt kept me in place.

The backside of our car swung around, and smashed into the bumper of the vehicle in front of us, jolting us both hard again. I could hear screeching tires, and the smell of burnt rubber filled the air.

We headed straight for the wall of a store, my foot still burying the gas pedal until I slammed on the brakes as the front end crashed through the building. Both air bags deployed as debris rained down in loud, giant thuds against the roof. I raised my hands protectively as it dented in, expecting it to collapse on us at any moment.

And then there was silence.

Carefully, I turned toward Roberta. Her eyes were closed, and she was slumped against her seat. Her right arm was twisted at an odd angle, and she was bleeding from her head. The gun was on the floor at her feet, and I wasn't taking any chances. Reaching caused me to groan in pain, but the tips of my fingers managed to hook the trigger guard. Dragging the weapon toward me, I picked it up and tossed it out the driver's side window.

Several people ran up to the vehicle. "Are you okay?" a concerned man shouted.

"We need an ambulance and the police. Call 911 and tell them this is a hostage situation involving Officer Wilcock's wife," I instructed, rubbing my arms, which were already beginning to bruise. "My phone is broken."

"Yes, ma'am. Right away." He ripped out his phone and dialed the number right there, relaying the information I'd given him correctly.

"Miss?" the man spoke again. "The dispatcher wants to know if you're hurt?"

"I'm sore, but as far as I can tell, nothing appears to be broken."

He peered farther into the vehicle and began relaying Roberta's condition to the dispatcher. My head was spinning and I closed my eyes, waiting.

"Ma'am? They want me to hold the phone to your ear. Is that okay?"

"Yes," I replied feeling dizzy. I leaned back against the seat. "Hello?"

"Hi, Mrs. Wilcock, this is dispatch. I'm relaying a message to you from Officer Wilcock. He's en-route to your location.

"Cami! Cami!" Dylan's frantic voice suddenly piped through the phone. "Can you hear me?"

"I'm okay, Dylan. I promise. Roberta's not doing too well, though, from the looks of things.

We need help."

"Hang on. I'll be there soon. I love you."

"I love you too," I whispered.

"I've dispatched two ambulances to your location since this is a multi-vehicle accident," the woman's voice came again over the radio. "The fire department is on the way also."

"I'm sorry. I hope I didn't hurt anyone else. She had a gun on me, and I didn't know how else to stop her." I started to cry.

"Don't worry about it, Mrs. Wilcock. We'll take care of everything. Just relax as best you can."

The sound of multiple sirens filled the air, and I sighed in relief, knowing what it meant. Help was coming, and Dylan was on the way.

Finally . . . it was truly over.

EPILOGUE

Cami-
Two Years Later

"Russ, can you help me with these boxes?" I called, and he appeared in the doorway.

"Sure. Where do you want them?" he asked, coming to my side.

"These are all my glass dishes, so in the kitchen please."

"Will do—if I can find my way to the kitchen in this new castle of yours. This place is huge! And have you seen the pool? I can tell where I'm going to spend my summer's from now on." He grinned.

"I'd hardly call it a castle—it's only five thousand square feet—but it is lovely, isn't it?"

"Five thousand square feet," he grumbled as he bent to pick up a box. "You could fit two of my parent's houses in this place."

I laughed as he disappeared from sight. I heard the front door in the foyer open and close. "Dylan? Is that you?" I called out.

"Yeah, it's me, Goody. Where are you?"

"In the living room."

He came around the corner—white smile shining in his dirty black face. Shrugging out of his turnout coat, he flung it over his shoulder, revealing his sweaty dark-blue department t-shirt and red suspenders on his turnout pants.

"Did you get the fire put out?"

"We did!" He grinned and quickly grabbed me to him. He kissed me hard, and the acrid scent of smoke and sweat assailed my nose.

I laughed and shoved him away. "Ugh! You reek! Go take a shower!"

"You're supposed to hail the conquering hero," he teasing, pulling me back against him and shimmying up and down against my body.

"What are you doing?" I cried as I tried to shove him away again, but he held onto me tightly.

"Now you're filthy too! Shall we take a shower together?" He grinned widely. "You've got to have a fireman fantasy somewhere in that pretty head of yours."

"You're terrible!"

"I am, but you love me anyway."

"I do," I replied, giving in and letting him kiss me in earnest.

A groan from the doorway caused us both to glance at Russ standing there with a disgusted look on his face. "Get a room," he griped.

"We did," Dylan replied, sweeping his arm in arc as he gestured toward the house. "Several, in fact."

I couldn't help giggling as he leaned over

and rubbed his dirty black nose against mine before he kissed me again.

Russ crossed the room behind us, grunting as he picked up another box. "I'm surprised the two of you don't have a dozen kids running around already the way you're constantly going at it."

"A dozen?" I laughed. "Isn't that a little extreme? We haven't had enough time to have that many kids."

"Besides, Cami has to finish school, and of course there's her brilliant theater career to consider too," Dylan smiled and lightly kissed my lips again.

"You just want to keep me to yourself a while longer, and you know it."

"You're right. That's exactly what I want." He grinned and swept me off my feet. "See ya later, Russ," he called out as he carried me off toward the bedroom.

Russ appeared around the corner and waved as I stared over Dylan's shoulder. "Have fun!" he said. "I'm off to find new friends—preferably single ones."

Dylan and I laughed again. "Good luck," he replied loudly to Russ. "Come back when you're married!"

"Jerk!" Russ hollered back as we disappeared around the corner.

"We love you, Russ!" I shouted.

"Yeah, yeah. I know."

Dylan and I smiled at each other again, and he kicked the bedroom door closed behind us.

I sighed as he kissed me. Life was good.

About the Author:

Lacey Weatherford is the bestselling author of the popular young adult paranormal romance series, Of Witches and Warlocks, and contemporary series, Chasing Nikki. She has always had a love of books and wanted to become a writer ever since reading her first Nancy Drew novel at the age of eight.

Lacey resides in the beautiful White Mountains of Arizona. She lives with her wonderful husband and children along with their dog, Sophie, and cat, Minx. When she's not out supporting one of her kids at their sporting/music events, she spends her time reading, writing, blogging, and visiting with her readers on her social media accounts.

Visit Lacey's Official Website:
http://www.laceyweatherfordbooks.com
Follow on Twitter:
LMWeatherford
Or Facebook:
Lacey Jackson Weatherford

3748028R00195

Printed in Great Britain
by Amazon.co.uk, Ltd.,
Marston Gate.